FIRST
GIRL TO
DIE

BOOKS BY HELEN PHIFER

FIRST GIRL TO DIE

HELEN PHIFER

bookouture

Published by Bookouture in 2021

An imprint of Storyfire Ltd.
Carmelite House
50 Victoria Embankment
London EC4Y 0DZ

www.bookouture.com

ISBN: 978-1-80019-603-2
eBook ISBN: 978-1-80019-602-5

For Emily Gowers, thank you for being so amazing.

PROLOGUE

2016

The sky from the patch of damp, mossy grass outside of Rydal Caves looked as if it was cloaked in thick, black velvet. Tiny stars glittered throughout, as if they were diamanté that had been painstakingly sewn across it by hand to make it sparkle. The group of teenagers were huddled not too far from the entrance to the caves. Gusts of wind kept carrying away the tinny music playing from a mobile phone, distorting it, but they didn't care. They giggled and huddled closer to keep warm. The vodka they were drinking straight from the bottles warmed their insides enough to heat their hands and make their thoughts fuzzy.

The circular edge of the full moon as it appeared at the very tip of Loughrigg Fell cast a silvery glow down onto the caves and the teenagers. As it rose slowly above them it was as if they were the characters of a play on the centre stage, the moon their spotlight. As the alcohol diminished, so did their inhibitions. Brad, the only boy amongst the four girls, stood up. Stumbling and crashing his way through the bracken, he clambered up the hillside until he reached the top of the cave. He was so glad he'd come tonight. He very nearly hadn't, but he was having a great time. As he stumbled towards the edge of the cave, he heard the voices of his friends carried towards him, and he teetered on the edge, grinning down at them. Cupping his hands to his mouth he yelled, 'Look at me I'm the king of the world.' A loud noise from behind startled him and he turned to see what it was. The grass was slippery and then he was sliding, unable to stop himself, his trainers not holding traction. He looked back to see her watching him and then he was flying through the air to a cacophony of high-pitched screams as the wind carried the sound towards him. The ear-piercing screams echoed around the fells and then he hit the rocks with such speed and force that they stopped in a split second, and he heard nothing more.

CHAPTER ONE

Detective Constable Morgan Brookes had woken up early to the sound of the dawn chorus and had taken her morning coffee out into the garden to drink, along with the newspaper. It was so lovely to hear the blackbirds and song thrushes chirping and calling to each other. This was more like it. As much as she loved the dark autumn nights it was nice to see the sky bright in the morning; it made her early starts a little more bearable. She scanned the paper to see if there was any sign of Gary Marks's capture, but there was nothing. He had managed to escape from his prison guards back in October, while on a visit to the hospital, and hadn't been seen since. A part of her hoped he was dead, that he'd fallen foul of an accident and because he had no ID on him, hadn't been identified. She wasn't a bad person, but he was, and her life would feel so much safer if she knew there was no way he could come back to hurt her or anyone she cared about.

When she reached Rydal Falls police station, she wondered what the day would hold in store for her. Thank God the small town had been relatively quiet since they had arrested that horrid man for the murder and kidnap of two little girls. Morgan still had bad dreams about not being able to save Charlie Standish, but it helped a little knowing that she had rescued Macy Wallace from the same fate. Sometimes she wondered if Macy had saved her and given her a spark for life she hadn't felt since her mum's death. The kid was tough and relentless. Morgan still saw her every couple of weeks. She would turn up at the police station with a packet of biscuits or some home-baked fairy cakes covered in pink icing and sprinkles for Morgan, who repaid the favour by giving her lots of chocolate in return. Every day since Macy's case Morgan went to work hoping that there had been no murders. She would be quite happy to never have to work a murder investigation ever again. As she walked up the back staircase to the third floor and the CID office, she heard Amy's and Des's voices as they bickered with each other, and she smiled. That was good; it meant nothing too serious had come in overnight. Life was pleasant at the moment; she was happy working and spending time with her friends. Together with Ben, her boss, and Amy and Des, she had taken to attending the weekly quiz at The Black Dog and they were still to come higher than last, but it wasn't about the winning, as Ben regularly told them, it was the taking part. Before she could step onto the third floor, she heard a flurry of heavy boots below as officers rushed out of the back door to answer the latest emergency call which had come in. As she walked into the office, she was surprised to see Ben's office empty.

'Where's the boss?'

'No idea. I thought he might have been with you?'

Amy grinned at her, and she shook her head. 'Why would he be with me?'

'Because he left the pub with you last night. I thought you might have been consoling him over him getting that question wrong about what year England won the Rugby World Cup. He looked pretty devastated about it.'

'He looked pretty drunk more like it. No, I didn't go home with him. I dropped him off at his house though. Do you think he's okay?'

Morgan's phone began to vibrate in her pocket, and she pulled it out to see Ben's name flashing across the screen.

'Morning, are you having a day off?'

'No, I slept in. My alarm never went off. I'll be in soon.'

'No worries. Do you need a lift?'

'That's what I was phoning for. I left my car at the pub.'

'Right, well I'll come get you, but you can buy the coffees.'

She hung up, and Amy smiled.

'I'll have a hazelnut latte, and Des will have a semi-skimmed giraffe milk skinny cappuccino.'

Des glared at her. 'Sod off, Amy, I told you I'm not vegan. I'm not even vegetarian now. I'll have a normal cappuccino, please, Morgan.'

Morgan turned and made her way back out to the stairs, wishing Ben had phoned a few minutes earlier, before she'd found a parking space and trudged up three flights. As she reached her car, the radio in her other pocket began to ring. She looked at it, somehow knowing that her morning was about to get a whole lot worse than having to fight for a parking space.

'Hello.'

'It's the control room. We can't get hold of Sergeant Matthews. Do you know if he's around?'

'He might not have his radio. I'm about to see him. Should I give him a message?'

'Yes, please. Can you ask him to attend Priory Grove? He's the only negotiator working today for South. There's a teacher threatening to jump out of a window.'

'Blimey, they must be having a bad day. Yes, I'll let him know.'

'Thanks, Morgan.'

Morgan ran the last few metres to her car and drove off towards Ben's house a lot faster than she would have usually, wondering what had happened to tip the poor teacher over the edge.

As she turned into Ben's street, he was already walking towards her car. She pulled over, and he opened the door and got in.

'They need a negotiator. You're the only one on for South.'

The look of horror on his face didn't go amiss. 'Where?'

'Priory Grove School.'

'What? Are you winding me up? Isn't that a junior school?'

'Yes, it's a primary school and no, I'm not. There's a teacher threatening to jump out of a window.'

'Christ, and I thought I was having a rough morning.'

She glanced at him. He had a five o'clock shadow and his eyes were watery. He looked sad, weary, or maybe was he just hung-over. He'd been drunk last night, but not steaming; he'd still been able to walk without falling over and had managed to open his front door without too much of a fight.

'Are you okay, Ben?'

'Cindy's birthday.'

He didn't say anything else, and Morgan didn't ask. His wife had been dead for six years, and he still carried the guilt around his shoulders like a heavy, leaden cloak that he couldn't shrug free.

CHAPTER TWO

The school, which was situated behind a busy road and looked out onto a funeral home, was a hub of activity. There were no children around, which was a blessing. There were two police vans with lights flashing and a car. Ben jumped out of Morgan's car and shouted at the huddle of officers who looked unsure of what to do.

'Turn those bloody lights off, now.'

The drivers of the vehicles ran towards their respective vans, and the flashing blue lights died one after the other, returning the street to seeming normality.

Ben looked at Morgan. 'Christ, some poor bastard is having the worst day of their life and they're illuminating the street and putting them under the spotlight. Could they draw any more attention to the plight of whoever this is?'

He strode towards the front gates. Cain was inside the entrance to the school, talking to a tall woman who Morgan recognised from a previous case as the head teacher, Andrea Hart. She hurried to keep up with Ben. He was on a mission. As they got closer, she saw Andrea look at her with an expression of relief on her face and she hoped she wasn't expecting her to be the one to end this.

'Morgan, thank you for coming.'

'Andrea, this is Ben, he's a trained negotiator.'

Andrea looked at him, then held her hand out, shaking his.

'I'm not sure what to do. Brittany is a lovely girl and a very highly thought of teacher.'

'Where is she now?'

'In the staffroom, upstairs by the window. She's acting really strange; she's mumbling and talking rubbish. To be honest with you, I think she may have taken some kind of recreational drug because this is completely out of character for her.'

Morgan felt a chill settle over her shoulders. Her friend from school was a teacher here, and there weren't a lot of Brittany's in Rydal Falls. 'Brittany Alcott?'

'Yes, do you know her?'

She nodded, feeling her throat constrict. 'Yes, she was one of my best friends at school.'

Ben glanced at Morgan. 'You might be better speaking to her then. Normally, I like to talk to people on the phone at first, but if she's taken something then it's going to have to be face to face.'

Morgan shook her head. 'I don't know what to say.'

'I'll tell you.' He asked Andrea, 'Can you take us to the staff-room?'

Andrea nodded and led them into the school. Ben turned to Cain. 'Get fire and rescue here ASAP, they might be needed.'

A loud crash followed by a heavy thud came from above them. Morgan followed Andrea through the long corridor until they reached a door that Andrea pulled open. There was a steep staircase. Morgan took the stairs fast and then stopped on a landing where a blonde-haired woman, the same age as Morgan, was standing outside the door to the staffroom.

'Paige, this is Morgan, she's a policewoman. She went to school with Brittany.'

Morgan realised that Andrea was now pinning all hope on her shoulders, as if by knowing Brittany she could save her. There was another loud crash from inside the room, and the two women looked at each other, fear etched across their faces. Morgan reached out with a hand that was trembling to open the door and pushed the handle. The door moved a few centimetres but wouldn't open any further. Brittany had put something in front of it to stop anyone getting inside. Ben stepped forward and tried to push it. It gave slightly and that was it.

'Who is it? There's no one in. Stop looking for me. I'm not here. It's my baby.'

Paige was wringing her hands. She whispered, 'Brittany went out for a run this morning and when she came home, she looked awful. She practically collapsed onto her bed. I gave her some paracetamol, but she wouldn't let me call the doctor. I told her I'd put a sick day in for her and came to work. Then she turned up twenty minutes ago, talking and mumbling about no one being home and something about a baby. She's hallucinating or something.'

Ben asked, 'Does she take drugs, Paige? Is she pregnant?'

She turned to Ben and shook her head. 'Not that I know of, and for all I know she isn't pregnant. I don't understand what's happening.'

'Morgan, try and engage with her, get her attention.'

Morgan turned to the small gap in the door and called, 'Brittany, it's Morgan Brookes, from school, please can I come in?'

The sound of Brittany dragging furniture stopped. The silence felt heavy as Morgan pushed her ear to the door. She could hear Brittany whispering to herself.

'Brittany, we're worried about you. Let me in. I can help you. Whatever is wrong we can sort it out. Would you like me to phone for a doctor? Are you ill?'

Brittany didn't acknowledge her, but instead began dragging the heavy piece of furniture again. Morgan turned to Ben. 'Now what?'

The deafening sound of breaking glass filled the air, and Morgan heard screams from outside. Ben threw himself at the door and she joined him, pushing frantically. Between them they managed to move the door just enough to squeeze through it. A cool breeze from the broken window blew through the staffroom, making the blinds rattle as they swung from side to side. Bile filled Morgan's throat as she realised the staffroom was empty. She ran towards the window and stared down into the playground and the crumpled body on the floor with a large pool of dark-coloured liquid forming around her head. Morgan's knees buckled and she almost swooned out of the window herself, but Ben's hand grabbed hold of the back of her coat, yanking her away from it. She heard him mutter, 'Shit.' Then watched as he rushed back out the way they'd come moments ago. Paige was crying, and Andrea looked as shocked about what had just happened as Morgan felt. All three women stared at each other, then Morgan's instincts kicked in and she ran towards the gap in the door. Squeezing back through, she turned to Andrea.

'I'm sorry, I need you and Paige to come out of there and not go back inside. Until we can figure out what the hell just happened, this is a crime scene.'

Andrea nodded. Taking hold of Paige's arm she led the crying woman out of the staffroom. 'Yes, of course.'

Morgan made her way outside. She heard the sirens of an ambulance turning into the street. Cain was standing by the front gates to the school with the student he was training, waiting to direct the ambulance inside. Ben was kneeling next to Brittany's broken, lifeless body. Morgan didn't need a paramedic to tell her it was too late. There was nothing they could do. Brittany's glazed eyes told her all she needed to know. She felt a wave of sadness. How had this happened? Morgan thought back to their school days, picturing Brittany as the tall, attractive teenager who, she remembered, had been the sensible one at school, the best friend who never tried to lead her astray and, out of all her friends, she'd had a bit of a girl crush on Brittany; she'd looked up to her. And now she was dead. Morgan swallowed the lump in her throat and turned away. She couldn't watch this. She needed to do something useful. Andrea was standing on the step staring, her face as white as the crisp cotton shirt she was wearing. Morgan took hold of her arm.

'I'm sorry, there's nothing we can do out here at the moment. Let's go inside and you can talk me through what happened before we got here.'

Andrea nodded. 'Is she…?'

'Yes, I'm afraid she is.'

Sandra, the school secretary, was standing peering out of the small window in her office, her back to them.

'Sandra, I need you to send a message out to parents that we've had a serious incident that is being dealt with and there is no need for them to panic. The children are all safe and well; they are to be collected at the usual time from the rear of the school.'

Sandra turned to them, a sheepish expression on her face.

'Is Brittany okay? I'll do that now, Andrea.'

Andrea shook her head. 'No, she's not.' Before Sandra could begin to ask a barrage of questions, the phone began to ring, and Andrea turned to walk away. Morgan followed.

'I need to tell the staff. God, I hope we don't get parents turning up, but it's only a matter of time before the Chinese whispers start.'

'It's okay, we'll take care of that. We will get a scene guard put on, and we'll move Brittany and get her to the mortuary. We won't leave her out there on full view of pupils and their parents.'

'Thank God for that. I don't even know where to begin, Morgan. We have never had an incident of this nature in the history of the school.'

Morgan followed Andrea into an empty classroom. 'Excuse me whilst I go and find Paige. I can't have her wandering around crying; it will scare the pupils.' She didn't get very far before another, much older, teacher came in with her arm around Paige's shoulder.

'Mrs Hart, what's going on, is Brittany okay?' Paige's voice quivered as she whispered. Morgan knew she had to push all her thoughts and feelings about it to one side. She had to do her job.

'I'm afraid not, Paige. I know this is a terrible shock for you, but we need to find out what's happened to make Brittany act this way. How well do you know her?'

'I… we… we share a house together with another girl. She's so lovely. She doesn't drink much or take drugs, but she was acting as if she was on something, wasn't she?'

'Does she take any regular medication, or has she recently been prescribed anything that she could have had an adverse reaction to?'

She shrugged. 'I don't know. I gave her paracetamol this morning. Oh God, was it me, did I cause this?'

The look of horror etched across her face was almost unbearable to look at. Morgan shook her head.

'I doubt that paracetamol could have caused this, Paige, and even if they did it's an over-the-counter tablet available to buy at every shop in England. It wouldn't be your fault. I take them all the time and have never heard of them causing the kind of behaviour that Brittany was displaying.'

Paige nodded.

'Mrs Hart, I'm going to need Brittany's personnel file with her next of kin's address and her doctor. Is she married or in a relationship?'

Paige answered while Andrea exited the room. 'Not married, said she wasn't ever going to commit herself to that. She's been seeing a woman on and off for the last six months.'

Morgan didn't know if her parents still lived in the same house they had when she used to go and call for her when they were at school.

'What's her name? Do you have any idea where she lives?'

She nodded. 'She's called Fleur Collins. She used to share the house with us but moved out into a flat on the high street. Oh God, who's going to tell her?'

'I will. Do you think she'll be at home now?'

'No, she's a dental nurse. She works at the surgery on Main Street.'

Mrs Hart came back in with a thin blue file and passed it to Morgan.

'I've photocopied the relevant stuff. You can keep hold of that. I need to call an emergency governors' meeting. Please excuse me, Morgan. You know where to find me.'

'Thank you, yes. I need to go and inform Brittany's parents.' She opened the file to check they were still living at the same address.

By the time Morgan returned outside, Brittany had been taken to the hospital mortuary. There were officers at the entrance to the school, and Wendy, the on-duty CSI, was already on scene. Wendy smiled at Morgan, and she waved back crossing towards where she was documenting the scene. Her eyes were drawn to the large, dark pool of congealing blood that was littered with broken glass.

'Please could you photograph the staffroom and have a look around for anything that might be drug related? She may have a locker as well. Mrs Hart, the headteacher, will be able to show it to you if she does.'

'Yes, of course. This is just awful, the poor woman, what a horrible way to die.'

Morgan stared down at the blood once more and shuddered, it was horrific. She looked over to where Ben was on his phone, and he beckoned her over as he ended the call.

'Are you okay? How well did you know her?'

She nodded. 'We were friends at school. She was one of the nicer girls. I saw her a little while back to say hello to and we had a brief chat, but we haven't been close since school. One of our close group of friends died in a tragic accident but we all drifted apart after that, and I haven't really kept in touch with any of them. I have her next of kin details; do you want me to go and pass the death message?'

'I'll come with you. I've sent a patrol to guard her home address. I want it searching for anything that she could have taken to make her act like this.'

'I've asked Wendy to search Brittany's locker and the staffroom for drug paraphernalia.'

Morgan walked towards her car, glad to be escaping from this devastating scene. Not that she wanted to face Brittany's parents or her girlfriend; she knew too well the pain she was about to wreak on them would change their lives forever and it tore at her heart. At least it meant she was keeping busy and doing all she could for her friend now she was no longer here. There was little else she could do but find out what had happened to make her act this way.

CHAPTER THREE

Morgan drove to the address on the next of kin form that Mrs Hart had given to her. Brittany's parents had moved since high school. The address was a small two-up two-down cottage on the outskirts of Rydal Falls, with the cutest front garden she had ever seen. It was tiny. The small patch of grass was a rich, lush green and it was only when she opened the gate and looked closer did she realise it wasn't real grass; on closer inspection the brightly coloured pots of flowers weren't real either. Ben whispered, 'Well, there's a brilliant way to save time gardening.'

Morgan stood on the small step, her hand raised to knock on the door, but she couldn't move it any further. Her knuckles were reluctant to make contact with the wood because once they did there was no going back. She felt the warmth of the sun on the back of her neck as it broke through the haze and wished she could start this morning all over again. Wished she could have got to the school a few minutes earlier, been able to engage Brittany and talk her away from that window. She heard a loud knock on the door and stared at her hand. It was still mid-air. She realised Ben had stepped forward to do it. The door opened, and her hand dropped to her side. Brittany's dad hadn't changed a bit, apart from a few more wrinkles around the corner of his eyes which lit up when he saw Morgan.

'Morgan Brookes? How lovely to see you. Look at you all grown up. You know we were just talking about you the other day. Brittany said she needed to get in touch with you.'

Morgan swallowed the lump in the back of her throat. 'Hello, Mr Alcott, Sam.'

'Why are you here? Has something exciting happened in this street? Are you doing some of those enquiries they're always doing on the television?'

Ben saved her having to answer. 'Mr Alcott, may we come inside?'

Morgan saw the light in Sam's pale blue eyes dim a little as his expression changed from one of delight to pure panic.

'Of course, what's the matter, something is wrong, isn't it?'

Morgan felt a slight pressure on her back and realised that Ben was pushing her to move forward and go into the house. Her feet were stuck to the floor, and she had to force them off the step and through the open doorway.

'Yes, Sam, I'm afraid it is.'

Sam didn't turn to look at her. He pointed to the brown leather chesterfield, and they both sat down.

'Is Ava around?'

He shook his head. 'She died last year, had a massive stroke.'

Morgan felt the coldness seeping through her veins at what she was about to put this poor man through and wished she could be anywhere but here. She could feel Ben's eyes staring at her.

'I'm so sorry, Sam, I had no idea.'

She was trying to figure out how the hell she'd missed this and realised that last year had been a complete whirlwind of case after case. She'd suffered enough problems of her own to take much notice of anyone else. Ben took the conversation into his own hands, and she realised he'd given her a chance, but she'd blown it.

'Mr Alcott, I'm afraid we have some bad news about Brittany.'

Ben paused to give him a moment to take in what he'd just said. Sam Alcott was staring at him, his eyes wide, his mouth open.

'There was an incident at the school first thing, and I'm afraid to say that Brittany is dead.'

Sam looked confused, and Morgan could understand why: how does your daughter go to work one day in a primary school and end up dead?

'Brittany wasn't acting herself and there was an accident. She fell out of the staffroom window.'

Sam flinched, his hand covering his mouth. 'Oh my God, is she okay? I need to get to the hospital to see her. She hates hospitals. She's going to need some stuff taking up.'

Morgan stood up and crossed to the chair where Sam was sitting. She knelt down, taking hold of his hands.

'She died from her injuries, Sam. She sustained a massive head injury. I'm so sorry.' The words felt alien, as if she was speaking a different language, they felt so wrong on her tongue.

The man in front of her began shaking; the blood rushed from his face as the shock registered and he let out a small gasp falling forwards. Morgan tried to catch him, and they both ended up on the floor in a heap. She let out a screech.

'We need an ambulance.'

Ben was already on his radio asking the control room operator for paramedics. Trapped beneath Sam's dead weight, Morgan wanted to scream. Ben rushed over. Taking hold of Sam's arms he managed to manoeuvre him off Morgan. Sam's eyes were fixed in an expression of horror and sadness. He wasn't moving. Morgan began to check his airways so she could start CPR. There was nothing, but she didn't care, she couldn't leave him without at least trying. She began to do chest compressions, followed by two short breaths – still nothing. After five minutes, she heard Ben's voice.

'He's gone, Morgan, it's no use, he's dead.'

Morgan looked up at Ben, wild-eyed and bewildered. She turned back to the man on the floor and continued. Ben didn't try to stop her; she wouldn't even if he did. She might not have been able to save Brittany but she sure as hell would try and save her dad. She owed it to the pair of them to do her best.

CHAPTER FOUR

Morgan could have cried when the paramedics arrived. Her arms were aching, and she knew deep down that Sam was dead, but she couldn't seem to stop. This time Ben reached down and grabbed hold of her shoulder.

'Let the professionals do their job, Morgan.'

His hands were pulling her to her feet, and she felt herself standing up. Ben pulled her back so the paramedics could work on Sam in the tiny space they were all filling. Nick, one of the paramedics who had attended to Morgan a few times, turned his head to look at her.

'Sorry, there's nothing.'

Ben took over. She felt as if her mind had been completely blown. In less than an hour she had seen Brittany die and now her dad.

'Thank you.' Ben began to give them what scant details they had for Sam Alcott. Morgan looked around at the multitude of family photos of Sam and Ava, and Brittany, their only child, from childhood holidays to weddings, Brittany's university graduation and a photo of her with a group of teachers. Morgan recognised Andrea Hart standing next to Brittany. Her eyes filled with tears, and she turned to go outside; she couldn't cry in front of everyone despite her heart tearing in two with grief and sadness. She felt as if she was the grim reaper, maybe she should change her name to Officer Death. Outside, the sun had completely burned through the clouds, the mist had cleared; it was going to be a beautiful spring day. The kind of day that filled your heart with hope and your soul with joy that better days were coming after a long, dreary winter. The contrast between her feelings this morning as she'd drunk her morning coffee to now were like a huge, black chasm inside her chest. She walked towards the car, her eyes full of unshed tears for both Brittany and Sam.

Finally, a police van appeared at the corner of the street. Some student officer needed a sudden death to mark off their list of assignments, so they would take over here and accompany Sam to the mortuary. She felt exhausted beyond belief. Ben came out of the house and got into the driver's seat. Reaching out his hand he took hold of Morgan's.

'You're freezing.'

She nodded.

'That could have gone a lot better.'

Looking at him she couldn't believe the small chuckle that came out of her mouth and felt terrible, but then she laughed even louder, hysteria threatening to take over.

'Do you think so?'

'It's not our fault, Morgan, it's no one's fault. You didn't push Brittany out of that window, and you certainly didn't cause Sam's heart to decide to stop beating.'

'I know, but I still feel like shit.'

'Yeah, me too. Christ, it's not even dinner time and look at the carnage we've left in our wake.'

She smiled at him, but she couldn't make it reach her green eyes that usually crinkled and shone with mischief. She wondered if Ben had wished he'd died when Cindy had. The thought of her not ever knowing him gave her a cold shiver.

'Where are we going now?'

'Well, I guess we should go to Brittany's house and see if there's any evidence of drug taking there. There's nothing we can do here. Cain and his student are here to deal with the formalities.'

'I don't think she would have taken drugs, Ben, especially not before going to work. She works with kids, and that's not the Brittany I knew. She was always the sensible one: whenever we came up with really stupid ideas, she was the one to ask if we thought we were going to die or something. I feel awful. The last time I saw her was only for a fleeting chat. I didn't even know about her mum.'

'You're not a teenager any more, Morgan, with nothing to worry about other than your English homework. You're a busy person with a full-time job that takes up more of your spare time than it should. Brittany would have known that. I'm sure she was a busy woman herself.'

She nodded. 'She was the only one of my friendship circle to go to uni. The rest of us didn't bother. I went to college to get the exams to apply for this job but that was it. Most of them were working in Morrisons or Sainsbury's the last I'd heard.'

'Do you wish you hadn't become a police officer, Morgan?'

She shrugged. 'Today, yes. The day we had to deal with Charlie Standish's broken little body, no.'

'Why not when we found Charlie, what was so different then?'

'Because as sad and awful as that was, I knew I wanted to help her more than I could when she'd been alive. I knew we would find the person who did that to her, and I wanted to more than anything.'

He turned and smiled at her. 'Remember that, Morgan, remember that you do this because you want to help people when they can't help themselves and you'll be okay. Maybe you might need a stiff drink to help you blot out this morning when you go home tonight, but tomorrow you'll be ready again to help Brittany and find out what happened with her.'

'You should definitely write a motivational book for coppers; you know that it would be a bestseller.'

Ben chuckled. 'Somehow I doubt that, but thanks for the vote of confidence. Although I've always fancied myself as an author.'

*

They arrived at the quiet street where Brittany lived. There was a PCSO standing outside the garden gate. Ben stopped the car in front of her and they got out.

'Morning, Cathy, is anyone inside?'

She shook her head. 'No, apparently they all work at the school.'

'Do you know which is Brittany's bedroom?'

'No, my psychic abilities aren't turned on this morning. I was told to wait outside and not to let anyone in, although if she lives with two women it might be hard to figure out which is her room. Maybe look for the one with a little nameplate on it that says Brittany's Room.'

Morgan wasn't getting drawn into this conversation. She took the scene guard booklet from Cathy and signed them both in.

'Are we suiting and booting?'

'Gloves for now; if we find anything interesting then we'll suit up.'

Slipping on some blue nitrile gloves, Morgan let Ben lead the way. She was stalling for time. She didn't want to go in and start looking through Brittany's personal stuff. Ben turned to her as if sensing her reluctance.

'I can go in if you want to wait out here.'

She thought about it for a split second. 'No, I need to stop thinking of her as a teenager and do the only thing I can to help her now.'

He walked inside and she followed him into the gloomy hallway. The house smelt of stale curry and her stomach lurched a little.

'If I take a look down here, do you want to find her room?'

She didn't answer, instead she climbed the stairs; on the landing she could see four doors. All of them were closed except one, which was thrown wide open, and the room was in total disarray as if it had been ransacked. She walked towards it. Brittany had been acting strange, had she messed up her room like she had the staffroom? Stepping into the large double bedroom she looked at the row of framed photos on top of a pine dressing table. She was right: there smiling back at her was the same photograph from Sam's house of Brittany's graduation. Three beaming faces full of life stared out. She crossed towards it and picked it up. All of them were gone, wiped out in the blink of an eye. How cruel life could be at times. Placing it back down she looked around for any pills, baggies, wraps or bottles. There was a glass of water on the bedside table. No blister packs of tablets though. Morgan began to open drawers and rifle around to see if she could find anything. There was nothing, not even a packet of painkillers. She checked under the mattress and everywhere else she could think of where you could hide drugs. Satisfied that there wasn't anything, she went to the shared bathroom and began to look through the medicine cabinet which had an assortment of birth control pills, some condoms and two tubes of toothpaste. She had no reason to look in any of the other bedrooms, the other occupants weren't being investigated, but she couldn't help opening the doors to see what their bedrooms looked like. Both of these were the opposite to Brittany's: both beds were made, no clothes strewn across the floor. She closed them and went downstairs to where there were sounds of kitchen cupboards being opened and closed. As she walked in Ben turned to her, waving a small glass bottle full of dried herbs.

'Only weird thing I've found is this.' He unscrewed the lid and sniffed. 'What the hell is it? It stinks.'

Morgan felt a wave of dizziness come crashing over her. She knew exactly what that was. She had a very similar one in her cupboard at home. It was a jar of Ettie's herbal tea. Morgan's was to help her sleep; this one looked slightly different though. Ben stepped towards her, waving it under her nostrils.

'Sniff that, it's vile. What the hell do you think it is?'

Morgan shrugged and for the first time felt as if she didn't know what to do. She knew it was only harmless herbs picked from Ettie's garden and dried out, but when she told Ben he would have it bagged up and sent off to forensics. Then they would have to bring Ettie in for questioning because that was the nature of this job, and up to now this was the only thing they had found that was questionable, and she couldn't do that to her; she didn't want to do that to her. Finding her voice she whispered, 'It looks like herbal tea.'

'You're kidding me, this is drinkable? It smells disgusting. I bet it tastes even worse. Why the hell would anyone put themselves through that?'

'Because it's good for you. There are lots of health reasons.'

He grimaced. 'I think this would be the cause of health problems. I want it bagging up. Where the hell did it come from?'

Morgan's chest felt tight, her heart was racing and she knew she should tell him. But she knew Ettie wouldn't give someone anything harmful on purpose. A voice whispered *are you sure about that? After all it can run in the family.* Morgan let out a gasp, and Ben turned to stare at her.

'What's up?'

It was no good, she couldn't lie to him, and she was sure this could all be cleared up in no time at all.

'I know where the tea comes from.'

'You do?'

She nodded, feeling miserable, as if she was about to commit the ultimate betrayal, but where did her loyalty lie? To her job, to Brittany and Sam, or to Ettie, her long-lost aunt?

CHAPTER FIVE

Ben parked in the small public car park which led onto Covel Woods, he had insisted on speaking to Ettie about the contents of the jar. Neither of them had spoken much since Morgan had told him where she thought the tea came from. She felt awful, she didn't want to do this, but Ettie couldn't possibly be the reason that Brittany had jumped out of the window. She had been giving away or selling herbal teas and remedies for years without anyone coming to any harm but there was this niggling feeling inside her that was making her doubt all of the above facts, unless something toxic had got into it accidentally. She got out of the car, slamming the door a little too hard. The noise echoed around the trees, sending a group of birds squawking and screeching into the air.

'I'll let you lead the way.'

She glared at him. 'I don't actually know if I'll find it from here. I only found it by accident when I was at the Potters' house across the river.'

'Surely, it's not that difficult to locate. How many houses are there in these woods? I didn't think they were particularly big.'

She felt miserable and wished she hadn't told him now or at least asked him if she could do something else and let Amy attend with him. There was a wooden style that she climbed over. A number of small paths led away from it into the woods, and she took the one which might lead to the river, not that she knew if it did; she was completely guessing. If she found the river she could follow it upstream to where Ettie's fairy-tale cottage was, with its lilac front door and a drystone wall surrounding the herb garden. She hadn't been here for a while, and she wondered how Ettie was and if she was going to be furious with her for even asking her about the jar of tea. She charged on ahead of Ben, whose leather loafers were struggling to keep up with her sturdy Dr Martens. After ten minutes Morgan realised she was getting hot and out of breath, although not as out of breath as Ben who sounded as if he was wheezing behind her. She paused, waiting for him to catch up, and heard the sound of water babbling in the distance.

'Do you even know where you're going, Morgan? I don't have time to spend hours tramping through the undergrowth. Or even worse getting lost. We'll be the laughing stock of the station.'

'Yes, actually I do.' She sounded a lot more confident than she felt, but she continued until she reached the riverbank and breathed a sigh of relief. It was uphill from here, so they had to come across the cottage sooner or later. She heard Ben let out a huff from behind her and ignored him, forging ahead now, determined to find it and not let him think she didn't have a clue when actually she didn't.

*

A faint whiff of acrid, bitter smoke filled the air, and Morgan hurried even faster until she saw a thin grey plume rising through the tops of the large oak trees and knew she was almost there. Her legs were aching from the uphill climb wearing heavy boots. As the cottage came into view a sinking feeling filled her stomach. She didn't wait for Ben to catch up. She wanted to warn Ettie they were here. She pushed open the gate. A huge raven was perched on the kitchen windowsill, and she smiled to see it staring back at her. Not in the least bit interested or intimidated by the panting stranger, instead it bent its head and began to pick at its feathers, cleaning itself. Before she could knock on the door, Ettie opened it. She stood there smiling at Morgan, her arms open wide. Morgan smiled back and stepped into them for the biggest, warmest hug she'd had in a very long time. It felt so good, and it made her feel even worse for the havoc she was about to wreak on this lovely woman.

'Well, I thought my eyes were deceiving me but no it's definitely you. Come in, sweetheart, and tell me how you are.'

Ettie let her go and stepped back just as Ben made it to the gate of the cottage. Her head tilted and she frowned, glancing at Morgan who cast her eyes towards the floor, too embarrassed to even know where to begin.

'You brought company. Haven't we met before? Is he your supervisor?'

'Yes, Ettie, this is Sergeant Ben Matthews.'

Ben held out his hand. 'Hello, it's great to see you.'

By the look on Ettie's face Morgan could tell she didn't share the same sentiment.

'Well, you both better come inside and tell me what this is about. I get the feeling this isn't a social visit.'

Morgan followed her into the cramped living room full of books and shelves of herbs in jars similar to the one inside the evidence bag that Ben had in his pocket.

'Please sit down whilst I put the kettle on. You have time for a drink, don't you, after your walk through the woods to get here.'

'Thank you, that would be great.'

'Sit yourselves down then and catch your breath. I'm not sure which way you came but by the look of you I think you took a detour around Heron Pike to get here.'

Morgan laughed. 'I got lost.'

Ben stared at her. 'I knew you had, but you kept on as if you knew where you were going. I wondered why it took so long to get here.'

Ettie winked at Morgan. 'You made it, quit complaining.'

Ben laughed. 'Yes, we did. Eventually.'

'So, are you going to tell me why you are here, or do I have to get out my crystal ball and guess?'

Morgan looked at Ben, she didn't want to be the one to do this, and he nodded.

'There's been a very serious incident today: a teacher from Priory Grove threw herself out of the staffroom window.'

Ettie turned to face them in slow motion, her hand covering her mouth as she whispered. 'Brittany?'

'How could you know that?'

She blinked a couple of times, dabbing the corner of her eye with the end of the apron she was wearing.

'She came to see me a few times about a herbal remedy for the stomach aches she was having. I can't imagine why else you would be here. She's the only teacher from the school I've seen these last few months. What happened to her? Is she okay?'

'I'm afraid not, she suffered fatal injuries. We found a jar of tea in her kitchen, and I needed to ask you what was in it.' Ben tugged the plastic evidence bag from his pocket and placed it on the pine tea chest that served as a coffee table.

Ettie shook her head, her eyes moist with tears. 'That poor girl. I can tell you exactly what is in it. I can also tell you that there is nothing inside it to make her throw herself out of a window. It is purely to ease the symptoms of bloated stomach and bowel problems.'

Ben smiled at her, and Morgan could tell that despite himself he liked Ettie. She felt relieved, but she knew it wouldn't stop him from taking it further. Ettie turned back to the boiling kettle, and they waited for her to make the pot of tea. She carried a tray over and put it on the chest. There were three mugs, a milk jug and sugar bowl. She pointed to it, and Morgan busied herself pouring out tea for her and Ben. She passed one to Ben, who took a sip.

'Can you tell me what's in it?'

She crossed to the shelves, running her finger along the glass jars until she reached one and plucked it from the shelf. Turning to face them she crossed the room and passed it to Ben.

'This is the exact same one that I gave to Brittany. I always make up three batches whenever anyone asks for something specific. That way if they come back for more I have it ready prepared. Inside this one is a mixture of belladonna leaves, mugwort, camomile and lemon, to take away some of the bitterness. It is beneficial to those suffering from stomach cramps, bloating and irritable bowel problems. The belladonna and mugwort are very good at soothing bowel spasms, which is what Brittany came to me for. She'd been having problems for some time which conventional medication wasn't helping with.'

Ben nodded. 'Do a lot of people come to you for your tea? I don't mean to be rude but that one smells awful.'

She smiled. 'You'd be surprised how many people like my special blends of tea. They are purely medicinal and yes this one does smell a bit odd, but I suggest adding a slice of lemon at the same time as the leaves are being steeped, to add a little burst of something tarty to take away the smell. When you're desperate and have tried everything for a problem, then drinking a small cup of tea in the morning or before bed to help rid you of those pesky symptoms is a small price to pay.'

She never once acknowledged that she'd given Morgan a tea to help her sleep, and Morgan felt a fierce loyalty towards her aunt. She wanted to stop Ben's questions, but she knew that someone was going to have to ask them, and it was better it was him.

'What other kinds of tea do you make?'

Morgan glanced at him, realising he was being genuine and not sarcastic.

Ettie stood up and walked back to her impressive glass jars full of an assortment of dried herbs and flowers.

'Lavender tea to help with sleep; rose tea for confidence, love and luck – that is my bestselling tea; it's amazing how many people come to me for that. Strawberry leaf tea is also very popular in aiding with luck and fertility; apple tea for creativity and abundance. I have a feeling this one will be taking off very soon now that everyone and their dog are getting on the manifesting your soul's desires boat. The list is endless. I also prepare more prescriptive teas, like Brittany asked for, to help with medical problems.'

'Wow, that's impressive and do all your customers have to come trailing on a five-mile hike to buy it?'

She tutted loudly. 'Only the ones who are in need of serious help.' Her eyes fell on Morgan then looked directly back at Ben. 'Of course not. I have a stall on Kendal market every fourth Saturday, and there's a small gift shop on Finkle Street that carries a selection. People know where to find me if they need me in between.'

'Oh, that's very good. Well I'll have to send this off to be forensically examined. I hope you can understand that I mean no disrespect to you, but according to witnesses Brittany was acting completely out of character, as if she was on drugs, and this is the only thing we found inside her house that is questionable.'

Ettie shrugged. 'You must do what you must, detective, but I have been making herbal tea for over forty years and have had no complaints or anything like this happen up to now.'

Morgan interrupted, 'And I'm sure that this has absolutely nothing to do with the tea, Ettie, we are just following procedure and wanted to let you know. Thank you for being so open and honest with us. How are you, have you heard from...?'

She couldn't say his name; every time she tried it felt as if the words were too heavy for her tongue to pronounce. Ettie was shaking her head.

'I was good until you broke the news about poor Brittany, and as for my brother I haven't heard a peep. Let's just hope it stays that way. Have you heard from him, dear?'

It was Morgan's turn to shake her head.

'Good, he's bad news. Now, will there be anything else?'

Ben put his mug down and stood up. 'No, not at the moment. Thanks for talking to us and thank you for the tea.'

Ettie beamed at him. 'You're very welcome and see, it didn't taste too bad, did it? You didn't even notice that wasn't a cup of Yorkshire Tea.'

Morgan glanced at Ben and watched as the colour drained from his face as he stared down at the almost empty mug, then looked up at Ettie who began to laugh, a real belly laugh that made Morgan chuckle.

Ettie shook her head. 'I'm kidding, honestly your face is a picture. What's the matter, did you think I'd poisoned you like some wicked witch from a fairy tale?'

He leaned down, grabbing the evidence bag whilst visibly trying to compose himself, and Morgan felt bad that she was grinning at his discomfort. She turned and walked out of the front door. Ben followed but she heard Ettie's voice as she whispered to him, 'I'm sorry, that was a poor joke. If you'd like something to help you with the weight of that grief that you carry around with you, I do have something that could assist with that, and it tastes quite nice too.'

They were outside in the garden now; Ettie was standing in the doorway. She smiled and nodded at Morgan then closed the door gently. Ben was staring towards the door, his mouth open. The raven was still perched on the windowsill, watching them. He let out a loud squawk and then took off into the air, his wings flapping magnificently as he soared higher and higher. Ben turned to Morgan.

'What the hell was that about?'

'She's good, she knows things. Maybe you should take her up on that offer?'

'What, and end up jumping out of the canteen window at the nick? No thanks, I'm okay. Did you tell her about Cindy?'

His tone was accusing, and Morgan felt a spark of anger ignite inside her chest at the cheek of his suggestion that she spoke about him on such a personal level.

'No, I did not. I told you she's very intuitive and knows things. It's just the way she is.'

He shook his head and began walking in the opposite direction to the one she had brought them, and Morgan followed, hoping that this was a quicker way to get to the car because she needed something to eat before she passed out with exhaustion.

CHAPTER SIX

2016

Brittany smacked her lips together and pouted once more. Her birthday present from Sienna, the nude MAC lip gloss, looked amazing. She had no idea how her friend could have afforded it and wondered if it was stolen. Sienna was quite the magpie, but who was she to question its origin when she loved it so much? As soon as she was old enough she was going to get lip fillers so she had a pout worth posting on Instagram. She was almost ready to go camping, but there was just one problem with her plans for the night which included hiking up to Rydal Caves with a tent, a bottle of vodka, a sleeping bag and her friends from school. Although it had been warm today she knew it would be really cold tonight, but they had planned this night forever and it was what she had wanted for her birthday present more than anything. Her group of friends, together to party, where there were no strict parents to spoil things. It was the last Friday of the Easter holidays; they would all be back to school on Monday and then the exams would start. They might not be all together in school ever again because all five of them had taken different options and their exams were on different days. Brittany wanted to be a primary school teacher; Sienna wanted to be a police officer, although God knows why she'd want to do that. Morgan wanted to join the police too; personally, Brittany couldn't think of a worse job than having to deal with drunks and dead people all the time. Brad wanted to be

a professional rugby player. He was pretty good, and she thought
he'd look amazing in the England kit one day. Everyone fancied
Brad, he was funny; his brown hair was very similar to Harry
Styles's, although he wouldn't admit he probably went to the barber
and asked for a similar cut and blow dry. He was kind, and always
stuck up for his friends. Brittany pretended she didn't fancy him,
but she did, although not as much as Sienna who was obsessed
with him. Out of all their friends, though, it was Morgan who
Brad tended to drift towards. Yet she was the most different out of
them. They were all into the Kardashians, and Morgan was more
The Craft: she always wore black and a pair of Dr Martens. They all
paid a fortune to have long, wavy curls, and she straightened her
natural red hair to get rid of her curls. By rights they were polar
opposites. Morgan always had her nose in a book and generally
one about some awful, sick American serial killer, while the rest
of them swooned over celebrity fashions in *Heat*, *Hello!* and *Elle*
magazines. But Brittany liked Morgan. She didn't pretend to fit in,
she was just herself, and Brittany felt sorry for her after her mum
had been found dead. Much to the disgust of the others at first, she
had taken Morgan under her wing, bringing her into their small
group. The big problem was that Brad also liked her more than
the rest of them, and it had Sienna, Jessica and Lara all frothing
at the mouth, they were so jealous. But she knew that Morgan
wasn't aware of any of this; in fact she was pretty oblivious to boys
in general and it had crossed Brittany's mind that maybe as well
as being a Goth she might be more drawn to girls than boys. Not
that it mattered to Brittany, and she was pretty sure if that was
the case then the others would be relieved they could fight over
Brad between themselves.

She had already stashed her backpack, tent and sleeping bag in
Sienna's shed a few days ago, as well as some warmer clothes. She
gave one last twirl in the mirror, blew herself another kiss and ran
downstairs.

'Oh, look at you. You look beautiful, Brittany. I hope whoever you've gone to all this trouble for appreciates it.'

'Mum, I haven't gone to any trouble. I always look like this but thanks for the compliment.'

Her mum laughed. 'You know what I mean, you look far too nice for a sleepover at Sienna's house, that's all. Is Brad going to be there? I hope he isn't sleeping over too?'

'As if, Sienna's mum would go mental. She's stricter than you and Dad. No boys allowed in her house; God would be mortified.'

'Brittany, don't be mean. She's a lovely woman. She just has a stronger bond towards God than most of us. I hope you don't say anything like that to Sienna.'

'You should hear what Sienna says about her, it's definitely not very Christian like.'

'Well, have a lovely evening. I suppose if you're at Sienna's house there won't be any alcohol involved, so I don't have to worry about that. Did you like your presents, love? I'm sorry we couldn't get you the Chanel bag of your dreams, but it costs the same price as a second-hand car and well, you know we don't have that kind of money spare.'

'I love them, thank you. Michael Kors bags are just as good, and I was only joking when I said about the Chanel bag. One day when I'm working I'll buy us both one.'

Her mum laughed. 'You better get a bloody good job then, love. Have a good night. I'm going to catch up on my soaps before your dad gets home from work. I might even have a glass of wine. Do you need picking up or are you definitely sleeping over?'

She crossed the room and hugged her mum. 'I'm definitely staying over, have a bottle of wine.'

Kissing her mum's cheek, she grabbed her jacket and left her, excited to be free for the night. Not that her mum was too bad; it was her dad that was really strict, and she just wanted a bit of freedom from being watched all the time.

CHAPTER SEVEN

Alan, Mike and Dave had decided upon a gentle ramble today because Dave had sprained his ankle two weeks ago on their descent down Heron Pike and done nothing but complain about it. They decided on a leisurely walk from the north side of Loughrigg Fell to Rydal Caves. It was just under five kilometres and Alan was hoping Dave would manage without grumbling too much. As they rounded the path, the opening of the cave came into view. The shallow lake in front of the opening to the cave made for a picture-perfect photograph, and he lifted the camera from around his neck to take some shots. Dave and Mike sat down on a patch of grass, and he could hear them unzipping bags containing their packed lunches. As he zoomed into the entrance to the cave he paused, what was that? Lifting the camera away from his eyes he squinted to see if he could see it. He could make out the pale figure of a woman as she stumbled out of the entrance to the cave. She was holding on to the side of the dark, grey slate walls and she was naked. He felt a rush of warmth as his cheeks turned red, and he turned to the others.

'Hey, can you see a naked woman in the entrance to the cave?'

Mike and Dave burst out laughing; Mike guffawed. 'You bloody wish there was a naked woman. What's up? Debs not letting you have any fun?'

'Arsehole, I'm being serious.'

He lifted his camera and zoomed in, then quickly put it down again. She was definitely naked apart from a pair of pink knickers and matching socks. Where were her clothes? It was a lovely spring day, but it wasn't that bloody warm.

'Look, there she is on the right-hand side. She's clinging on to the side as if she's scared or something.'

Both Dave and Mike stood up. They stood next to him, and Dave muttered, 'Jesus Christ, what's she doing? Where are her clothes?'

They turned to look at each other. 'What are we supposed to do? Maybe she's a model on a photoshoot or something?' offered Mike.

'There's one small problem with that, where's the photographer?'

Mike shrugged. 'No idea, but do you think she's okay? What is she doing?'

Alan didn't know, but he did know that they couldn't leave without at least asking if she was okay.

'We can't leave her like that.'

'It's none of our business, Alan, some things are best left alone.'

He turned to look at Dave. 'Seriously, what if she's in trouble? She might need help.'

'And she might start screaming blue murder if you go by her.'

'We should leave.' Alan turned to Mike.

'I can't, not without at least asking if she needs help.'

He took off his camera and turned it on to record, passing it to Mike.

'Just record me, so if anything happens we can show the police that we were trying to help her.'

Dave and Mike shrugged. Mike took it from him, and Alan began walking towards her.

'Hello, are you okay? Do you need help?' He wondered if she had had an accident or maybe got lost. As he got closer he could hear her mumbling. She was facing the wall, her cheek pressed against the cool, damp slate.

'Hi, I'm Alan. I just wanted to see if you were okay. Do you need a hand?'

She turned her head slowly to look at him, and he realised that she wasn't very old. She also looked as if she didn't understand a word he was saying to her. Her eyes were darting from side to side, and she had a look of what he could only describe as wild etched across her face.

He waved at her, making sure he kept looking at her face and not anywhere else.

'Where're your clothes, lovey? It's not warm enough to be undressed. Are you lost?'

She let out a loud screech, making Alan jump and slip off the dark green, mossy stepping stone he was balanced on. He landed with a loud splash, feet first, in the shallow lake and swore loudly as the freezing water began seeping into his boots and up his trouser leg. The girl then turned back to the wall and began to scramble back inside the cave, leaving him standing there wondering what the hell had just happened. Behind him he could hear Mike and Dave laughing at his misfortune, and he turned around to face them. Giving them the finger, he stepped out of the icy water back onto one of the stepping stones and squelched his way back towards them and their laughter.

'That was class. I have it all on camera. You shit yourself, Alan, when she screamed.'

'Sod off. I'm phoning the police. She needs help, and I'm not chasing her into the cave.'

He sat down on the grass, took out his phone and dialled 999. He didn't know if this qualified as an emergency, but something was seriously wrong, and he didn't want to see her get hurt. When he finished explaining to the voice on the end of the phone exactly what his emergency was he felt stupid. Dave and Mike were still sniggering, a lot quieter than before, but he was now so annoyed with them when he ended the call he looked up and said, 'Grow up, you goons, it's not funny at all.'

They must have realised how angry he was because they both did shut up, and Alan hoped it wouldn't take the police forever to get here, although it was quite some distance from the roadside. All he could do was keep watch and hope she was okay whatever she was doing inside that cold, damp cave.

CHAPTER EIGHT

Morgan and Ben had made it back to the car in a quarter of the time it had taken them to reach Ettie's cottage. Neither of them spoke. Morgan's radio, which she had left in the glovebox, came to life as an emergency call for Rydal Caves came over the airwaves. She looked at Ben, hoping he'd say yes. He hadn't teased her about his way back being quicker, so she didn't feel quite so annoyed with him.

'We could go to that, we're probably the nearest patrol.'

'We could, but we're not.'

'Why? It's an immediate response.'

'We have too much on.'

'Please, I hate to think of someone needing help and we didn't go.'

'Morgan, you drive me insane at times but yes, you're right.'

The control room operator put out a call for the nearest patrols to start making their way; the only problem was the nearest patrol was at least twenty minutes away. He shook his head but started the engine, and she picked up her radio.

'Control, show myself and DS Matthews on route. We're around six minutes away from the road nearest the cave then another ten-minute walk.'

'Brilliant, thank you. If you can make your way another patrol will back you up.'

Morgan put the radio into her jacket pocket and glanced in Ben's direction. He was all over the place today, and she didn't know if it was just with her or the world in general.

'Thank you.'

'For what?'

'For agreeing to go. I know you don't want to.'

'Morgan, stop. I'm sorry, I'm not mad at you, I'm just having a crappy day, okay, and you're right, it's our job to go. I wasn't thinking straight.'

She nodded and looked out of the window. The scenery was a passing blur of green because he was driving a lot faster than anyone should in a Vauxhall Corsa around winding country roads. Without realising it she'd clenched hold of the car seat, her knuckles white, to keep herself from flying all over the place as he took the sharp twists and turns to reach the small car park near the scene. Abandoning the car at the side of a grass verge in the car park, they got out and began to hurry along the footpath to the caves. Morgan took the lead; she knew the way there blindfolded, as she'd spent a lot of evenings here with the small group of friends she hung around with at secondary school. It was where they came to drink and smoke without the worry of getting caught. The memory made her think of Brittany. And Brad. She pushed the thought aside.

'Do you think it's a bit weird?'

'What?'

'Another call about a woman acting strange in the space of a few hours? Despatch said she's been reported as naked and had run into the caves. That's not normal behaviour.'

Ben paused for a moment, and she looked behind to see his cheeks were red and he was breathing heavily. This was a steep rocky path and it wasn't the easiest to climb in a hurry. He nodded. 'Just a bit, but you know how this goes. You get one road traffic accident and then the next few jobs are all accidents, a sudden death and another two or three come in one after the other. Maybe it's that kind of day.'

She didn't answer; instead she carried on, picking up the pace even more. There was this lead ball which seemed to have formed in the pit of her stomach since the scene this morning, making it difficult to breathe. She had a bad feeling about this, a really bad feeling. She rounded the corner and saw three men all standing around looking in the direction of the dark mouth of the open cave, and her mind flashed back to her teenage years and to Brad, who had been found dead on the rocks just in front of her. She pushed that memory away again; she needed to focus on what was happening now.

'Detective Brookes,' she gasped. She was breathing hard. It wasn't easy climbing and running in Dr Martens. All three men turned to stare at her, and the youngest of them pointed to the cave.

'I have no idea what she's doing in there, but she ran away screaming, and I didn't want to scare her any more than we already did. Are you really a detective?'

Resisting the temptation to roll her eyes she nodded, then carried on walking towards the stepping stones that led into the cave.

'Be careful on those stones they're really slimy. Mind you don't slip.'

She glanced back at the man who had just asked her if she was a detective and nodded her appreciation, noticing that his trousers were soaking wet, just as Ben came crashing around the corner. He stopped at the group of men, bending double to try and catch his breath. Morgan leapt onto the first stone; there were an assortment of sizes leading into the entrance. Morgan took a large step onto the second one, and Ben, who must have recovered sufficiently to talk, shouted.

'Morgan, wait for patrols.'

She didn't turn around. They had no idea how long another patrol was going to be, and she didn't want to waste any time. An image of Brittany's broken, bleeding body lying on the tarmac in the school playground filled her mind. She had no idea what was going on here, but she wasn't about to let another person get hurt if she could help them. As she got nearer to the large black opening, she shouted, 'Police, are you okay? We're here to help you.'

There was no reply apart from the sound of her own voice as it echoed back towards her. She knew Ben was going to be furious with her and then she heard a loud thud as he landed on the stones behind her. Stepping off the large flat stone she balanced on the smaller ones and deftly moved from one to the other until she was at the entrance of the dark cave. Morgan ran inside. There was no noise from the outside world: no birds chirping, no sounds of Ben's breathing behind her, nothing could penetrate the oppressive darkness that waited inside except for the drip, drip of water as it ran down the slate walls of the cavern. It didn't bother her; she liked the dark and had always enjoyed the solitude it brought her. And she knew these caves well from her younger days. There was another, smaller one situated further back, past the pool of stagnant water that was alive with insects skimming across the surface. She carried on walking around the edge of the cave when she heard a dull splash. Ahead of her through a sliver of light she saw a partially naked woman's body lying face down in the water. Forgetting all about trying to stop her feet from getting wet she took the quickest way to get to her and splashed into the perishing water. It quickly seeped through her boots, soaking her feet, but she carried on until she reached the woman. She bent down, grabbing her as best as she could under her arms and dragging her out of the black water. The woman was a dead weight, and Morgan was struggling when all of a sudden another pair of hands were there, ready to carry her and Morgan realised that Ben was here helping.

'We need to get her out of this cold and into the sunlight.'

She nodded, agreeing with him. They couldn't leave her in here, on the wet slate floor that was absolutely freezing. Between them they managed to hike her up and carry her roughly out of the cave, trying their best to keep her already frozen body out of the pool of water. They splashed through it and were rewarded by the feel of the warm midday sun as they neared the entrance to the cave. Morgan felt a burst of energy course through her. There was no way they could balance the woman on the stepping stones: they were going to have to wade through the water. Suddenly she heard splashing as the three men who had watched her go inside all waded in to help them carry the woman to safety. When they reached the side, they laid her gently down and Morgan quickly shrugged off her jacket, covering her as best as she could. Alan did the same, passing his coat to Morgan who spread it across her lower body. It was only when she looked at the pale face that Morgan recoiled in shock.

'Oh my God, I know her. It's Sienna Waters.' She knelt down next to her and felt for a pulse. There was one, but it was weak. Reaching out she pressed the palm of her hand against Sienna's head and then snatched her hand back. The skin on her forehead was burning hot despite the fact that the rest of her body was covered in goosebumps.

'We need paramedics. What's going on, Ben? First Brittany and now Sienna?'

'How do you know her?'

'From school.' She looked up at him. She knew she was panicking; she could feel her heart beating way too fast.

'We were all in the same friendship circle; Brittany and Sienna were really close.'

More heavy footsteps sounded along the path and two uniformed officers appeared, as out of breath as Morgan and Ben were.

'Paramedics are on the way. How are we getting her to the car park?'

Ben shook his head. 'We can't carry her, it's a long way and far too dangerous.'

'One of you needs to go back and bring the paramedics here. Once they've assessed her they can get the air ambulance travelling.'

Morgan was staring at Sienna's face. She looked as if it was already too late, and a cold fear lodged itself at the base of her spine. What had happened today to make two women act this way? How had one of her old friends ended up dead and another unconscious? And why was she here, in the place they'd found Brad's broken body? None of this made any sense. There had been three more including herself in that circle. Was someone trying to tell them something? She didn't know but she was going to do her best to find out.

CHAPTER NINE

They made a sombre party on the descent back to White Moss car park. The paramedics had said they had no idea what was wrong with Sienna, and because she was unresponsive they had intubated her and an air ambulance was now flying her to the nearest hospital, Westmoreland General, in Kendal. When they reached their cars, the two officers left to greet the air ambulance at the hospital, leaving Morgan and Ben still trying to figure out what had just happened. The three guys who had found Sienna were huddled in a group by a car.

'We better get brief statements before they disappear.'

Ben shook his head. 'No, get their names, addresses and phone numbers. We'll send officers to get formal statements if we need to; hopefully, she'll make a full recovery, and this will all be fine.'

Morgan didn't argue. Taking statements was time-consuming, and if she'd thought she was hungry when she left Ettie's cottage, after that mammoth hike to and from Rydal Caves in record time, she was near enough done.

'Good, because I stink like someone who doesn't know what deodorant is, and I'm famished.'

Ben laughed and his eyes crinkled at the sides, which she loved. The dark cloud that had been hanging over him since this morning seemed to have lifted, despite them dealing with two sudden deaths and now this. Morgan joined in and the group of men turned to look at them, then turned away quickly. Which made her laugh even more. Ben crossed towards the car. 'Come on, sweaty Brookes, let's get you freshened up.'

'I'll just grab their details.' She headed over to the men, keeping a bit of distance between them in case they could smell her as well, although she did think she might be being a touch oversensitive.

'Thanks again for phoning it in and making sure she was okay, that's very good of you. Can I get your details? Officers may need to come and see you to take a statement if that's okay.'

All three nodded. It was Alan who seemed to be the general spokesperson for the group.

'I really hope she's okay. If we hadn't been there, who knows how long she would have lain in that cave? Hypothermia would have set in pretty quick, it's so cold and damp in there, and where were her clothes? Did you spot any inside or do you think she got undressed on the way to it?'

Morgan could have kicked herself. Of course, where were her clothes? She hadn't even looked around in the cave; she'd been so worried about getting her out of there and medical attention.

'I don't know, but we'll be looking into it.'

She listed down each of their details. 'Thank you.'

Then she walked back to the car where Ben was on the phone. She opened the passenger door and leaned inside. She knew he was talking to Amy; she could hear her voice on the other end. When he ended the call he looked at her.

'Get in then.'

'I can't.'

'Why not?'

'She was naked, Ben. We forgot about that; we were so busy trying to save her. But why was she wandering around a cave in her panties and socks? Where the hell are her clothes? I'll have to go back and have a look before other walkers arrive and begin tramping all over it. What if it's a crime scene?'

She shut the door, let out a sigh and headed back in the direction they'd not long come from. As she reached the path to the bridge through the second set of woods she'd been in today, she heard a car door slam shut and footsteps behind her. Morgan turned and smiled at Ben who was shaking his head.

'Every bloody time we leave the station together, I could put a bet on at the bookies that it all goes tits up, Morgan. Why is that?'

She grinned at him but carried on walking in her squelching boots, ignoring the dull ache in her legs as she made her way back up the path towards Rydal Caves.

*

She left Ben trailing behind, thinking that if she got up there first she could meet him on the way back down. There were a few more people on the path now and she wondered if they should be sealing it off as a crime scene. But there was no sign of any foul play when they'd first arrived, it was literally just Sienna collapsing. Self-inflicted, drug-induced behaviour maybe? Perhaps she and Brittany had both taken something to cause this. Then she remembered they'd found no evidence except for Ettie's herbal tea. Christ, she hoped that they wouldn't find any of that at Sienna's home if they had cause to search it. That would be awful, for them, her and Ettie. She reached the crest of the hill, crunching her way through the slate and rocks to get to the entrance before the family with four kids that was trailing behind her did. Out of breath, she looked around to see if there were any clothes, but she couldn't see anything. Once more she stepped onto the large flat stepping stones, crossing quickly because at this point her feet and boots were so wet it didn't matter if she slipped in the water. She strode from stone to stone and jumped off the last one, landing in the water with a loud splash. Then she was on the dry stone floor of the cave using the torch on her phone. She looked around: there were no discarded items of clothing, no shoes, nothing. She snapped photos of every part of the cave, then she hit the record button to take a video she could show them at the station if she needed to. The only thing in this cave was a duck perched on one of the large stones protruding out of the shallow pool, watching her with its head tilted to one side. She smiled at it. 'Hey, did you see where that woman put her clothes?' The duck looked away from her, bored.

'Why don't you bring it in for questioning?'

Ben's voice echoed around the cave behind her, and she turned to look at him. His cheeks were flushed with the exertion of climbing the steep path for the second time, and she laughed.

He perched on a large piece of slate, loosened his tie and shrugged off his suit jacket, undoing the top three buttons of his crisp white shirt. She had to look away as she wondered what it would be like to undo the rest of them for him.

'I went to school with Sienna as well. She was in my group of friends until she fell out with us all.'

'I'd hate to be a teenager again, although it wasn't too bad for me. I loved rugby so it kept me on the straight and narrow, but the raging hormones and spots were a nightmare.'

She laughed. 'Yeah, I can't say I particularly enjoyed it. I was a little bit out of most people's comfort zone; I was a bit of a Goth, and they were more like the Barbie dolls, but we got on okay.'

Ben laughed. 'You were a Goth? I'd never have guessed.' He laughed ironically as his gaze cast down towards her sodden boots. 'I like that about you though, Brookes, you're not afraid to trail your own path. Mind you, it gives me heartburn at times, not to mention shooting pains in my chest, but...'

'But you get to work with me, so totally worth it, yeah?'

'I suppose so. Right then, what now?'

'I guess we go back to the station.'

'You don't want to scour the fells looking for our victim's clothes? Although I have no idea if she is a victim or what the hell happened here to be honest.'

'No, but don't you think it's strange? Where are they? Did she really wander up here naked with no one seeing her?'

He shrugged. 'Your guess is as good as mine. Maybe she's been up here for hours, wandering around.'

'Surely, she drove here. She must have a car in the car park. How many cars were there when we arrived?'

'I'm not going to lie, Morgan; I didn't even look.'

'Come on, we can go back and check to see how many there are and PNC them.'

'I love your enthusiasm; I honestly think it's refreshing.'

'But?'

'Nothing, I'm just stating the obvious. For the record I'm also knackered, hungry and thirsty. Write down their vehicle registrations and you can PNC them back at the station.'

She held out her hand and he took hold of it, then she heaved him to his feet and they began to make their way back down Loughrigg Fell once more.

CHAPTER TEN

Ettie picked up the basket she used for gathering herbs and flowers, pushed her feet into her fur lined boots to protect them from the nettles and brambles in the woods, and left her cottage. She hadn't been able to settle since Morgan had left. She didn't like that the police had come calling to question her about her herbal teas and what she put into them. That was her business, not theirs. As she closed the gate behind her, she heard the swooping of wings and saw her pet raven land on a tree in the distance, watching her. He wasn't actually her pet; he was a wild bird, but for some reason he spent an awful lot of time perched on her windowsill. On the days the weather was much cooler she would leave it open for him, and he would sometimes hop inside and sit on the ledge. He never moved off it. He didn't fly around the cottage or make a mess. He just liked to sit there in the warmth and watch her. She didn't mind. He was a handsome bird and very good company. He never complained about her chattering to him. She knew what they thought of her in Rydal Falls, that she was some kind of witch or crazy woman, and she didn't care. She supposed she *was* a witch of some sorts, but all she did was try to help people with her teas and crystals. A few kind words here and there made all the difference. It was what the world was sadly lacking in: compassion and kindness seemed to be in very short supply. Making her way through the woods along the narrow path that got smaller the deeper she went, she found herself in the small clearing where the muted sunlight broke through the dense shade of the huge beech trees and the beautiful but deadly belladonna plants thrived. She stood and looked around, something felt off, had someone been here messing around with things they shouldn't? It was possible. She was good at reading people's tea leaves and sometimes their minds, but she wasn't very good at detecting if they had been trespassing where they didn't belong. It didn't seem as if anything was out of place, though; there were no trampled plants, and it didn't look as if there were any missing. Good, because this was all hers. Only she knew about the dangers of these particular plants, which were deadly if consumed in the wrong amount. Tugging on a pair of thick leather gloves, she busied herself picking some of the leaves and big, juicy dark berries on the plants that were nearest to her. Even the leaves could sometimes have a nasty effect on you, and she didn't have time to become ill.

Standing up, she noticed something white flapping in the distance. Her eyes followed the movement and she realised it was a piece of material. She made her way around the periphery of the clearing until she reached the tree with the low branches that it was caught on. She realised it was a white T-shirt that was now ripped along the short sleeve. Leaning forward she plucked it from the branch and threw it into her basket. What was the world coming to? First of all the police were hanging around, pointing fingers and all but accusing her of poisoning someone, and now there was a discarded woman's T-shirt in her sacred clearing? Turning, she began to walk back to her cottage, feeling a little angry that this item of clothing had been left so casually, discarded without a thought. It was fresh, she knew this because it was still dry and very clean.

Back at her cottage she went into the kitchen and began pulling the fresh berries from the plants. She liked to dry the leaves and berries separately. Ettie worked quickly, a feeling of uneasiness settling over her like a heavy cloak and she knew it was the item of clothing she'd picked up from the clearing. It was giving off a bad vibe very similar to the woman who had come to see her a few weeks ago. She had turned up out of the blue and asked for help, begging her for a spell to make her true love fall madly in love with her. Ettie had to send her on her way; the darkness in her aura had scared her a lot more than she would readily admit. She had only ever seen one other aura so black it was like an empty void and that had been the one surrounding her brother, Gary, on the day he was led into court. Ettie believed this darkness around them meant that their souls were no longer present. She shuddered, staring at the T-shirt she had draped on the back of the chair. She knew it might be of some importance, what for she had no idea, but she could not, no she would not have that thing inside her house. Taking a brown paper bag from out of the cupboard, she picked it up and deposited it inside, then she took it outside and put the bag on a hook in her small shed out the back of her cottage. Closing the door, she went back inside and instantly felt better. She locked her door, then went back to her stash of belladonna.

CHAPTER ELEVEN

The hospital was busy. Amy and Des arrived at the emergency department, at Ben's request, to see what was going on with the casualty from the caves. Amy showed the receptionist her warrant card and was directed to the police waiting room. It had been a while since she'd been there. Des was in a grump for a change. He hadn't shaved and looked as if his suit had been thrown on the floor at the back of his wardrobe for weeks. She hadn't approached him yet; sometimes he was best left alone with his moods which seemed to be ever increasing lately. She took a seat and picked up a *Good Housekeeping* magazine that was a couple of years out of date, flicking through the glossy pages. She wasn't really paying attention to them, but it saved having to make conversation with Des, who was staring out of the small window that looked onto the ambulance loading bay. The door opened and one of the ward sisters walked in.

'Hiya, you're here about the woman brought in from the caves?'

'Yes, how is she?'

'At the moment, unconscious. She's been intubated and will probably be taken around to ICU very shortly to be monitored. The doctors are rushed off their feet at the moment, and I can tell you now they are completely baffled by her condition.'

'Aren't we all. Is she likely to wake up soon? Is it worth us waiting here to speak to her?'

The nurse laughed. 'Crikey, I'd say that's a definite no. She needs help to breathe, and her bloods have been sent to the lab to be fast tracked. The consultant is concerned that she may have ingested something poisonous, but we won't know until the blood results come back.'

Des turned to Amy. 'She's on a ventilator, Amy, how well do you think you'd be able to talk on one of those?'

Amy gave him one of her death stares. She was too polite to tell him to piss off in front of a complete stranger, but the look on her face said it for her. He didn't say another word.

'They'll be in touch with you when she's awake. There's really nothing you can do. I'm sorry.' The nurse walked out and in walked a uniformed officer with a plastic cup of vending machine coffee. He looked at them both and nodded.

'Not much happening here. Do you know what I'm supposed to do?'

Amy shrugged. 'Better check with your supervisor, not for me to tell you. Come on, Des, let's go back and see what Ben wants us to do next.' She stood up and walked out, Des following behind.

'What are we doing then?'

'I don't know, do I? And what's wrong with your face? You look as if you're in pain. Have you got a stomach bug or something?'

'I'm not ill, I'm just fed up with all this drama.'

She stopped walking and turned to look at him. 'Are you being serious? You're a seasoned detective working in the criminal investigations department, do you not think that drama is part of the job description?'

'You know what I mean, Amy, aren't you tired of it all?'

'No, it's our job, Des, we chose to do this.'

'I know but that woman this morning when we turned up to help out, I can't get the image of her bloodied, crumpled body out of my head. She went to work and ended up dead, then the bloody grim reaper went to pass on the death message to her dad and killed him off too. I'm telling you now, if something bad happens to anyone in my family, do not send Morgan to pass on anything; she's like an angel of death.'

Amy began to chuckle and shook her head. 'Is it your age? Do you think you might be going through the male menopause, Des?'

'Piss off, Amy.'

'You seem to be super sensitive lately. I just want to help.'

He shook his head and got inside the car. Amy's phone began to ring, and she saw Ben's name flash across the screen.

'No news at the hospital, boss, they're waiting on bloods. The consultant is thinking she might have ingested something poisonous.'

'*Really? We're on our way back to the station to get some lunch. Do you want anything?*'

'No thanks, we're good. We'll get something on the way back. How did you get on at Ettie Jackson's?'

'*Not much there either.*'

She realised he couldn't say much in front of Morgan: the woman was her aunt, and he might be feeling a bit awkward.

'Are we all meeting back at the station? And why are you getting the post-mortem so quick? Isn't it a suicide?'

'I don't know. On the face of it, yes. But if she was acting strange and out of character, I just want to see what Declan has to say about it, especially if the doctor is thinking the woman we found at the cave has consumed something toxic and yes, see you soon.'

Amy didn't know what was going on but knew that whatever it was it wasn't right. Maybe they had eaten some magic mushrooms but the wrong kind or taken some drugs that had come from a bad batch. It wouldn't be the first time. It happened sometimes. Heroin could be too pure or mixed with potentially dangerous ingredients so the dealers could make more money out of dodgy stuff, resulting in a flurry of overdoses and sudden deaths although the teacher at the school didn't seem the type to be a secret drug taker, but, she reflected, you never really knew someone as much as you thought. Everyone had their secrets and lies.

CHAPTER TWELVE

The station was buzzing with officers. There seemed to have been an influx of them after a stint of barely enough to staff a shift. It was like that in this job: it was either a feast or a famine. Morgan hardly knew any of them. A few of them occasionally spoke, but not many of them seemed to know how to interact with colleagues from other departments. Amy came strolling in behind them, calling 'Hello' to the group of officers standing around the brew station in the corridor, who just ignored her. Morgan found herself sniggering like a teenager, and Ben shook his head at the pair of them as they all climbed the stairs up to their office. Once inside Morgan opened the bag of sandwiches they'd picked up from the small Sainsbury's on the high street and began offering them around.

Amy shook her head. 'I'm good, thanks. Des is on his way up with bacon butties.'

Ben looked down at his chicken salad sandwich on brown bread, and Morgan, who had already ripped open the cardboard packet of her cheese savoury sandwich and taken a bite, smiled.

'Why didn't we think of that?'

He nodded. 'It's all good. I'm sure my body will thank me for this wet, brown piece of lettuce; it needs some nourishment.'

She snorted and almost choked on the mouthful of sandwich. Des walked in surrounded in a cloud of bacon grease, and she put her sandwich on the desk.

'Where did you get those?'

'Canteen.'

She didn't wait for Ben to ask her. She nodded and walked out, heading in the direction of the canteen. Cain was also heading that way. He waited for her to catch up to him.

'What a morning. I've never known anything like it. Well, actually, I have but not for a while. I can't get that teacher's smashed up body out of my head.'

'I went to school with her. She was one of my friends.'

'Oh, Morgan, that's awful. Are you okay?'

She looked up at Cain. He towered over her, and the look of genuine concern etched across his face made her eyes want to water. She liked him, he was funny and a very good officer. She blinked a couple of times; she didn't do crying in front of people.

'Yeah, just shocked and saddened. Then her poor dad when we went to tell him, it's just awful.'

Before she could do anything, she felt his big bear arms around her shoulders as he gave her a quick hug. She froze for a second then hugged him back, not remembering the last time she'd actually hugged someone and realising she quite liked the feeling of warmth that radiated from his body.

'Brown sauce, Morgan, oh.' Ben's voice echoed over the railings, and she realised he could see her. She pulled away, looked up at him and stuck up her thumb.

'Thanks, Cain, I needed that, it's been a long time.'

'Really, you have no one to give you a hug when you need it?'

She studied his face, he was so nice, and then she shrugged.

'I guess not.'

'Well, that's no good, from now on I'm your official hug buddy. I might not be much good at anything else but hugging I can do. Just throw your arms around me whenever you need a quick one. I'm more than happy to oblige. I honestly thought that you and—' He lowered his voice as his eyes lifted upwards and whispered. 'That you and Benno were an item.'

'Absolutely not, friends and work colleagues, yes, but nothing more.'

'Judging by the look on his face just then I'd have said it went far more than friends, but who am I to judge? I'm not a relationship expert, just ask my ex-wife.'

They walked into the busy canteen, Morgan wondering who else thought that she and Ben were an item. Cain went over to a group of officers who were already sitting down, eating, and began chatting to them.

*

A few minutes later she was back in the office passing a paper bag containing the last bacon bun in the canteen to Ben.

'Where's yours?'

'They only had one left.'

He held it back to her and she shook her head. 'No, it's okay. I don't like brown sauce. I'll stick with my sandwich.'

They ate in silence, and then Ben stood up.

'I don't know what's going on, but whatever it is it's not your usual morning in Rydal Falls. Did they say how long the blood tests would take at the hospital, Amy?'

'No, boss, I would say a couple of hours depending on what they're testing for.'

'What are they looking for I wonder? Did the woman from the caves gain consciousness at all?'

Des, who was blotting his mouth with a serviette, spoke first. 'No, they had intubated her and were taking her to ICU. Amy didn't quite understand that part, did you, Amy?'

He ducked as a pencil flew across the room, just missing his head. 'You're such a dick, Des.'

Ben held his hands up. 'Behave kids, someone will lose an eye.'

Morgan smiled. Stan, her dad, used to say that to her when she was younger and messing around with her friends. A sharp pain in her chest took her breath away. Just thinking about Stan and everything she'd lost hit her like a bolt of lightning. Grief and guilt were a heavy burden to carry around. She saw Brittany's head, a sea of crimson leaking from the side of it where she had landed, crushing her skull. She didn't need to be a forensic pathologist to tell them what her cause of death had been; it had been plain for everyone to see. Brittany had been so pretty at school. Her icy blonde waves and eyes the colour of the palest blue agate made her look like some teenage goddess. The boys had liked her a lot; Morgan had liked her a lot. She had been kind to her after her mum's death, and she'd been thankful for that because she'd always felt out of place in school. But Brittany had helped her to fit in those last few months. Sienna was pretty too, but not in the same league as Brittany. Her hair had been more straw coloured, with sapphire-coloured eyes, and she had a jealous streak. They'd all fancied Brad Murphy who had been quite the catch back then. Poor Brad, he'd almost asked her out a couple times and each time she'd deferred the question because of Sienna and Brittany, who both had a massive crush on him. Morgan needed to know what had happened this morning to end in so much tragedy with her friends. She owed it to them to find out what had gone so terribly wrong.

'So, I think we should speak to Declan about the post-mortem and see what he thinks about toxicology, and then someone needs to speak to Brittany's girlfriend. I really want to know what's in the jar of tea. You can ask Wendy to get it sent off for testing.'

Ben stopped talking and she looked up, realising they were all looking at her.

'Sorry, drifted off there. I was thinking back to my school days.'

He arched an eyebrow at her. 'I suppose it's a lot easier for you to remember yours. I can barely remember what my teachers were called it's that long ago. Is that okay, Morgan, can you take the jar of tea to Wendy?'

He pointed to the clear plastic evidence bag on the desk containing Ettie's tea, and she nodded. There was no way this had anything to do with her aunt, no way at all, but she couldn't argue with him when he was only doing his job.

*

The door was wide open when she arrived at the large Crime Scene Investigation office down the corridor. She rapped her knuckles on the wood all the same.

'Knock, knock.'

'Who's there?'

Wendy's voice broke into laughter, and Morgan grinned at her as she walked in. She was sitting at her desk, surrounded by *Star Wars* memorabilia.

'Ben asked if you would send this off to be tested.' She held up the bag.

'What is it?'

'Herbal tea from the victim's kitchen.'

Wendy crossed the room, taking the bag from her and holding it up to the light.

'It's herbal all right, wonder what flavour it is? I'm partial to a herbal tea. It looks like the stuff from that little shop in Kendal. I can't remember its name now, but it sells nice candles, tea and coffee.'

Morgan sighed. 'Whatever it is I don't think it had anything to do with her death. I've had some very similar tea and it worked a treat, helping me to sleep better. My aunt makes them. She lives in a small cottage in Covel Woods and grows all her own herbs and fruits for them.'

'Oh, how awful for you. Have you asked her about the contents?'

'Yes, and she's adamant there's nothing in it that would send someone off the rails and make them jump out of a window. She's been making them a long time and now I feel awful because Ben has it in his head that this is the cause of death.'

'Yikes, that's awkward. What are you going to do?'

'Not a lot I can do, except hope that Ettie didn't unintentionally poison it. I can't see it though; she's so lovely and gentle.'

Wendy nodded. 'Well, let's get it fast tracked and prove it had nothing to do with her, eh.'

'Thanks, Wendy, that would be great and very much appreciated.'

She left Wendy still looking at the contents of the bag, a sinking feeling inside her stomach that things were on the verge of going spectacularly tits up in a big way.

CHAPTER THIRTEEN

Declan waited for his assistant, Susie, to come back from her lunch break and then he was going to start on the sudden death that had come in this morning. Technically it was a suicide; the woman had jumped to her death and there had been plenty of witnesses. However, according to her work colleagues, she had been acting strange and way out of control. While waiting for Susie, he went back to his egg mayo and tomato sandwich, his feet on the desk as he read the latest instalment in the Detective Kim Stone series by one of his favourite writers, Angela Marsons; although he reckoned that their very own Morgan Brookes was giving Kim a run for her money with all the disasters and murders that she seemed to attract to their relatively rural part of Cumbria. His mobile began to ring and reluctantly he picked it up.

'Yes?'

'*Good afternoon to you too. Wasn't it not that long ago you were telling the lovely Susie off for her awful phone manners?*'

'Yes, but this is my personal phone, and you are interrupting my reading, so I can be as rude as I like, especially to you, Ben. Please, don't send me any more bodies today. Can you both hold off from passing death messages until I've cleared my current caseload?'

Ben's laughter filled his ear, and he held the phone away until he stopped.

'*What a morning, sorry about that.*'

'Hmm, are you though? And what about Morgan, is she okay? Bless her.'

'*She's fine, at least I think she is.*'

'Have you actually asked her that, Ben? I worry about her. She's so young and ends up smack, bang in the middle of things she shouldn't.'

There was a pause from Ben, then he continued, '*There was another woman found acting really strange at Rydal Caves this morning. By the time we got there she was unconscious inside the cavern.*'

'What do you mean acting strange?'

'*Like naked apart from her knickers and socks kind of strange, talking rubbish according to the walkers who came across her.*'

'That's interesting, how is she now?'

'*On a ventilator in ICU. She collapsed and had to be airlifted to hospital.*'

'Did you see her?'

'*Yes.*'

'Describe her appearance to me.'

'*I already said she was naked.*'

'No, her skin colour, tone, feel.'

'*Her face was quite flushed, red cheeks, but then so were mine by the time I'd climbed up that bloody fell to reach her.*'

'What did her skin feel like, smooth, soft?'

'*Hot, she was really hot, and I suppose you could say it felt a bit rough.*'

'How so? Sandpaper rough as in scratchy or just dry?'

'*Jesus, Declan, she was almost naked and unconscious, I didn't really touch her more than I needed to.*'

'What did it feel like where you did touch her?'

'*Like she needed to slather some body lotion on.*'

'Hmm, this is very interesting. How would you describe her behaviour? I know you didn't see it but from what the eyewitnesses have said?'

'*I'm not sure, delirious maybe.*'

'Judging from what you're describing I'm thinking that it's some kind of poisoning or ingestion of a highly toxic forest plant or fruit. Ben, you need to speak to the doctor looking after her and ask them if they know or have identified anything.'

'We've been trying. They're still running tests. I was thinking some kind of recreational drug?'

'Do either of them have a history of drug taking?'

'Not as far as I'm aware, although we don't really know anything about the woman found at the cave, except that both of them were friends and went to school with Morgan.'

'And there go my early warning alarm bells: the very mention of Morgan's name and the fact that they weren't known drug users. If they'd taken something like pure heroin they would have died straight after injecting it. They wouldn't have been acting as they did beforehand.'

'What could do that though?'

'I've only ever come across something similar to this once before, and I might be way off course, but did you know that the plant *Atropa Belladonna* grows abundantly in this area? The dark, damp conditions that some of our countryside provide make it thrive.'

'What's belladonna?'

'Deadly nightshade to me and you; it's a highly toxic plant with small green leaves and the sweetest black fruits. It contains extremely high levels of the alkaloids atropine, scopolamine and hyoscyamine, which are used in modern medicine but obviously in the correct doses.'

'Right, can we pretend that I haven't got a clue what you're talking about please?'

Declan laughed. 'Sorry, basically if it's ingested it can cause serious problems, even death. Consuming a high enough dose can cause anticholinergic syndrome from the effects of the alkaloids it contains. Some antipsychotic medicines can present with these side effects as well, so we can't rule those out just yet. It can present with blurred vision, hallucinations, loss of short-term memory, agitation, respiratory failure and cardiovascular collapse. It causes delirium,

agitation, redness of the face and neck, dry skin and urinary retention – which I'll check in the post-mortem. The symptoms that
both of these women were displaying are very similar. If neither
of them are taking prescribed psychotic medicines then you need
to find out how and where they ingested a quantity of enough
belladonna to cause this.'

*'Thanks, sounds easy enough, right? Jesus, Declan, what if it's not
deadly nightshade or a prescribed medicine?'*

'Then you have a bigger problem of finding out what it is. What's
the name of the woman you found and which hospital is she in? I
need to speak to them and tell them what I think it is. If it is this,
then hopefully she will make a full recovery and she will tell you
exactly what happened.'

*'I hope so, wouldn't that be something? The second victim is called
Sienna Waters and she's at Westmoreland General, thanks.'*

Declan ended the call without a goodbye. He needed to speak
to the consultant in ICU about Ms Waters urgently. He had a gut
feeling that when he opened up the woman who had fallen to her
death, he would find that her oral mucosa would be much dryer
than it should be and there would be signs of urinary retention. He
had a bad feeling about this. In all his years working as a pathologist
he had only ever come across one case of belladonna poisoning
and the woman had ingested a large quantity of the fruit without
knowing what it was whilst foraging in a forest, and she had done
this accidentally; however, two women in the space of twenty-four
hours consuming belladonna was extremely worrying.

CHAPTER FOURTEEN

Morgan waited for Ben to get off the phone. He was having a rather animated conversation with someone in his office: his hands were flying in the air, and he was now sitting with his head buried in his arms on the desk. Amy leaned over to whisper to Morgan.

'He's not having a good day, is he?'

'It's Cindy's birthday, I don't think that's helping.'

'Oh, well there you go then. Why doesn't he take the day off if it gets him like this? Go visit her grave, go out and get drunk, see his mates and take his mind off it like I would.'

'I think we are his mates and coming to work is probably the best thing to keep him busy.'

'Poor bastard if we're all he's got.' Amy laughed, a little too loud, and Morgan frowned at her as Ben's door opened.

He walked in and looked at them both. 'What's so funny?'

Morgan shook her head. 'Nothing, Amy was just talking about—'

Ben's phone began to ring, saving her the embarrassment of having to make up a blatant lie to save the pair of them. He finished speaking as Detective Chief Inspector Tom Fell strode into the office.

'Does someone want to explain why no one has passed a death message on to the teacher's partner yet? I've just had to deal with a very angry, upset woman downstairs called Fleur, who is demanding to know if it's true that her girlfriend is dead. What the hell is going on?'

Amy stood up. 'Sir, trust me you don't want those two delivering any more death messages. They just keep adding to the body count.'

She grinned, and Tom stared at her. Morgan could tell he was wondering what she was talking about, and she stood up.

'Sir, we were told that section were going to pass the death message. Have they not done that?'

His arms were now folded across his chest as his head moved slowly from side to side.

Ben muttered, 'Bollocks,' under his breath.

Morgan winced and asked, 'Is she still here? I'd like to talk to her.'

'No, I had Cain drive her home and told her someone would be along to speak to her very soon. So, can I ask that you two.' He stabbed his index finger in Morgan's direction. 'Can you and Amy go see her imminently? Ben, a word.'

Morgan glanced in Ben's direction, wondering if he was okay, but he never looked back at her. Amy grabbed her jacket and Morgan's sleeve, almost dragging her out of the office away from Tom and the anger he was radiating. They never spoke until they were outside in the car park. Morgan's stomach was in knots. She could feel the awful cheese sandwich she'd eaten lodged inside her like a piece of rolled-up card. Amy took one look at her and smiled.

'His bark is far worse than his bite. He's not going to sack Ben if that's what you're worried about. Today has been so messed up, it's just one of those things. We're all human and make mistakes.'

'I know but that poor woman; hearing about her partner's death from everyone before we told her is just terrible.'

'It is, and we have a lot of apologising to do but it's not all our fault. If section were supposed to do it they can hardly blame us, can they? Oh, and Morgan, for the love of God, let me do the talking.'

Morgan glared at Amy, who winked at her, and she felt the corners of her mouth begin to turn upwards.

'I wish I could start today over again. My morning was pretty nice and chilled. I was just thinking how wonderful and quiet it had been.'

'And there you go, why did you say the Q word? You should know by now that whenever anyone at work mentions the Q word that it all goes horribly wrong in no time.'

Morgan lifted her hands in the air. 'I give up. Honestly, I can't do right from wrong. How was I supposed to know that?'

'Chill, it's like code 101 in the police regs, Brookes. Who tutored you again?'

'Dan and, in case you've forgot, he's in prison for murder.'

Amy glanced at her. 'Shit, no I haven't forgot at all, sorry. You really have had an awful time, haven't you, since you joined up? I'll give you this though, you have staying power because if it was me, I'd probably have handed my notice in and be working somewhere a lot less stressful.' She reached out and patted Morgan's arm.

Neither of them spoke until they reached the address of Fleur Collins. Her flat was above the chemist on the high street. There was a police van parked on the pavement outside, and Morgan wondered if Cain was as fed up with chasing around after her and Ben today as she was. As she got out of the car she felt a twinge in the back of her calves and lower back. All that rushing up and down Loughrigg Fell was taking its toll on her, and she was going to need a long, hot soak in the bath when she finally got home tonight.

The door to the side of the shop window opened, and she smiled at Cain, who nodded. 'We're going to have to stop meeting like this, Morgan, tongues will wag.'

He stepped out. There was no way they could squeeze past his large, muscular frame in such a narrow space without touching. Amy shook her head at him and muttered 'dick' under her breath. She followed Morgan upstairs to the spacious flat that was like something off an Instagram influencer's feed. It was all blushed pinks, navy and rose gold and Morgan had an instant twinge of flat envy, and then she saw Fleur sobbing into what looked like a sweatshirt, curled up on the sofa, and felt bad. This woman had just lost the love of her life and she was wondering what shade of pink the kitchen cupboards were painted. This was so different to Brittany's bedroom in the house she shared. Morgan crossed towards Fleur. She wanted to hold her close, hug her like Cain had hugged her when she'd needed it, but Amy was watching and she knew that she'd disapprove, so she didn't. Instead, she took a seat on the sofa nearest to the crying woman and reached out to take hold of her hand, which was so cold it felt as if it had been inside a bag of crushed ice.

'I'm Morgan.'

'I know who you are.' A sob stopped Fleur mid-sentence, and Morgan felt a cold chill settle over her. The crying woman took a deep breath and dabbed at her eyes with what she realised was the leavers sweatshirt from the year they had left school; it must have been Brittany's because she didn't recognise Fleur and she had a few more lines around her eyes than she did.

'Brittany talks about you a lot; every time your picture is in the paper she'd bring a copy home to show me.'

Morgan didn't know if she'd ever felt this uncomfortable. She hadn't really given any of her friends from school much thought since the day they'd left and yet obviously Brittany hadn't forgot about her, but was that because Morgan seemed to get herself in all sorts of newsworthy bother and garner lots of unwanted press attention?

'I'm so sorry for the mix up. We should have come straight here to see you.'

'They said that-that Brittany threw herself out of a window and killed herself. Please, what happened to her, because I know she wouldn't do that?'

Morgan glanced at Amy, and then she looked up at the ceiling, asking for a bit of divine guidance to get her through the next thirty minutes.

'First of all, Fleur, I'm so sorry for your loss. I can't even begin to imagine how much you're hurting. Brittany was a lovely, lovely girl and very kind to me at school. I'm sorry to tell you that she did fall from a window at the school, but we don't know why yet. According to her friend and other teachers she was acting really strange, mumbling and muttering in her final minutes.'

Fleur was shaking her head. 'I don't understand why she would be like that. It's not her at all. Did she suffer? I can't bear the thought of her lying like a rag doll on the playground, bleeding to death, all alone.'

Hot tears pricked at the corners of Morgan's eyes. 'It was very quick; I'm not medically trained but I ran outside as soon as it happened, and she was gone.'

The woman opposite her closed her eyes, then buried her face into the sweatshirt to stifle her sobs. Amy had her head bowed. Even she was uncomfortable with so much raw grief, and this shocked Morgan even more. Finally, Fleur lifted her head and began to talk.

'We met out running. I hated it, but my friend kept telling me it was good for my soul, so I went with him one morning really early. By the time I reached the river I was bent over double, heaving my guts up and he was laughing. I told him to leave me alone. He carried on, the next thing this gorgeous woman was crouching down asking me if I was okay and needed help. I looked up and stared into those pale blue eyes and I was smitten. Obviously, I didn't say anything because you know it's a small town, people talk and people like me aren't really the norm around here, but we just kind of clicked. I told her I was fine, she carried on running but kept turning back to look at me and, well, I couldn't stop staring. She was the most beautiful woman I'd ever seen. After that we kept bumping into each other, and a week later she came into the dentists to book a check-up and I asked her out for a drink. I didn't care if she was into me or not. I just knew I wanted to have this Amazonian goddess in my life. I can't believe that she's gone, it's not real. We had so many things to look forward to, so many plans.'

'Had she ever expressed suicidal thoughts? Was she on any medication? How was she the last time you saw her?'

Fleur shook her head. 'Absolutely not. She was happy, we both were. We booked a holiday at the weekend to New York for her birthday; a suicidal woman wouldn't do that.'

'How about yesterday, how was she? And what about medication?'

Fleur paused. 'She was a little distant yesterday when she got home from school. She mentioned bumping into an old school friend and had a bit of a minor disagreement, but she said it wasn't anything serious.'

'What did you say to her?'

'I told her to tell them to piss off, whatever it was was in the past and didn't need dragging up now.'

'Did she mention the name?'

'No, I don't think so, she said it wasn't important.'

Morgan wondered who had upset Brittany and what it could have been about.

'What about drugs, medication?'

'None that I know about. She wasn't into taking stuff from the pharmacy. She did suffer with her tummy, and she liked to drink herbal tea; she used to buy some from a woman who lives in the woods and swore it was the best thing ever to help with her stomach spasms. I mean, she said it tasted like shit, but it worked much better than anything she'd ever taken that the doctor prescribed.'

'Do you have any of the tea here?'

'No, she always took it home with her if she wasn't staying here.'

'You didn't live together, was that planned for the future? And, I'm sorry to ask such a delicate question, but could Brittany have been pregnant? She mentioned a baby just before she fell.'

'What? No, absolutely not. Well not without having sex with a man and I don't think she did. She wasn't cheating on me. Oh God, was she?'

Morgan felt her cheeks turn pink. 'I'm sorry, not that I'm aware. I'm just trying to get to the bottom of why she was acting so out of character. I couldn't help noticing but this place is amazing, and her house share is a bit…'

'Of a shithole?'

'Not that bad.'

'She had two months left on the contract and then we were moving in together. I kept telling her to just come here, but she wanted to make sure that Sam knew first about the pair of us. I think he does deep down and honestly doesn't care. All he wants is for Brittany to be happy. Oh, poor Sam, how is he?'

Before Morgan could say anything, Amy said, 'I'm afraid he died this morning after he was told about Brittany.'

Fleur stared at Amy, her face a mask of confusion. 'I don't understand, are you telling me he's dead too?'

'I'm afraid so. The paramedics think he had a massive heart attack. He didn't know anything about it.'

If Fleur's face wasn't pale enough at the realisation of what Amy was saying, she looked as if she was about to faint, and Morgan whispered, 'I'm so sorry.'

Amy took over. 'Is there anyone we can call for you to come and sit with you? You've had a massive shock. You really shouldn't be on your own.'

Fleur shook her head. 'My mum is on her way from Barrow. Do I need to identify Brittany?'

'No, you don't. Morgan and the witnesses at the school were able to do that, but if you'd like to see her once the post-mortem has been carried out you'll be able to.'

'Thank you, Morgan. I wouldn't want to see her like that.' She began to cry again, and Morgan wished again that today was over and done with. That she could turn back the clock and make it to the school before this catastrophic series of events had begun, to put a stop to them. Amy took out a pen and some crumpled Post-it notes from her pocket. Scribbling down contact numbers on them she placed them on the coffee table in front of Fleur.

'If you think of anything or have any questions, don't hesitate to get in touch.'

Footsteps on the stairs made them all turn to face the door, and an older woman who was the image of Fleur but with cropped grey hair walked in, mascara trails down her cheeks. She ran over, hugging her daughter fiercely, and Morgan realised how much she missed her own mum's hugs. She felt a tiny spark of fury inside her chest for the injustice of it all. For herself, for Brittany and now for Fleur, she was ready to get to the bottom of what had happened now that her job here was done. She wasn't going to stop until she had answers for everyone.

CHAPTER FIFTEEN

2016

Morgan screeched at her dad. She'd taken to calling him Stan since her mum had died and their relationship had deteriorated. Her voice now was reaching some previously unknown high-pitched realm of loudness.

'I hate you. Why didn't you die instead of Mum? You're a waste of space. All you do is drink and ruin my life.'

She turned and ran upstairs, his words slurred, echoing behind her.

'Well take a ticket and get in line, kid, because I hate myself more than you ever could.'

She slammed her bedroom door, making the whole house rattle. She knew Stan would be clenching his fists downstairs but didn't care. God, she despised him at times. Throwing herself onto her bed, she pounded the pillows with her fists and let the tears flow. All her friends were going to be at the camp out tonight up at the caves. It was Brittany's birthday and she really liked her; she had been so nice to her after everything that had happened with her mum. And Brad was going to be there too. Not that she ever stood a chance with him. Brittany really fancied him, they all did. He was always nice to her as well, which made Sienna and Lara really pissed with her, but it wasn't her fault. A sharp crack against her window made her sit up. It was closely followed by another, and she quickly crossed to the old sash window that was rotten and draughty. She peered down to see Brad standing by the cherry tree, about to launch another stone at her window. She brushed her sleeve against her face to blot away any damp tears and pushed the heavy window up before he could launch another pebble and put the glass through.

'What are you doing?' she hissed down in his direction, afraid Stan would hear her and come to see what or who she was talking to.

'I've come to carry your stuff.'

She frowned at him. 'What stuff?'

'Your bags.'

'What are you talking about?'

He was grinning at her, and she felt the black cloud of anger dissipate as she grinned back.

'Your tent and sleeping bag, you goon. What did you think I meant?'

She shrugged. 'I'm not going.'

It was Brad's turn to frown. He shrugged the backpack off his shoulders and began to shimmy up the drainpipe to the flat roof below her window. She sucked in and held her breath, afraid to let it go. If the drainpipe was in a state of disrepair like the rest of the house it would come away from the wall, taking him with it. Thankfully it held.

'Why aren't you coming?'

'I'm grounded. Stan said I couldn't go anywhere. I have to study for the exams.'

Brad groaned. 'Did you tell him what we were doing? He knows my dad; they drink in the pub sometimes. I'll get in trouble.'

'No, I did not. I told him I was sleeping at Sienna's house, and he didn't believe me.'

'Shit, well you'll just have to sneak out a little bit later and meet us there. Or you could drag your drawers in front of your bedroom door or put the pillows under the duvet, so it looks like you're sleeping. If he's drunk, he'll never tell the difference.'

Morgan considered it for a few moments. 'I can't.'

'Why not? Come on, Morgan, it will be fun. You and me looking up at the stars and drinking cheap vodka, what more could you ask for?'

She looked down at his brown eyes and brown floppy hair. His nose was covered in freckles like hers, but he suited them and they made him look like a surfer dude, whereas she looked like a whiter than white ginger. She realised that she wanted to go with Brad and drink vodka more than anything else.

'I can't, you don't understand. As much as Stan is a dick, I still feel bad for him, and I worry about him. If I'm not here, he might burn the house down or choke on his own vomit.'

'Well, that's very noble of you, Morgan, but isn't it supposed to be the other way around? Isn't he supposed to be the one taking care of you? It's not your job to take care of him.'

She shrugged. 'I know, but I was really horrible to him just now. If he realises I've snuck out to go meet you all, he'll go and tell everyone's parents and ruin everything. You go, Brad, and have a great time. You can tell me all about the gossip tomorrow, if Brittany gets too drunk or Sienna finally lets rip and proves what a bitch she can be after a couple of vodka shots.'

Brad laughed. 'You're not really selling it to me, Morgan. I think I'd rather stay here all night.'

She smiled. 'Get away, go have fun for me. We can always go camping again when the exams are over.'

'You promise?'

'I promise.'

He looked up at her. Lifting his fingers to his lips he blew her a kiss and bowed.

'Well then, my little Morticia Addams, I shall go forth and endure a night of drunken stargazing to bring back the best gossip for you I can acquire.'

Morgan blew him a kiss back, her cheeks turning pink, but she didn't care. A smile spread across her lips, and she watched him scramble back down the drainpipe, wishing with all her heart that she was going with him. Bloody Stan and his stupid rules. Her mum would have let her go without a moment's hesitation and she wished she was here to ask. A pain gripped her chest at the thought of her lovely mum. She had never envisaged a life without her in it and now that she was gone she hated it. The bleakness and loneliness was hard to get used to, and Stan's drinking made it even harder.

CHAPTER SIXTEEN

As they walked out into the fresh air Morgan inhaled deeply. 'That was tough.'

Amy nodded. 'What now?'

'I want to try and find out who upset Brittany yesterday; maybe she told her friends she lived with. Paige didn't mention it at the school but there's another woman we could ask.'

'Your call. You lead and I'll follow.'

Morgan drove to Brittany's house, hoping someone could shed some light on what had happened yesterday to give them the slightest reason for her behaviour. The door was ajar, and Morgan called in. 'Hello, it's the police, can I come in?' She knocked and then a pale-faced woman, much older than both Paige and Brittany, appeared. 'Hi, I'm Detective Morgan Brookes. I'm following up with Brittany's death. Is it okay to have a quick word?'

The woman nodded, and Morgan followed her inside. She turned to beckon Amy to follow, but she was on her phone in the car and gave her a thumbs up. The house seemed as though it was cloaked in a heavy atmosphere of dread and confusion, which it probably was. She was led down to the kitchen where Paige was sitting at the table nursing a mug. The woman pointed to the large pink spotted teapot.

'Would you like a drink?'

'No, thanks. I just wanted to ask you a couple of quick questions.'

They both nodded. Paige's eyes were so red and puffy Morgan felt awful for her.

'I'm Debbie. I work at the school too, so I know what happened.'

'It must be a terrible shock for you both. I've been speaking with Fleur, and she said that Brittany had a bit of a run-in with an old friend yesterday that had upset her. Did either of you speak to Brittany? Did she mention it to you?'

Paige shook her head. 'No.'

Debbie nodded. 'She told me; she didn't say what it was about or who it was, but she came home a little pale yesterday after she'd nipped to the Co-op for some milk. She said she'd got into a bit of an argument over something that happened a long time ago.'

'Did she say who with?'

'No, she was really vague about it, like she wanted to get the confrontation off her chest but didn't want to give any details. She said it wasn't her fault and she'd done what she had to do. I'm not going to lie; I had no idea what she was talking about. Then I gave her the letter. I bloody knew there was something odd about it, because there was no postmark; it had been hand delivered, and the handwriting looked creepy, but it was addressed to her, so I had no right to keep it from her.'

Paige was staring at Debbie. 'What letter? When was this?'

'Yesterday.'

Morgan felt a glimmer of hope deep inside her that just maybe they were about to catch a break. 'Do you know what was in the letter or even more important, where it is now?' She hadn't found a letter when she'd searched Brittany's bedroom earlier.

'No, she read it, her face went pale and then she ripped it into tiny pieces and threw it in the bin.'

'Which bin?'

Debbie pointed to the kitchen bin. 'I'm sorry, I emptied it yesterday and threw it in the wheelie bin. It's rubbish day; they were emptied first thing.'

Morgan, who had been sitting straight up since the mention of the letter, felt her shoulders slump back down. She had been so close – she should have checked the bloody bins.

'Oh, shit.'

Both Paige and Debbie nodded in agreement.

'She didn't say what it was about?'

'No, I can only tell you that whatever was written inside it can't have been very nice, because the blood drained from her face and she went as white as that.' Debbie was pointing to the linen tablecloth.

'Thanks, that's a shame but useful to know. Did she say if the conversation happened inside the Co-op?' Morgan had her fingers crossed, because if it had it would be captured on CCTV.

'No, I think it was on her way there. She'd gone for a walk by the river and bumped into whoever it was there.'

'Okay, thanks. If you can think of anything else, can you let me know please?'

'Of course, but that's it I'm afraid.'

She gave them her card and left them to it, returning outside to where Amy was ending her phone call. Morgan got back inside the car with every ounce of enthusiasm wiped from her.

'Well?'

'Nothing. She got a letter yesterday which made her go very quiet, but she ripped it to shreds and threw it away.'

'Did you check the bin?'

'No point, it's bin day. They were emptied earlier.'

'Always a point, Morgan, there might be some fragments of it left behind.'

'You be my guest, Amy.'

Amy took some gloves from her pocket and tugged them on, then she got out of the car and made her way towards the bin at the side of the house. She lifted the lid, wrinkled her nose then let it slam shut and came back to the car.

'Well?'

'Nothing.'

Morgan didn't speak to Amy all the way back to the station; she couldn't find the words. The fact that two of her school friends had ended up this way was really gnawing at her mind; what did it mean? The incidents had to be connected, but to what?

As they got back into the office Ben was nowhere to be found. Des was still hanging around. Amy threw her jacket onto the back of her chair and flopped down onto the desk chair.

'Well?' Des asked her, and Morgan knew what was coming next.

'Well, what?'

'How did it go?'

'Are you for real? It wasn't a physio appointment, Des, it was a death message and a double one at that. How do you think it went?'

'Awful.'

Amy looked across at Morgan who was waiting for her computer to load. 'He's perceptive today, isn't he?' She jerked her head in his direction. Des tutted loudly.

'I was trying to be nice, Amy, you should try it occasionally.'

Ben walked in. His cheeks were flushed, and he looked as stressed as Morgan had ever seen him. She let Amy do the talking and began typing Sienna's name into Google. She couldn't remember the name of her shop, but an instinct was telling her that she needed to pay it a visit. She had to see what products were on the shelves and by that she realised that she meant whether any of Ettie's products were stocked there. Clicking on a link, a picture of a happy, smiling Sienna filled the screen along with a shot of her shop on Finkle Street on the day it opened. She was pretty young to open a shop, but who was Morgan to judge? Maybe she had a business partner. The shop was called Tea Leaves and Reads. She wondered if Ben had already sent someone there to check it out.

'Message passed?' he asked the pair of them, and they nodded.

'Good, thank you. That can't have been easy, anything interesting?'

Morgan nodded. 'Brittany had a run-in with an old school friend yesterday. She wasn't pregnant or at least Fleur didn't know if she was, and she was excited about a trip to New York that they'd just booked. Like everyone else, Fleur said this was way out of character for her. Also, she received a handwritten letter yesterday morning which upset her because she ripped it up and threw it straight into the bin. Unfortunately, the bins had already been emptied.'

'Bugger. That's interesting though. Who wrote her and what about? Keep asking if anyone was aware of it. Declan was going to speak to the consultant taking care of Sienna. He's taken a personal interest and is absolutely fascinated with this case. He thinks it's some kind of toxic poisoning.' He disappeared inside his office, and Morgan knew she had to go to the shop. She followed him, knocking gently on the door.

'Sarge?'

'Come in, Morgan. What's with the sarge?'

'Ben, I want to pay a visit to Sienna's shop. Have you sent a search team there yet?'

His eyes opened wide, and she knew then that he hadn't. He was far too distracted today; it wasn't like him at all.

'Christ, no. I sent them to check out her flat. There wasn't anything that stood out though. I didn't think about the shop, that's a good idea, Morgan. Should I come with you? I need to get out of here. I can't think straight.'

She had never heard him ask her for permission and it sounded strange.

'You're the boss, ask yourself?' She smiled at him, trying to lift him out of the funk he seemed to be lost in.

His laughter echoed around the small office. 'Yes, I suppose I am. I'll come then.' He stood up and she led the way, Ben following behind. It wasn't until they got into the car that she turned to look at him.

'I'm sorry that you're having a rubbish day and that it's Cindy's birthday, but are you okay in yourself? You seem a bit…' She didn't know what to say.

He was staring at her, holding her gaze and she felt her cheeks begin to turn pink it was so intense.

'I seem a bit distracted, is that the word you're looking for?'

She shook her head. 'No, I was going to say weird.'

He began to laugh, and she added, 'But weird is good, you know how I feel about weird. In fact, weird is the norm in my life. Welcome to the weird club.'

He reached out his hand and touched her cheek, his fingertips stroking the skin with a touch that was almost featherlight and for a fleeting moment she wanted to reach up and hold his hand, but she knew that would definitely be weird. He snatched his fingers back as if he'd realised what he was doing.

'You're not weird, Brookes, you're a very good person and don't tell yourself otherwise. Thank you, I'm tired today. I drank too much straight vodka on an empty stomach last night, but that's no excuse for my shitty behaviour today. I'm okay, I'll be okay, which is more than can be said for Brittany and Sam. I feel as if I've made far too many fuck-ups in the space of today's shift. Thank you for steering me in the right direction. Now, drive me to this shop so we can take a look around and see if there's anything there we can recover for forensics to solve the case and find out what has pushed two perfectly sane women over the edge.'

The shop was in darkness when they arrived. Morgan pressed her face to the glass and could see shadowy movement at the back. She knocked on the window and a woman appeared, shaking her head and pointing to her watch as she mouthed the words 'sorry we're closed'. Ben pulled his warrant card from his pocket, pressing it against the glass and shouted, 'Police.'

The expression on the woman's face was one of pure panic, and she rushed towards the locked door, where she began to unlock and slide bolts across. She pulled the door inwards for them to step into the gloomy shop, which smelt of tea, incense and something Morgan couldn't put her finger on.

'Goodness me, I'm sorry, I didn't know you were police. I'm afraid my boss isn't here, it's her day off. How can I help you both?'

Morgan realised that the woman who seemed to be visibly trembling had absolutely no idea about Sienna. This day was like something from a nightmare.

'You are?'

She looked at Ben. 'Marilyn. I work here two days a week, but it's Sienna who owns it.'

Morgan smiled at her. 'I'm afraid there's been an incident involving Sienna.'

Marilyn's hand flew to her mouth as she let out a gasp. 'Oh, my, is she…?'

'No, she's taken ill and is currently in Westmoreland General. Do you know if she has a husband or boyfriend? An address for her next of kin?'

Marilyn shook her head. 'As far as I know her mum is in St Cuthbert's Nursing Home, advanced dementia. She hasn't got a partner that I'm aware of. They split up quite some time ago. She's started seeing someone called Brad, but it's early days or so she said, and I have no idea who he is or where he lives. Is she okay, what ward is she on? I'll pop over and see her after tea.'

Ben let out a sigh. He gave Marilyn the information he had and then turned to begin looking around the shop. Morgan looked at the woman; the name Brad felt like a shock to her mind. It struck her as odd; something was off with all of this, and what were the chances of Sienna seeing someone called Brad?

'Well, she's unconscious at the moment, so you might be best to ring them before you go there.'

'What happened?'

'At this precise moment in time, we don't actually know. That's what we're trying to find out.'

Morgan turned to look at Ben. Her stomach dropped when she saw what he had picked up off a shelf: a jar of what looked like Ettie's herbal tea. He unscrewed the lid and let out a loud noise of disgust.

'Urghh, why do people drink this stuff?'

Marilyn stared at him, then turned to Morgan. 'Is he always this rude?'

'No, sorry, it's been an awfully long day. Do you mind if we take a look around?'

'Of course not, I'll switch the lights back on.' Marilyn disappeared somewhere out the back of the shop, and Morgan tried her best not to glare at Ben as he was picking up various jars and bottles. The shop was bathed in a warm glow and Morgan found herself admiring it. She would never have pegged Sienna as the kind of woman who would enjoy selling these kinds of products; she would have turned her nose up at them when they were at school. There was even a bookshelf with books on meditation, magic, moon magic and several decks of tarot cards next to baskets of brightly coloured crystals. A fridge was stocked with lots of fresh produce with a large handwritten 'Organic, Grown Local' sign taped to the glass. Marilyn came back to see what they were doing.

'Those crystals, herbal teas and tarot cards are what keeps this shop open. Everyone can't get enough of them.'

Morgan nodded, understanding why. Who didn't want to believe in a little bit of magic when the world was so brutal, unforgiving and cruel? She turned to the jars of tea and began reading the handwritten labels. None of them were the same as the tea they found in Brittany's kitchen, but then Ettie said that she'd made that one specially. Ben was still wrinkling his nose as he studied the labels.

'What do you think? Should we take a jar of each to send off for testing, and does Sienna drink this stuff?'

Before she could answer Marilyn interjected, 'She does, we both do, and testing for what?'

He looked at her. 'For illegal, toxic or deadly substances.'

A look of anger flashed across her eyes. 'Now look here, we have been selling these teas since last year and there have been no complaints. We only stock those four blends from that particular supplier and no one has ever been ill from them. How dare you come in here and insinuate that the products we sell are deadly. Are you insane? We both also eat the fresh fruit and veg, the bars of chocolate and anything else that takes our fancy, are you going to take the whole stock away to be tested?'

Morgan watched, fascinated to see what Ben's reaction was going to be. He paused for a moment, glancing in her direction, but she wasn't going to rescue him this time. He needed to sort his act out and maybe Marilyn was the person to force him.

'Of course not, but we need to make sure and it's specifically the tea that we're interested in. Would you know if they'd been tampered with?'

'Yes, there's a seal on each jar like the one you broke when you opened it.'

'Oh, are all these jars sealed?'

She nodded. 'Of course, I add the security stickers myself as they come in.'

'Right, that's good. Can we take a jar of each to send off for testing? Please?'

Marilyn finally cracked a smile. 'Well, yes, of course you can.' She picked up a jar of each blend of tea including the one Ben had opened, wrapped them in tissue paper and popped them into a brown paper bag with handles.

'That will be twenty-two pounds please.'

Ben's mouth fell open, and Morgan had to turn away to hide the grin.

'It's evidence.'

'I don't care what it is, you come in here, give me awful news about my employer and friend then damage goods that I can't resell. If Sienna is poorly, I'm going to have to run the shop, and we don't give away free things to anyone. Will that be card or cash?'

Flustered, Ben shrugged. Pushing his hand into his pocket he pulled out a twenty and a five-pound note. Marilyn took it from him, rang it up and passed him six fifty pence pieces back.

'Sorry, I've cashed up the pounds and two-pound coins. Will there be anything else?'

Morgan smiled at her. 'Not right now, thank you. We may have to come back tomorrow with a crime scene investigator, but we will let you know if we do.'

Marilyn nodded at her, strode across to the front door and opened it wide for them to walk out of.

As Morgan got back into the car she started to laugh. Ben's expression was still one of confusion and he looked at her.

'What's so funny and what the hell just happened in there?'

'Sorry, it's just your face is a picture and I think that you just got served by the world's savviest shop assistant. Actually, you were kind of rude in there.'

He lifted the brown paper bag in the air and stared at it. 'I think I just got conned more like, what the hell?'

Morgan stifled her laughter all the way back to the station, whilst Ben sat cradling his bag of expensive teas.

CHAPTER SEVENTEEN

Morgan accompanied Ben to the CSI office. Wendy had her coat on and let out a groan when she saw them both.

'It's finishing time. Do you two not have homes to go to?'

Ben grabbed her hand and dropped to his knees. 'Please, Wendy, help a guy out, no one can do it like you.'

Wendy giggled, pulling her hands from his. 'Get up, you arsehole, have you been drinking?'

He shook his head. 'After the vodka I consumed last night when we lost at the crappy pub quiz, I don't think I'll ever drink again.' He got to his feet beaming at Wendy. 'Please, Wendy, these need sending off now.'

'You'll be lucky; you'll have to find someone to drive them to Penrith to get them looked at tonight.'

He nodded. 'I will. Can you bag them up and arrange it?'

'Bloody hell, Ben, the things I do for you.' But she was shrugging her coat off and took the brown paper bag from him.

'Let me go find a PCSO. They're always up for a jolly; one of them will do it.'

Off he wandered, leaving Morgan and Wendy, who had now slipped on a pair of gloves and was taking the jars out of the bag. She lifted one up, looked at Morgan and asked. 'Oh, no, is this more of your aunt's tea?' Morgan nodded. 'Oh crap, he's really got a bee in his bonnet about it, hasn't he?'

'It would seem that way, yes. I just hope he's wrong. I feel so bad, she's such a lovely lady and so kind.'

'Yeah, but you know maybe if it is, it's just accidental. I'm pretty sure she wouldn't intentionally sell tea that sends people nuts.'

Morgan smiled, but behind the smile was a niggling feeling. Ettie was Gary Marks's sister, a brutal killer's sister. His son, Dan, was even more sadistic than Gary, so where did that leave Ettie? How connected could Ettie be? Could something have emerged from deep inside her? And if so, what did it mean for Morgan, with her own relation to Gary? Her biggest fear was that she might one day cross the line from being the person chasing the monsters to becoming the one being chased. Could an entire family be bad to the bone and kill for pleasure without remorse? All these things were playing heavily on her mind. She was tired. It had been one long, sad day; she needed to go home and relax. Try to take her mind off it for a little while.

Ben walked back in with Cathy Hayes, who also had her coat on. Wendy took one look at her. 'You too?'

Cathy grinned. 'He made me an offer I can't refuse.'

Both Morgan and Wendy arched one eyebrow, and Ben laughed.

'Steady on, ladies, I offered her a bottle of wine and a takeaway if she would deliver the samples to HQ on her way home.'

Cathy interjected. 'It's nowhere near my way home, but I have nothing else on and I can't say no to a takeaway and wine, or Ben.' She fluttered her eyelashes at him, making him blush and grin at the same time.

Wendy finished writing up the evidence bags and labelling them and laughed. She put the individual bags into a brown paper sack and passed them to Cathy. 'I'll ring them and let them know you're on your way.'

Ben pulled a twenty-pound note from his wallet and passed it to Cathy. 'Is this enough?' She took it and smiled.

'This close to payday, I suppose it will do, you cheapskate.'

He laughed but took the last note out of his wallet and gave her the tenner. 'Buy yourself a decent bottle of wine.'

She took it from him and stuffed the notes into her pocket. 'Thanks, I will, and this will help.' Then she took the bag from Wendy and left them to it.

'I didn't get offered anything for my services.' Then she laughed. 'I'm only joking, Ben. Right, I'm going before you decide you want a whole house forensically searched from top to bottom. If you do be warned the on call is from Barrow tonight. If I were you, I'd go home before you get yourself in any more trouble.'

She put her coat back on and walked out of the door. Ben looked at Morgan.

'I think she's right: I need food, sleep and painkillers. You look a bit washed out too. Let's call it a day and we'll see how things look in the morning.'

'Fine by me, I'll drop you off.'

As they walked out of the station Morgan looked around. It was desolate, everyone was out on patrol or attending jobs. She glanced towards the heavy grey steel door that led into the custody suite and hoped that tomorrow wouldn't see them bringing Ettie in. She couldn't bear the thought of her kind, gentle aunt having to go through the indignity of being booked in, searched and put into a cell.

Morgan stopped outside Ben's large Victorian semi-detached house. It really was a beautiful house, and she wondered not for the first time why Cindy had chosen to take her own life when it seemed she had it all. A gorgeous, kind husband and an amazing home. He got out of the car and shut the door then turned around before she could drive away. He opened the door.

'Hey, do you want to come in for something to eat?'

'No, thanks, I better get home. I'm shattered. I just want to change into my fluffy pyjamas and chill.'

He shrugged, shut the door and lifted a hand to wave at her.

She drove off before she changed her mind. There were all sorts of emotions that ran through her head whenever she thought too much about Ben. She did think they'd had a chance not too long ago to move their friendship into something more, but neither had acted on it. She knew when he showed her affection that he was mostly being nice; he was probably the kindest man she had ever known. But messing up their friendship would make things too complicated and right now all she wanted was straightforward. Whilst he was still grieving and so messed up over Cindy, he was going to struggle to move on with anyone. Which made her sad because he was one of the good guys and he deserved a second chance at love, at life, because all he seemed to be doing at the moment was existing and working. As she drove away that last thought made her chuckle *and what about you, Morgan, are you classing this existence as living or are you also just working and doing nothing else?* The smarmy face of Fin Palmer, the last guy she'd dated, flashed across her mind. After that last disaster with him she was off men for the foreseeable. It was much easier to keep it that way; there was only one person she would ever let close to her again and it wasn't likely to happen anytime soon.

CHAPTER EIGHTEEN

Morgan had spent all night tossing and turning, finally drifting off in the early hours when she'd dreamt about the last time they'd been together at school. She lay in the dark, staring out of the window. She'd been dreaming about the day before Brittany's birthday. She hadn't made it to the camping trip that had turned into an absolute disaster, and she'd been so glad that she hadn't. At the time she'd hated Stan so much for not letting her out that night, but as the years had passed, she realised it had been for the best. It was all still a mystery to her that what should have been a fun night could have ended in such tragedy. They'd all drifted apart after Brad's death: her, Brittany, Sienna, Jessica and Lara. And now Brittany and Sienna had come back into the picture in such awful circumstances. Hot tears pricked at the corner of her eyes. She'd never found out what had happened that night. It had all been hushed up, but as she lay there now, thinking about it, she didn't think that it could have been so straightforward. Someone must have known what had happened; someone must have seen something. And as far-fetched as it sounded, could it be connected to the current case?

Morgan threw her duvet back and swung her legs out of the bed. She glanced at her phone and saw the time was 04.25. *Oh hello, insomnia my old friend, tell me you're not back for a long stay. I thought we'd parted on good terms*, she whispered to herself. She shivered and realised the heating had turned itself off again. Looking at her warm bed she was tempted to climb inside, but she knew she wouldn't be able to go back to sleep. Instead, she went into the bathroom, grabbing her super soft dressing gown from the hook on the back of the door and wrapping herself up inside it. Her stomach felt like a mass of churning snakes. Something was wrong, she knew that it was, and she had a feeling that it might all stem back to what happened that night. She needed to speak to Jess and Lara today. If she could get them to tell her what really went on the night Brad died, then maybe she'd be able to figure out what Brittany and Sienna were mixed up in now.

As she boiled the kettle she wondered about Brittany and Sienna's relationship; they had been so close at school, but what about now? Had their friendship stood the test of time, or had they drifted away from each other like the rest of them? Maybe yesterday's events were some kind of weird suicide pact? You read of stuff like that happening and a few years ago there had been a spate of teenagers attempting it. But that was before she joined the police and Brittany and Sienna were in their twenties. Pouring the boiling water into the mug, Morgan stirred the hot liquid and shook her head. That didn't make sense at all. If Brittany was in a happy, loving relationship and had just booked a break to New York, it didn't seem like she was feeling suicidal. She stopped stirring, realising she knew a lot more about Brittany than she did Sienna and realised too that because she was still alive, they hadn't paid quite as much attention to her background. Well, that was today's action plan: she would try and dig into Sienna's life a little more, then pay Jess and Lara a visit. She knew from social media that Jess had a nail salon in Kendal, and Lara worked at the hospital, but that was about it. She didn't want to pay them a visit at work though, so she'd get their home addresses. She took her mug of coffee and sat on her oversized chair, looking out into the garden. Opening the curtains she saw that the sky was turning from inky black to muted grey and purple; the birds were starting to chirp away on the branches of the huge oak tree and despite feeling as though another couple of hours' sleep would have been nice, she felt energised and ready to face the day. She might even get some flowers and take them to the churchyard to lay on Brad's grave. It had been a few years since she'd done that. Work had been so utterly crazy the last eighteen months; she hadn't even given him a second thought.

As she stared out of the window, feeling guilty, she thought she saw a shadowy figure disappear behind the huge oak tree, and her heart skipped a beat. Fear began coursing through her veins, turning her blood cold. It felt as if she'd been picked up and dunked into an icy bath. She forced herself to step to the side of the window, cloaked behind the curtains out of sight but still able to see the tree. She waited and watched to see if the shadow moved again. As much as she loved living in this ground-floor apartment, too much had happened here and sometimes the smallest thing could set off an irrational anxiety; she wondered if it was time to find somewhere else to live. She'd been attacked here and so had Ben; the newspapers had printed photos of the gates to the house, and if you were local, it wasn't so hard to figure out where the big converted Georgian mansion was. Her heart racing, Morgan looked around for her phone and realised it was still charging in the bedroom. Focusing on the tree she stood perfectly still waiting for any signs of movement, but there was none, and as the sky began to get lighter and she could see the surrounding area, it was clear there were no signs of anyone loitering around. Who would want to be watching her? She closed her eyes and whispered his name. *Gary Marks*. Then she opened them again. She was being ridiculous. He had managed to evade capture all this time since his escape from prison. Why would he want to come back to Rydal Falls where everyone recognised him? *Because he has an axe to grind, a grudge to bear, that's why, Morgan. You betrayed him by joining the police and then you betrayed your brother. He is not the kind of man to take that lightly. He could be watching and waiting for the right time to take his chance. One, two, Gary's coming for you, three, four, better lock your door.* 'Shut up.' She screeched the words out loud, scaring herself. Having an overactive imagination really sucked at times and now she was singing the stupid nursery rhyme from the film *Nightmare on Elm Street.* Only it wasn't Freddy Krueger she was afraid of. No, she was scared of her own father, a real living and breathing nightmarish monster, and no one knew where the hell he was. She grabbed the curtains, drawing them shut again and double-checked that her front door and windows were all secure, even though she knew they were. It was all a bit too much and she wondered if she needed to speak to someone about everything that had gone on. Maybe she needed to see a counsellor. Amy's cousin's boyfriend, Isaac, had helped her briefly with her insomnia, although she didn't know what he could do about her weird family connections and the worry that she could carry some morbid killer gene inside her that was just waiting to explode. She didn't know if anyone could help her with that.

CHAPTER NINETEEN

Morgan walked into the office and looked around; it stank of stale curry. It was so annoying that response officers would eat in here and leave their mess for them to clean up when there was a perfectly decent canteen on the floor below they could sit in. She crossed the room and opened the windows as far as they would go. There was a tikka-stained plate on her desk along with a dirty fork and Morgan felt her blood boil, as if they hadn't even had the good manners to wash their pots. Talk about adding insult to injury. Taking them to the kitchen along the corridor she opened the bin and dropped it inside. She wasn't washing that. The sink was also full of dirty mugs and cutlery, but they were CID's. Rolling up her sleeves she began to fill the bowl with hot, soapy water. As she began washing up her mind wandered to her aunt Ettie. What would happen to her if those jars of tea came back containing the toxic substance that both Brittany and Sienna had ingested? Could her kind, gentle aunt possibly be involved? By the time she had boiled the kettle, washed the pots and then wiped down her desk, the office smelt fresher, the cool breeze chilling the stuffy air. Amy walked in and took one look at the open windows.

'Are you having a hot flush or something? It's bloody freezing in here.'

'No, someone ate a curry and left their dirty pots on my desk. It stank the whole room out.'

'Ah, let you off then, mate. I hate it when that happens. So what's happening, anything more on those two cases since yesterday?'

'I have no idea, I walked in and have been cleaning up ever since.'

Ben walked through the door and straight over to close the windows.

'Morning, it's a bit chilly in here.'

Morgan looked at Amy who was in the process of logging on to her computer.

'Who wants to go to the hospital for an update on Sienna Waters? I have a meeting in twenty minutes with Tom I can't get out of.'

Morgan's hand shot up. 'Me, I will.' She noticed that Amy hadn't even bothered.

'Calm down, you're not at school now, Brookes. I bet you were a right swot; teacher's pet and everything.'

She glared at Amy. 'No, I wasn't actually.'

Ben nodded. 'That's great, update me when you get back.'

'What are we doing about Brittany?'

'There's little we can do until we get some tox screens back, but you can go see if Sienna is in a fit state to talk to you and maybe explain what the hell happened. If we can get to the bottom of that it might help us with Brittany. We know that they both ingested belladonna.'

She didn't need telling twice, glad to be out of the office which still smelt faintly of stale food.

The hospital was busy, but Morgan knew where intensive care was and made her way to the stairs. She avoided lifts if she could; she hated being stuck inside them on the best of days, and the thought of one breaking down with her inside was more than she could bear today. Outside the unit, she pressed the buzzer and a grainy voice asked, 'Can I help?'

'Yes, I'm from the police. Detective Morgan Brookes to see Sienna Waters.'

There was a pause and then the intercom went dead. Morgan stepped away from it, wondering if something bad had just happened inside the unit, when the heavy wooden door opened, and a nurse stuck her head out.

'Morgan?'

She nodded, pulling the lanyard out of her shirt so she could see her warrant card.

'She's not here. We did all that we could for her.'

A sense of impending dread washed over Morgan at the thought of losing another school friend in the space of twenty-four hours, and the thought sucked all the air out of her lungs.

'Oh, no.'

'Oh God, sorry, she's not, well, you know she's not dead. She woke up is what I meant. She doesn't need to be in here; she's been moved to Ward Four.'

Morgan's head snapped up. 'Oh, thank God for that.'

'Yes, sorry about that. I guess I need to work on my communication skills.'

Morgan laughed. 'Yeah, me too, mine aren't wonderful either, but thank you that's great.'

She wandered off back to the stairs in search of Ward Four, feeling a little bit of hope for the first time since yesterday morning, when she'd realised that it had been Brittany at the school.

*

Ward Four was a scene of bedlam. There were nurses and patients everywhere. Morgan stood at the empty nurses' station waiting for someone to point her in the right direction to where Sienna was. Bells were ringing all over the place, and she turned to look on the television screen behind her, to see if she could spot her friend's name. Near the bottom she saw it: room twenty-five. Looking up and down the corridor at the little signs above the doors to the bays and rooms, she saw twenty-five at the very end of the ward. There was no one to ask, so she figured it would be okay to start walking down that way. If she got stopped, she'd tell them it was official police business. She checked herself; it *was* official police business. For some reason her stomach had begun to churn and suddenly she was transported back to her school days: geeky Goth Morgan was about to show her friend how far she'd come, that she'd made it past that awkward teenage phase and was now a detective with a whole career ahead of her. She paused outside the door, smiling to herself. She had come a very long way. The only thing that was the same as her teenage self was her love of the same footwear. She knocked, waiting for a reply.

'Come in.'

Opening the door, she smiled to see Sienna sitting up in the hospital bed, thankfully wearing a hospital gown and looking much more alive than she had yesterday.

The woman looked at Morgan. 'I don't want a cup of tea, thanks.'

'Just as well because I'm not offering you one. It's me, Morgan.'

Sienna studied her for a few seconds then laughed. 'Morgan Brookes, no way. What are you doing here?'

'I've come to ask you the same thing.' She stepped inside, closing the door, and Sienna frowned.

'What do you mean? I was ill yesterday. The doctors think I ate or drank something that might have been toxic, but I can't think what. Anyway, what's it got to do with you?'

Morgan felt a prickle of uneasiness at the base of her spine. Had she really expected the girl who had been quite mean to her at school until Brittany had intervened to have changed because they were adults? She pointed to the chair. 'Do you mind if I sit down?'

Sienna shrugged. Morgan lifted the lanyard over her head. Leaning forward she placed it on the table next to the bed. Sienna picked it up, staring at it then at Morgan.

'Detective Constable, are you joking me? Is this some kind of prank?'

Morgan felt a sharp pain inside her like she used to get at school whenever someone looked her up and down for being herself.

'No joke, I'm a detective. I attended the call that came in yesterday to say there was a woman acting strange at the caves and found you. Do you remember anything about yesterday?'

Sienna was shaking her head. 'I don't, oh God, did you see me?'

Morgan nodded. 'It doesn't matter what I saw. What matters is figuring out what happened to you. Can you take me from how your day started to how you ended up at the caves?'

'Is this an interview? Shouldn't you have someone more experienced with you who knows what they're doing?'

And just like that Morgan's confidence in herself and her abilities was blown out of the water. For a split second she wondered if she was qualified enough to be doing this. Then she pulled herself back together, determined not to let Sienna see she was getting to her. She nodded slowly.

'More than qualified, Sienna. I'm usually working murder cases and catching killers.' She smiled at her, and the woman nodded, her lips pursed together, and Morgan wondered what her problem was and then she remembered: Sienna had always wanted to be a detective; she was probably fuming that Goth girl Brookes was the one doing what she'd always said she was going to do. She pulled her notebook out of her pocket, uncapped her pen and smiled at Sienna.

'If you could start from the beginning that would be great.'

'I, well, first thing yesterday, I erm, I got up and made myself a cup of herbal tea. I didn't eat anything because I'm trying to lose a few pounds.'

Morgan didn't look up at her or give away the fact that she'd mentioned herbal tea. She didn't acknowledge that Sienna was slimmer now than she'd been even at school.

'What flavour tea?'

'Don't laugh, but it's called Self-Love tea. I get it from a really sweet woman who lives out in Covel Wood. She supplies the shop – I have a shop on Finkle Street – with four different kinds.

Sleep Well, Self-Love, Abundance and I can't remember the name of the other, but they're really popular; in fact I sell more of that than anything.'

'Can you tell me the name of your tea supplier?'

'Yes, but what has that got to do with anything? She's been bringing her jars of tea to the shop for over a year.'

'I need to speak to her.'

'Ettie Jackson.'

There was a pounding inside Morgan's head, and she wasn't sure if it was the start of a headache or a blood vessel about to explode at the mention of her aunt's name.

'What else did you have?'

'A medium, decaff, almond milk latte from Costa and a salted caramel brownie.'

Morgan didn't mention Sienna's earlier comment about wanting to lose weight; she obviously had as much willpower as she did.

'What time did you go to get coffee? Did you sit in the café?'

'Around ten thirty, and no I got a takeaway.'

'Anything else happen that morning? Did you come into contact with any plants that might have been poisonous?'

Sienna laughed. 'No, I don't make a habit of going around touching deadly plants and flowers.'

'How did you get to the caves, do you remember anything at all about what happened that ended up with you being found unconscious. I mean it's a bit of a hike up to the cave and that path can be a bit tricky, how did you manage it?'

Sienna stared at Morgan and let out the loudest of sighs.

'I don't know for sure, I think I must have driven there because I'm too lazy to have walked from town. Is my car still in the car park? It's all a bit fuzzy.'

'When I visited the shop yesterday, Marilyn said you have a boyfriend called Brad. Can you tell me where he lives so we can speak to him?'

Sienna laughed. 'Oh, Lord, she's such a blabbermouth. No, I don't have a boyfriend, or a lover called Brad. I only told her that to stop her asking about my love life. It gets a bit embarrassing at times. I figured it was easier to make up a little white lie for some peace and quiet.'

Morgan stared at her, thinking that was just plain weird – of all the names to choose – but she didn't continue with that line of questioning.

'Did you know about Brittany?' Morgan wanted to see Sienna's reaction, to gauge her shock.

Sienna sat forward. 'No, what about her? Is she okay? She didn't get poisoned too, did she?' She was still grinning as if this whole thing was a big joke, and Morgan wanted to reach forward and slap the smile from her face.

'She's dead.'

Sienna let out a gasp, her hand clamped across her mouth. 'No, shut up.'

Morgan couldn't believe what she was hearing. 'Yes, she had a terrible accident and fell to her death at the school. She was acting strange before it happened; then when I arrived at the caves you were almost naked, mumbling and acting strange too, until you collapsed. How do you explain your behaviour? Do you or Brittany take drugs? Were you on some kind of diet pills maybe?'

'She's really dead?'

Morgan nodded.

'No, I do not take diet pills or drugs. The only thing I had yesterday was what I already told you about.'

'When was the last time you spoke to Brittany?'

'Let me see, about a month ago, she came into the shop to see if I had anything that could help with her stomach. She was having spasms and cramps that the doctors weren't doing anything for. She said they'd given her something, but it only helped once the attacks occurred. She wanted something more preventative and soothing.'

The sinking feeling of dread which was settling over Morgan felt too heavy to bear.

'Did you give her something?'

'Only a business card that I scribbled Ettie Jackson's address on. I said she might be able to help her.'

'How?'

'By mixing her a special blend of tea. That woman is a miracle-worker.'

'Do you know if Brittany went to see her?'

Morgan already knew the answer to this one: she had Ettie's statement and the jar of tea to prove that Brittany had visited her.

She shrugged. 'No idea, I haven't seen her since. It has been a bit crazy in the shop. It's really taken off with the teas and books on manifesting your perfect life and all that jazz.'

'Did you keep in touch with her after we left school?'

'Not really, we've stayed friendly, and she knew about the shop, of course, but we all kind of drifted apart after school. Oh, I did hear she was a lesbian though. I would have never guessed because she really fancied Brad. The last time I saw her was the first in a couple of years. Maybe she never got over him and decided no man could take his place.'

Morgan had always kept her distance from Sienna, who had a mean streak at school. She had just told her about her friend dying and she was eager to gossip about her, which was just awful. She stood up. 'What did the doctor say was wrong with you? Did they mention anything specific?'

'Apparently, it was anti-toxic syndrome or something like that. He's very nice and keeps referring to it as ATS. He said that there's a lot of prescription drugs that can cause it.'

'Are you on any prescription drugs?' Morgan wouldn't be surprised if she rhymed off a list of them, especially antidepressants or maybe antipsychotics, then she stopped herself for being so mean.

'No, not at all. I mean I take the odd painkillers for headaches, but everyone does. I try my best not to take anything other than natural remedies.'

'Then it's hardly going to be from a prescriptive drug, is it?'

'No, he said that the plant *Atropa Belladonna* is also one of the plants that can cause ATS. I think I need to check with Ettie that she is not unwittingly using deadly poisonous plants to make her teas with. I couldn't be selling teas that make this happen.'

She was smiling sweetly at Morgan, and Morgan knew that she needed to get out of there and fast. Her head was spinning at the thought of her aunt unintentionally killing people.

'Thanks. Oh, one last question: where were your clothes?'

'I don't know. I can't believe you found me naked. How embarrassing. But if you find them, I had a brand-new white Zara T-shirt on. I'd literally only just bought it a few days ago so I'd really like that back.'

Morgan had to get out of here; she couldn't be in the same room as this woman for much longer.

'Take care. I hope you feel better soon.'

She shut the door before she had to look at Sienna's smug face a moment longer. She needed fresh air and somewhere to clear her head to remove all the teenage angst and feelings that ten minutes with her old friend had managed to bring up, leaving her feeling as if she wasn't good enough to be doing her job. Before she went back to the station to tell Ben what Sienna had just disclosed to her and to check if the PNC bureau had sent her a list of the owners of the car registrations that she'd sent over. Maybe one was Sienna's.

CHAPTER TWENTY

Ben stopped in the small parking area, waiting for the police van to arrive. He was going to try his best to do this discreetly and without a fuss, but if it should all go wrong, he didn't want to be shouting over the airwaves asking for help and alerting Morgan to what he was doing. Amy hadn't spoken a word to him all the way here.

'Why didn't you ask Des to come with you on this shitshow of a job?'

She was glaring at him, and he felt his cheeks getting hotter.

'I needed a woman to search her should the need arise, hopefully it won't. I'm trying to do this as fairly and calmly as possible.'

'Really, then wouldn't it have been better to bring Morgan with you? I mean she's your first choice for everything else. Why me this time or do I only get the really crappy jobs no one else wants?'

'I'd have thought it was obvious why, Amy.'

'Yeah, too bloody obvious. You don't want to upset her, which is very noble of you, Ben, but I have news for you, she will go nuts when she finds out you sent her to the hospital in another town to get her out of the way so you could come arrest her aunt behind her back. It's sneaky and wrong. You should have told Morgan what you were doing first.'

'I didn't bloody know what I was doing until after the meeting, and both Tom and the Chief Super insisted that I bring her in for interview. So how could I have told Morgan?'

'Have you phoned her to discuss it?'

He didn't answer; he couldn't answer.

'See, I bloody knew it. I never pegged you as a sneak, Ben. This is so wrong and don't think Morgan is going to take it lightly. She is going to go into major meltdown mode.'

A police van drove into the car park, and he was glad to have a reason to get out of the small car and away from Amy's accusations. He got out of the car; he didn't need anyone to tell him that this was messed up, he already knew it, but just because Ettie was related to Morgan it didn't mean that he shouldn't do his job. At the moment the belladonna was all the evidence they had and it pointed towards that awful herbal tea as being the means of poisoning both Brittany and Sienna. This was his job; it was what he was supposed to do. He reached the van, and Cain rolled the window down.

'Thanks for coming, but I want this as low-key as possible unless it all kicks off. Is there anywhere you could park away from here but not too far so you can get here fast?'

'Where's Morgan?'

'Speaking to the victim from the caves yesterday, why?'

Cain shrugged. 'Just asking. There's a lay-by half a mile or so down the road. We'll go wait there.'

'Thanks, I appreciate it.'

Ben turned to face Amy who was now leaning against the car, her arms folded across her chest. She was still scowling at him. He wanted to tell her to pack it in because he already felt like a top-class arsehole for doing this. He'd thought he would be protecting Morgan by coming here whilst she was in Kendal, and she'd volunteered when he'd asked. He didn't know that everyone was going to be offended on her behalf. He closed his eyes. There was a throbbing pain in the side of his temple that he only ever got whenever anything involved Morgan Brookes. Why did she have this effect on him?

Ben led the way along the narrow footpath which led to the cottage in the woods and found his stomach was doing Olympic standard summersaults. Amy was behind him, giving him the silent treatment and no doubt still glaring at the back of his head. As they rounded the bend the small cottage came into view, and Amy whispered, 'Wow, that's so... it's like something out of a fairy tale.'

Ben didn't answer. That huge black bird was sitting on the gate staring at him with its beady eyes.

'Woah, that's one badass raven. Look at the size of him. He's not going to let you near and I don't blame him.'

Ben turned to look at Amy. 'It's a bird not a Rottweiler. It can hardly stop us from going through that gate.'

'Yep, it's a bird all right. It might not have sharp teeth but look at the size of that beak. It will peck your eyes out in less than a minute.'

'Jesus, Amy.'

She broke into a stifled giggle. 'Have you seen the *Omen II*, the original not the crappy remakes? Where that woman gets her eyes pecked out then gets hit by a truck? You can go face to face with that because I'm not going anywhere near it. I don't like birds and that's huge. I bet it would let Morgan in.'

Ben growled. 'Shut up, Amy.'

He took a step closer, and the bird actually ruffled its feathers and puffed out its chest. Amy was laughing behind him, the noise echoing around the woods.

'Oh, it's ready for you, boss. Have you got any CS gas in your pocket? You might have to use it.'

The cottage door opened, and Ettie saw the stand-off between the bird and Ben. She made a clicking noise with her tongue, and the bird turned to face her. For a split second it watched her. She nodded her head and it in turn tilted its head to the side and then it took off. Circling around Ben's head a couple of times, it then swooped and landed on the kitchen windowsill, where it proceeded to keep staring at Ben.

'Sorry about that, he's a bit protective. How are you? Is Morgan with you?'

Ben shook his head. 'I'm afraid she isn't, Ettie. It's me and Amy today.'

Ettie looked at Ben. Her eyes fell on Amy, quickly moving back to Ben.

'And what do you and Amy want? Have you come for some of my special tea?' She smiled, but it didn't reach her eyes, and he knew that she knew exactly why he was there. He had this awful, gut-wrenching feeling that this woman smiling at him had caused one woman to die and another to have a brush with death that was far too close for his liking. Regardless of who she was and whether it was intentional or not, it was too late.

'No, we haven't. Ettie there's no easy way to say this and I'm truly sorry to have to do this, but we've come to take you to the station for questioning.'

'Are you arresting me?'

'No. Well, yes, but not like that. If you come with me now then it'll be more of a voluntary interview.'

She nodded. 'I'll just lock my door; you never know who is around, do you?'

She didn't take her eyes off Ben when she said that, then she turned and went inside.

'What if she goes in and does something stupid or escapes out of the back door, Ben?'

'She won't. Why would she want to do that when I've given her the chance to come without a fuss?'

And then she was out of the front door, and Amy whispered, 'She's wearing an actual black velvet cloak; I think I love her. We should have Fleetwood Mac playing on our phones or something for her to flounce down the path to. What an absolute legend.'

Ben hissed, 'Shut up, Amy,' as Ettie turned to the bird.

'I might be a little while; you can get in the upstairs window if the weather turns bad.'

The bird let out a loud cry that filled the air, echoing around the trees, and Amy uttered one word, 'Epic,' as Ben gently shoved his elbow into her ribs. Ettie opened the gate and came out with her arms outstretched holding them out for Ben to cuff her.

'There's no need for handcuffs, Ettie. Hopefully, we can get this cleared up and have you back home soon.'

She nodded. 'The burning times may have passed but wise women and healers are still persecuted for their knowledge and love of nature. Death and healing go side by side, they always have and always will.'

Ben didn't know what to say to that, so he didn't say anything. He felt terrible and he knew that Morgan was going to be upset about this, but what choice did he have? He was convinced that somehow Ettie was responsible for this mess with her herbal teas, probably not intentionally, but he had to do his job. He would be letting Brittany down if he brushed it under the carpet as an accidental death or suicide without finding out why she acted the way she did. They walked back to the car in silence, Ettie leading the way through the woods with Ben and Amy following behind.

CHAPTER TWENTY-ONE

Fresh air hit Morgan's face and she had never felt so grateful to be outside. The hospital was stuffy and made even worse by the fact that Sienna had made her feel so crap about herself. There was a picnic bench around the side, and she had an overwhelming urge to sit down and take a few minutes. She did, feeling as if the weight of the world was pressing down on her. She let out a huge yawn. This morning's early wake-up call was taking its toll on her, but there was something else that she couldn't put her finger on. She had a feeling that something was wrong somewhere.

'Well, if it isn't the prettiest detective I know.'

Morgan turned to face Declan, who looked as if he'd stepped out of the pages of a men's glossy magazine. Gone were his usual dark blue scrubs and white wellies; he was wearing a pair of faded Levi's and a white shirt. His hair, which was normally slicked back or flattened under a cap, was freshly blow dried.

'Well, if it isn't the most handsome pathologist that I know. Or rather the only pathologist that I know. What are you doing here?'

'It's my day off and I have a hot date with an even hotter guy, but first I wanted to speak to the woman from the caves yesterday, who has made a miraculous recovery thanks to my intervention. I also wanted to speak to her consultant, who is actually my hot date.'

She laughed. 'Good effort. What do you mean your intervention?'

'I've waited so long for this kind of chance, to be the one solving the crimes. All those years of watching *Scooby-Doo* have finally paid off.' He winked at her. 'When I was back in med school there was a saying they taught us about looking out for the symptoms of the ingestion of toxins or poisons. "Hot as a hare, blind as a bat, red as a beet, mad as a hatter".'

'Well that pretty much sums up both Brittany's and Sienna's behaviour; both of them were mad as hatters. Sienna was really hot to the touch and her skin was red. I can't say about the blindness though; she collapsed.'

'Mmm, it's very interesting, isn't it, and quite bizarre really. It's not the sort of thing you hear about very often. In my opinion they were definitely poisoned, so I told her consultant, and it seems they managed to get her healed up in no time. It's all very Agatha Christie, and I'm sorry to say this, Morgan, but I'm finding this so intriguing. It's like some interesting murder mystery night.'

She laughed. He was so likeable and funny that you just couldn't take offence at anything he said.

'I suppose it is.'

'So, what's that handsome brute Ben doing about it all? And don't tell him I called him handsome, it will freak him out.'

'Honestly, I don't know what he's doing. Did he tell you about the herbal tea my aunt makes that they both bought from her? I have this terrible feeling that she may have accidentally put something in it.'

He was nodding. 'Yes, and I'm sorry to say this but it really does look that way. Like you say though, if she did it wouldn't have been on purpose. But what about other customers? Do we think there's a chance there's a whole contaminated batch out there lurking around?'

'Oh, shit. I don't know. We need to get all those bottles back from Sienna's shop Tea Leaves and Reads.'

'Does she own that? I love that quirky little place. I bought a few books and a deck of tarot cards from there last year; thank God I didn't try the tea. Sorry, Morgan, no offence.'

'None taken. You bought tarot cards? I wouldn't have pegged you for a card reader.'

'Not for me, for Susie. She's into all that kind of stuff. I wanted to get her something different for her Christmas gift, instead of the usual Lynx for Women gift set.'

'You're such a sweetheart underneath that grumpy exterior.'

He clutched his chest. 'Grumpy, me? How very dare you.' They both laughed, and Morgan felt a little bit lighter inside.

'You know, if it is your aunt's tea, then it would be a manslaughter charge at worst. As long as they can prove she didn't intentionally poison the pair of them.'

'That's true; you haven't met her, but she's such a lovely, gentle soul. I think she would be devastated to have caused anything like this.'

Declan reached out and took hold of Morgan's hand, squeezing it gently.

'You need to stop taking on the troubles of the world, Morgan. Not everything is your responsibility. How is your love life at the moment? I hope it's better than mine.'

And just like that they were back to small talk. She shrugged.

'What, you and the brute haven't got it on yet?'

'Declan.'

'Why not?'

'I don't know. We work together and he's my boss. It wouldn't be right.'

He was shaking his head. 'Not really a good enough reason, but I admire your morals.' He stood up. 'I better head inside before they discharge the patient. I really need to speak to her just to satisfy my own morbid curiosity. Take care, Morgan, and let me know if the two of you decide to get it on. I love a happy ever after.'

She laughed. 'What happened to your forensic scientist?'

'He found someone else who didn't work quite as long hours and wasn't as grumpy.'

'I'm sorry, Declan, you deserve someone nice.'

'Yeah, I do. Like Ms Waters's very handsome consultant maybe.'

He walked away grinning, and she watched him go. What a pair they made, both of them married to their jobs and couldn't keep a lover for very long.

She took out her phone and googled the number for Tea Leaves and Reads.

'Hello, Marilyn, this is Detective Brookes.'

'I know who this is, what do you want now?'

'I need you to take all the bottles of tea off the shelves now, please, just as a precaution.'

'And then what do you want me to do with them?'

'Can you box them up and keep them secured in the storeroom until we've had a chance to figure out if they need seizing or not?'

'I suppose so.'

'Whatever you do, please don't let anyone else buy it and do you have a list of the customers who have purchased, or do you know them personally?'

Marilyn muttered something about loss of earnings and she wasn't a walking address book then hung up. Morgan couldn't stop thinking about Sienna making up a fake boyfriend called Brad; it was so strange, was this all somehow connected to Brad's death? She wasn't sure where she was going with this train of thought but it was there inside her chest. That niggling feeling telling her there was something more to it and now she couldn't ignore it, she decided to go back to the shop now and get this over with.

Morgan left the car on the pavement outside Sienna's shop, not wanting to leave potentially poisonous jars of tea there, or evidence. She had driven there after leaving the police station. She walked in, relieved to see the shelves where it had been stocked were now empty.

'Are you happy now? I bet you didn't think I'd do it, did you?' Marilyn said as a greeting.

Morgan smiled at her. 'Thank you, it's a really difficult time for everyone at the moment. All we want to do is make sure everyone is safe and no one else gets hurt. I'll take the tea back to the station for now and get it booked in to the property store.'

'And what about the money Sienna is going to lose on it? It will never see the light of day again; you and I both know that.'

'Look, Marilyn, I know you're trying to keep the business afloat, but there is no price on a person's life, and Sienna would agree with me. She could have died. I don't think she would want to risk it happening to anyone else, do you?'

'I suppose not, let me go and get it for you.'

She went out the back of the shop, reappearing a few minutes later with a heavy box which Morgan took from her.

'Do you know of anyone who may have bought it?' she asked again.

'I've already spoken to the regulars who buy it that I know and told them to dispose of it or bring it back next week for a refund, not that Sienna is going to be very pleased about that.'

'It's the right thing to do, thank you. If Sienna is angry then you tell her to come and speak to me about it, not you.'

Marilyn walked her to the door, opening it for her. 'You're right, I will.'

Morgan balanced the box on one knee whilst opening the boot, where she placed the box and shut it again. She felt better knowing there wasn't a chance anyone could buy some potentially contaminated tea.

CHAPTER TWENTY-TWO

Morgan walked into the office and was surprised to see only Des sitting at the desk, blowing on a mug of coffee. She sat down at her desk opening her emails, scanning for one from PNC. She opened it and read down the list of registered keepers. None of them belonged to Sienna; how did she get to White Moss car park? They were going to have to wait and see if Sienna's memory came back to answer that question because the only other way was if she hitchhiked or was dropped off. She looked across at Des who looked as if he was trying to avoid making eye contact with her.

'Afternoon, where is everyone?'

His cheeks instantly began to glow a deep shade of red, and he began to stutter.

'They're, they, they're in interview.'

'Oh, who are they interviewing?' The question was asked in a casual, gentle manner and yet Des looked as if he'd just been caught cheating on his girlfriend, because his whole face was etched in misery and the penny dropped.

'Who are they interviewing?' More insistent this time. She stood in front of him, waiting for his reply, but she didn't need it. She knew it was Ettie, and a black rage was filling every molecule in her body.

'Ettie Jackson.' He looked so miserable she thought he was going to burst into tears.

She didn't answer because she was already out of the door and on her way down to the custody suite. She ran down the spiral staircase and almost sprinted down the long corridor to where the grey steel door was. She rang the buzzer, waiting for the door to click open like it should, but it didn't. Stepping back, she waved at the CCTV camera and pressed it again. The door still didn't click open, and she knew there was a chance they were busy, but this had never happened to her before. Generally an officer, the custody sergeant or one of the detention officers, was behind the desk ready to let her in. She hadn't heard any calls over the airwaves for an emergency in custody. She pressed the buzzer, and this time didn't let go. A voice crackled through the intercom.

'*Sorry, we're busy, can you come back later?*'

'No, I need to come in now.'

There was a long pause.

'*Can't let you in right now, Morgan. Come back in a little while.*'

'Tell Sergeant Matthews that I know what he's doing and who he's talking to.'

'*Yep, no problem. I'll pass the message on.*'

'No, you will go and tell him now.'

Her hands curled into fists by her sides as she waited for someone to come speak to her but no one came. Cain, who was walking past, nodded at her. His shift had finished, and he had his jacket on and a backpack slung over his shoulder.

'All right, Morgan, is the door stuck again?'

She looked at him. 'No, I don't think so. They won't let me in.'

His confusion was genuine. 'Why?'

'Because Ben is in there interviewing my aunt, who he didn't bother to tell me he was arresting, that's why.'

'Oh, shit. Look, if you want a bit of friendly advice, leave it well alone, Morgan. This isn't for you to get involved in. It's a conflict of interest, you know that, don't you? Get yourself out of here, take a few hours off and have an early finish. I'm going home now. Do you fancy grabbing a coffee?'

She looked at him. He was right, and she knew all of that, but it didn't stop the throbbing pain inside her chest that Ben hadn't been able to tell her what he was doing. She felt as if he'd betrayed her trust.

'Seriously, Morgan, walk away from this now. You can't do anything. It's out of your hands. It's not worth getting in trouble for.'

She nodded and turned away from the door. 'You're right, thanks, Cain.'

'Hey, what about that coffee?'

She paused, tempted to do just that: let Ben come find her and update her if he dared. How would he feel to see her sitting with Cain? And then she realised it was her who would feel crap and she wasn't going to be very good company the way she was feeling.

'Thanks, Cain, maybe another time.'

'Anytime, Morgan, just let me know.'

She walked straight out of the side door out into the car park and headed for her car. She was tired, angry and now in a brooding rage. It was time to get as far away from Rydal Falls police station as she could. She went home, changed into some joggers and a loose T-shirt, slipped on some trainers and went for a long walk, half run down to the riverside, where the air was clear and the sound of the babbling river would soothe her soul.

CHAPTER TWENTY-THREE

Ben leaned forward and paused the tape. Ettie had declined a solicitor and had also declined to speak many words apart from 'No comment'. They were in the first interview room nearest to the staff entrance, and he'd heard the banging on the custody door. He didn't need anyone to tell him who it was knocking to be let in. Amy kept glancing at him and shaking her head like he was some naughty schoolboy, and he was getting angrier by the minute.

'Would you like to take a break, Ettie?'

'No, thank you.'

He frowned; he wanted a break. He wanted just ten minutes to think.

'Look, I'm sorry that it's come to this. All I'm trying to do is figure out what went so horribly wrong. Even if it comes back that your tea was the reason for Brittany Alcott's death and Sienna Waters taking ill, we can work something out if you just talk to us about it.'

Ettie studied his face. 'I think you're telling the truth; I don't think that you do want to be here in this situation, but here's the thing, Detective Matthews, we are, and by the sounds of that commotion out there you didn't even have the courtesy to inform Morgan about your plans. Which in my humble opinion is really low. She deserved to know what you were up to. I'm extremely disappointed in you, Ben. I had high hopes for you.'

He felt as if he had just been told off by his grandmother for stealing money out of her purse. There was a knock on the door and Joanne, who was the duty custody sergeant, stuck her head in.

'Ben, a word, please.'

He stood up, excused himself and left the room, following her to her desk.

'Apparently you have to speak to Des. He's just taken a phone call from forensics for you.'

'Thanks, I'll go and see him.'

'Oh, and Ben, you need to calm Morgan down. She was hammering to get in. I had to send her away. Did you not inform her what you were doing?'

His cheeks which were already red burned even brighter. 'I thought I was protecting her. Jesus, does everyone know it's her aunt?'

'I don't know about everyone, but I do know that because I've bought some of her herbal tea in the past and she talked about her niece, Morgan, who was a police officer.'

'You bought her tea as well? What is wrong with everyone? Why do you all want to drink that crap?'

'Because she's good at what she does. Call me biased but I think you have this totally wrong.'

Ben turned away before his face gave away the fact that he was about to combust into a fiery inferno. He waited at the cold steel door for someone behind the desk to press the release button so he could escape, and it seemed they were taking an awful long time. He leaned his burning forehead onto the cold steel to try and cool himself down, when the catch finally clicked and he pushed it open, expecting to see Morgan standing on the other side. She wasn't, but there was a good chance she was waiting for him in the office, and he didn't want to see her just yet. He had no choice but to go up there, though. He needed to see what information Des had, so he braced himself and took the stairs two at a time. By the time he reached the third floor, he was breathing so hard he thought he was about to have a heart attack with the exertion and the stress. Inhaling deeply, he walked through the door ready for a showdown, only to be greeted by Des, who was pacing up and down, clutching a printout that he passed to him.

'Boss, you should read this, and you should also know that Morgan is pissed and on the rampage.'

Ben took the papers from him. 'Yeah, I know about that. What's this?'

'Some woman from the lab rang to say your test results from the sample of tea recovered from Brittany's house showed positive for a toxic plant substance called *Atropa Belladonna*.'

He looked up at Des and smiled. 'Yes, I knew it. I knew I was right all along, thank God for that.'

Des shook his head. 'I wouldn't get too excited if I were you. Apparently, it was a miniscule amount and not enough to cause any of the symptoms both victims displayed.'

Ben slumped onto the corner of the nearest desk as he felt all hope drain away of finding out what the hell was going on.

'She said that to have caused the symptoms that the victims displayed, the amount would have had to have been much, much more.'

'How much more?'

'I don't know, I'm not the scientist, but I've done a Google search and according to that just two to four berries would kill a kid; an adult would die from eating ten to twenty. Even the leaves are deadly in a large amount.'

'So, we're back to square one basically.'

'I suppose so, boss. Have you considered that they might have done this themselves?'

'Of course I have, Des.'

He took the papers, turned around and made his way back down to custody, where he was buzzed back inside.

Inside the interview room, Amy and Ettie were deep in conversation. As soon as he walked in, they both stopped talking. He sat back down opposite Ettie and pressed record.

'Interview reconvened at 16.27. Ettie, please can you tell me how much *Atropa Belladonna* you actually put into your jars of tea? I know that you do because the tests have come back with a positive result for it.'

'I never said that I didn't use it, Detective. Yes, I can tell you exactly how much I use. I pick the leaves and harvest some of the berries, but I dry them out and I use the tiniest amount of the leaf; sometimes less than a quarter of a berry in a batch of ten to fifteen jars, because as you now know they are deadly and can cause all sorts of problems if a large amount is taken. It is wonderful in helping soothe bowel and stomach spasms, but only in the smallest of quantities. Before you ask this isn't in the teas that I sell to the shop: these are in the specific teas that are requested.'

'And Brittany asked you for some of this special tea?'

Ettie let out a long sigh. 'Yes, she did and from what I can gather it was working very well. If she died from belladonna poisoning then it wasn't through me. You need to be looking very closely at whoever had access to her food and drink. Now, is there anything else you need to know, because I am afraid that's all I can give to you. Any further questions will be no comment.'

'Not at this moment in time. I have no further questions. You are free to leave. I'll get someone to give you a lift home.'

He reached over, stopped the tape and nodded at Amy, who stood up.

'Come on, Ettie, I'll take you home.'

'Thank you, dear, that's exceedingly kind of you.'

Amy walked out and Ettie followed. Ettie turned to Ben.

'If you want my advice, I think you need to speak to Morgan and smooth things over with her. She's going to be very upset with you.'

And then she was gone. The door shut behind her and he was left staring at the white walls of the interview room, wondering what the hell was going on and why he was having to take relationship tips from the woman he had just accused of poisoning her customers.

CHAPTER TWENTY-FOUR

Jessica was living off green smoothies, or any smoothies at the minute. She had a bridesmaid dress fitting next week and she'd be bloody damned if the dressmaker was going to pull and pinch her back rolls whilst muttering about how she was going to have to let the seams out again. She was fairly sure the woman lived to insult the poor bastards who needed to have their dresses made, because none of the shop-bought ones fit. When Lara had asked her to be her chief bridesmaid she'd been thrilled, until she'd realised that it would mean having to wear a long dress that would show off her bingo wings and back fat. So, she had bought a smoothie maker and a book of recipes which, if she was honest, tasted like crap. The only time they were okay was if she used ice cream instead of ice cubes, or a shot of vodka, which kind of defeated the whole trying to be healthy thing. Lara had told her to stop being stupid, that she didn't need to lose any weight because she looked amazing as she was. Yeah, she wished she did. Jessica stared at herself in the full-length mirror, in her mismatched bra and panties that had seen better days. God, she needed to go shopping. This was the thing when you were single and hadn't had a boyfriend for over twelve months. There wasn't much point splashing out on fancy lingerie when no one was going to see the stuff, and it was always so uncomfortable anyway. She turned to the side, sucked in her belly and let out a sob, wondering if she broke a leg or an arm if she'd be able to get out of being a bridesmaid. There were eight weeks to go to the wedding, surely Lara wouldn't want her hobbling around on a pair of crutches, spoiling the photographs. There was always the low blow; she could be a complete bitch and tell her that she thought hotshot Greg was having an affair with someone they both knew. She stopped for a second and realised that would be a really shitty thing to do just to get out of wearing a bridesmaid dress.

She threw the contents of her last remaining bag of frozen smoothie mix into the blender thing. Opening the fridge there was no milk left, and she let out a groan. She had meant to go to the shop for some on her way home from work and totally forgot. Opening the freezer she spied the half-eaten tub of Ben & Jerry's Cookie Dough ice cream and took it out. It had been there so long there were ice crystals on the top and it was frozen solid, so she took the lid off and put it in the microwave for a minute. When it pinged and she took it out all that was left was a gloopy, yellow mushy mess with balls of cookie dough floating around inside it like little balls of poop. It looked like milk. Taking a spoon from the drawer she fished out the bits of cookie dough and ate them, savouring the sweetness and wishing she had said no to the whole bridesmaid thing. Tipping the congealed mush into the smoothie maker she turned it on, watching it all blitz together into a purple concoction. Taking her supersized mug of violet-coloured slush, she went and threw herself onto the couch. Picking up her phone she opened the Facebook app and then snapped a photo of her tea. Uploading it she began typing...

What am I thinking Facebook? I'm thinking that this is ridiculous and does anyone have a discount code for Domino's?

She shared it then began scrolling through her newsfeed whilst sipping and grimacing at the same time. She stopped scrolling to see a picture of Brittany Alcott's smiling face and lots of comments saying, 'RIP Brittany, I can't believe you're gone'. A feeling of horror washed over her, and she sat up, thinking that she had read it wrong. Surely not. She clicked on the photograph to see hundreds more comments saying RIP and felt a wave of nausea roll up from her stomach to the back of her throat. She'd finished the goddamn awful smoothie and now thought she was going to puke it all back up. She dialled Lara's number and waited for her to answer. She did immediately.

'Hey, have you heard about Brittany?'

'*No, what about her?*'

'I think she's dead.'

'*What? Who told you that? You know what you're like, Jess, you told me Ashleigh Baker was dead the other month and she wasn't. You're not exactly reliable on the old gossip front. I told Greg who told his mum who only went and sent a sympathy card to her mum.*'

'That was a genuine mistake. I didn't know you'd tell the whole town. This isn't. It's all over Facebook, Lara.'

'*Oh, well it has to be true then, doesn't it?*'

'Where are you?'

'*On the toilet.*'

'Have a look now and ring me back.'

Jessica hung up. She felt physically ill. She was definitely going to throw up. Standing up, she began to walk to the toilet. She was so shocked her legs were actually trembling. She hated death or the thought of anyone dying, especially at their age; it wasn't right. She made it to the bathroom and leaned over the toilet, clutching on to the sides of the bowl as water began to fill her mouth. Then her phone began to ring, and she forced herself to stand up and go get it, pausing to splash cold water from the tap into her mouth then spit it out a couple of times. Her legs were still wobbling as she made her way back to the sofa to answer the phone.

'*She's dead.*'

'I told you. Oh God, poor girl. I feel awful. I haven't seen her in ages. Does it say what happened? I didn't really look; I was too busy panicking.'

'*Accident at the school apparently, but I've just messaged Paige who works there, and she said she threw herself out of the staffroom window.*'

'Nooo, oh that's awful. Why did she do that, Lara?'

'*I don't know. I don't know everything. Maybe she was depressed. What an awful way to go though, at work, and what about all those kids in the school?*'

'Do you think she was feeling guilty about Brad? It's his anniversary soon. Maybe she couldn't stop thinking about him. I get like that at times whenever I think about that night and how he died.'

Lara paused.

'*I don't know. I think we all feel bad about that night, Jess, but what were we supposed to do? We were kids, we had our whole lives ahead of us and it wasn't our fault. There was nothing else we could have done.*'

'I suppose so, but I feel sick, like really sick. I was about to puke when you rang back.'

'*What did you have for tea? Did you actually drink that disgusting crap you put a picture of on Facebook, because I was about to text you a Domino's code.*'

'Yep.'

'*Christ, Jess, I've told you a thousand times you look just perfect in that dress. You don't need to starve yourself to death.*'

Jess felt the room begin to blur around the edges. She felt really ill. 'I know, look I don't feel well. I'm going to have to lie down. Speak to you later.'

'*Yeah, let me know if you need anything.*'

Jessica hung up. Her face felt as if it was on fire, and she was definitely seeing double. She tried to stand up, but her legs gave way and she ended up falling back down onto the sofa. Curling into a ball, she grabbed a cushion and put it over her face to try and stop the room from spinning. God, had she given herself food poisoning off that awful bloody smoothie? That would really piss her off if she had. You just never got food poisoning off pizza or doughnuts, did you? Squeezing her eyes closed, she began to inhale deeply through her nose and out through her mouth to try and slow her breathing down. Her heart was racing, and she wondered if the shock of her school friend's death had caused some kind of panic attack or reaction, because she had never felt this dreadful before.

CHAPTER TWENTY-FIVE

By the time Morgan arrived back at her apartment it was getting dusky, and there was a cold nip in the air that hadn't been there when she'd set off. She had walked then run, then walked for almost eight miles and was absolutely shattered. She wanted to get in the shower, then eat and sleep, nothing more. Her brain was exhausted, and she had listened to *Morbid*, her favourite true crime podcast, interspersed with a playlist to keep her going and now all she could think about was the awful crimes of the killer the podcast hosts had been talking about; thankfully, they had taken place in Australia in the eighties. She'd thought she'd seen her fair share of sick, evil bastards but that one had been something else. She hadn't thought about Ben or Ettie or what was happening, refusing to let her mind dwell on it any longer. As she was opening the front door her neighbour, Emily's, Mini zoomed into the driveway, spraying gravel all over, and she let out a sigh and muttered *every single time I look a state she appears, as if by magic, to make me feel even crapper.*

'Hey, Morgan, long time no see. How are you?'

Morgan gritted her teeth. She wanted to reply *angry beyond belief, Emily*; instead she turned and smiled at her.

'I've had better days. How are you?'

'Oh, I'm good. Look, I've been wanting to ask you about Ben, how is he doing?'

'He's okay, why?'

'No reason, he's such a nice guy, I thought, you know, that you and him might…'

'Might what?' Why did everyone assume they were sleeping with each other? It was beginning to get on her nerves now. Could a man and woman not work with each other and be friends without everyone assuming they were having a quick leg over in the stationery cupboard when no one was looking?

'Nothing, sorry, I'm just being nosey. I guess I'm a bit lonely. I liked his company and, you know, he's kind of cute.'

'Well in that case you should send him a message, Emily, see if he wants to go for a drink. He's not doing anything or seeing anyone that I know of.'

'What, you wouldn't mind if I did?'

'Absolutely not, go for it.'

'Wow, thanks. I might just do that. Have a great evening, Morgan. If you're not busy, you could come up to mine for a glass of wine and we could put the world to rights.'

At this precise moment she couldn't think of anything she'd rather not do.

'I'm exhausted and I smell terrible, but thanks for the offer. I need a hot shower and my bed.'

The disappointment on Emily's face made her feel bad, but she was sticking to her guns and doing exactly what she said.

'Night, Morgan.'

She lifted a hand and waved in her direction, opening her front door and slipping through it before Emily came after her to barrage her with more questions. She was like a trained interviewer. She wondered if she had ever applied for the police. She remembered her talking about it a little while ago. It would be such a shame to let those interviewing skills go to waste. Closing her front door, she slid the various bolts into place, kicked off her damp trainers and began peeling off her running clothes on the way to the bathroom.

After a long hot shower, she went into the kitchen and opened the fridge. At least she had food that was still in date in there. Even though they were only microwave meals, they were better than nothing, and she picked out a butter masala with rice and popped it in the microwave. Still trying not to think about Ben's betrayal, she was sitting on one of the bar stools blowing her forkful of rice when her doorbell chimed. Picking up her phone she opened the app to see who had the cheek to be bothering her at this time of night, praying it wasn't Emily, and saw Ben's face peering into the camera. He stepped back and waved his hand at her.

Pressing the green button on the screen she said, 'Go away, I'm busy.'

'*No, you're not. Let me in.*'

'No, I'll speak to you tomorrow.'

'*She didn't do it, Morgan. We have proof.*'

Morgan felt the heaviness that had been pressing down on her shoulders lift.

'Good, now leave me alone.'

She turned her phone onto silent and began to eat her warmed-up curry. He didn't get to treat her like that and expect her to forgive him so easily. He had lied to her about going to a meeting and then gone to arrest Ettie without so much as a heads-up to what he was doing, sending her to Kendal, far away from Rydal Falls, so she didn't know what he was up to. Well he could sit and stew. Friends didn't act like that; she would sort it out tomorrow, but first she was going to have to speak to Ettie and apologise to her. She wanted her aunt to know that she had nothing to do with today's events. She glanced down at her phone and saw that she hadn't turned the app off. Ben was now standing against his car with Emily, who was dressed in what looked like the shortest pair of silk pyjamas, standing far too close to him, talking. She'd seen enough. They were consenting adults, let them get on with it. She pushed the rest of the plastic carton away from her. She'd lost her appetite. It was time to try and get some sleep. She wanted this day to be over with.

CHAPTER TWENTY-SIX

The vibrating was driving her insane. She had no idea where her phone was, but if this was Ben at this ungodly hour she would shove the phone where the sun didn't shine. Groping around under her pillows, her fingers wrapped around the smooth, hard case and she dragged it to her ear.

'What?'

'*Sorry to disturb you, Morgan, it's Pam from the control room. We can't get hold of DS Matthews and we need someone to attend a fatal accident on Riverside Road.*'

She sat up. They didn't get called to fatals; they had an accident investigation collision unit that dealt with them. 'Why do you need someone from CID?'

'*There was an eyewitness who said the victim was acting very strange in the moments before it happened. The Force Incident Manager wanted someone from your team to take a look because it's similar circumstances to the two calls the day before yesterday.*'

Cold creeping fingers of fear began to crawl up her back and she told herself not to ask, then heard her voice say, 'Do we have a name for her?' She knew before Pam answered that she was going to say Jessica or Lara, and she hoped that she was wrong, that this was completely nuts. A voice whispered inside her head, *you didn't speak to them yesterday and you should have warned them*. Her heart was racing, and her shoulders were heavy with the guilt that she had let one of them down.

'*Not yet, sorry. She's in her pyjamas with no shoes and no ID on her.*'

'I'm on my way. Keep trying to get hold of Ben, please.'

She ended the call, wondering if he was upstairs with Emily. Even though she told herself it didn't matter, she knew that it did; deep down it mattered a lot. But she didn't have the time to dwell on that now. One day she was going to have to figure it out, but not anytime soon. She dressed quickly, pulling on a pair of black leggings and a thick black roll-neck jumper. The flipping heating had gone off again and she was shivering. She ran a brush through her hair and tipped her head upside down. Wrapping it in a topknot she went into the bathroom to clean her teeth and splash cold water in her eyes to wake her up. That would have to do. It wasn't a fashion parade at this time in the morning. She didn't even know what time it was and went back into the bedroom to grab her phone and watch. It was almost three. No wonder she felt like crap.

She drove to Riverside Road, unable to deny the sense of relief when she had got into her car and there was no sign of Ben's car parked on the drive. That would have been awkward, having to knock on Emily's door and drag him out of her bed. So why wasn't he picking up? She was torn between driving to his house to see what was going on and going straight to the scene. Her sense of duty made her go to Riverside Road. She had that awful churning sensation in her stomach again. She wasn't prepared to see another of her friends dead in horrific circumstances.

She parked the car in front of the police tape that was sealing off the road and nodded at Sarah, who had been on the same intake as her.

'You got the short straw, Morgan?'

She smiled at her. 'Lately, I seem to get nothing but short straws. How bad is it?'

'Bad. Delivery truck versus human, who by all accounts was just standing in the bend of the road waving her hands around.

Poor woman got wiped out. The driver didn't stand a chance. He didn't see her until he hit her.'

Morgan felt a lump forming in the back of her throat. Two lives ruined in a split second. 'Thanks, I better suit up.'

Sarah nodded, and Morgan walked back to her car, realising that it was her own car, and she had no protective clothing in it apart from some gloves. She turned back, and Sarah pointed to her van. 'Plenty of kit in there.'

'Thanks.'

When she was dressed, she ducked under the tape, and began walking down the pitch-black road, illuminated only by the blue flashing lights, towards the van parked in the middle of the road with an ambulance behind it. Morgan inhaled deeply, staring in the distance at the lifeless figure in the middle of the road. There were paramedics and two police officers standing over it, looking helpless. She could hear the sobs of a man carried on the wind from somewhere and she looked over her shoulder to see where he was. An officer was with him in the back of the police van. The sliding side door was wide open so he could see the crumpled mess on the floor, and she wanted to scream *shut the sodding door, you moron*. She didn't, she turned back and began to walk towards the body, pushing one foot in front of the other. She knew instinctively there was a fifty-fifty chance of it being either Jessica or Lara, and she wasn't sure who she would rather see. In some ways she hoped the victim would be a complete stranger, because if another of her school friends was dead, then what did it mean for her? Her mind was a jumbled mess and then she was there, standing next to one of the officers. All she had to do was to look down and see who it was. It was simple, but she couldn't do it.

'Sorry we had to call you out, but there wasn't a lot of choice. The FIM said that CID needed to take a look. She isn't happy with three women in the space of twenty-four hours either dead or seriously injured. What do you think?'

'Oh, yes that's strange, isn't it?' She knew the strangest thing at the moment was her reaction, but she didn't want to look down, because whilst she wasn't looking at a corpse it meant that her friend wasn't dead, didn't it? Everyone was silent, and she realised they were all waiting for her to look. She coughed into the crook of her arm, trying to dislodge the lump that was forming in the back of her throat. Why the hell hadn't Ben answered his phone? This should have been him not her. The two officers were glancing at each other, and she knew they were wondering if she'd lost the plot. Casting her eyes down she looked at the bloodied, broken figure and sucked in her breath.

'Oh, my Christ, Jess.' She knelt down to look closer and make sure she wasn't mistaken. She wasn't. Her beautiful friend. She hadn't seen her since school, but there was no mistaking her. The officer was shining a torch onto her face that was a bloodied mess. Morgan turned to the paramedics. 'Are you sure she's dead? Can't you do anything for her, surely there's something?'

The older of the two knelt down. Taking hold of Morgan's arm he helped her to her feet.

'I'm sorry, love. She was dead before we even arrived. Massive head injuries and internal bleeding is my guess. At least it was quick. From what the van driver said, she wasn't breathing when he got out to check her. Did you know her well?'

She nodded. 'Yes, she was one of my best friends at school. They all were, the other victims.'

'Is there a sergeant on the way, so we can get her body moved?'

'I don't know.' And then she heard a car and prayed it was Ben coming to take over, because she didn't know how to deal with this without breaking down. They all turned to face the headlights driving towards them, and then a car door was slamming.

'Morgan, can you come here, please?'

His voice was hoarse, gravelly, and she knew he'd been roused from a deep sleep too. She walked towards him much faster than she'd walked towards the scene. He held the tape up for her and she ducked under. He grabbed hold of her arm.

'What's going on? Do you know this victim?'

She nodded. 'Yes. Ben, what's happening?' Her voice was trembling, and she knew it was taking everything she had to hold it together. He turned to the officer sitting in the van with the driver for the world to see.

'Mate, shut the door.'

There was a loud bang as the heavy door was dragged shut. 'Morgan, get in the car. I'll take over but don't go anywhere. Promise me you're not going to drive off. I need you here.'

He was staring in her eyes, pleading with her not to do anything stupid and for once to do as she was asked.

'I'll wait in the car.'

Hurrying to get inside the safety of the car, she couldn't stop shivering. She turned the ignition on so she could blast the hot air, and Ben turned to make sure she wasn't driving away, although God knows what he was going to do if she did, run after the car? When he turned back and ducked under the tape, she let out the soft cry that she'd been holding in and felt the warmth of her tears as they rolled down her cheeks. She didn't know what was happening or why her friends were dying so horrifically, but it had to end. She had to stop this now.

CHAPTER TWENTY-SEVEN

Ben phoned Declan. He didn't wait around for someone at head-quarters in the control room to try and get hold of him, because that could take a lot longer than him dialling him directly. They would have to go through the out-of-hours number, and he knew he was taking a liberty, but he was sure that his friend would forgive him when he knew why. This was an accident; the van driver had dashcam footage which he'd played back for Ben and the officers. The woman had clearly been standing in the middle of the road waving her arms around, but not in a stop, help I've broken down kind of way. She was just there. It looked as if she was doing some slow-motion dance in the dark seconds before the squeal of the van's tyres and brakes jammed on. The poor bastard hadn't stood a chance. The van was almost on her before she became visible. Ben had kept glancing over at Morgan to make sure that she didn't see this footage. It was bad enough she had been called here in the first place. He'd been so tired and by the time he'd got home he'd gone straight to bed and been out for the count.

'*What in the name of Mary, Mother of Jesus are you phoning me at this time in the morning for?*'

Declan's voice sounded even rougher than his.

'Sorry, there's another.'

'*Another what? Help a guy out here, Ben. You've just woken me out of a decent sleep, and I'm pretty rubbish at this whole psychic thing.*'

'Sorry, I mean another woman has been involved in a fatal accident and was acting really weird just before it happened.'

There was a lot of rustling from Declan's end, and Ben wondered if he'd fallen asleep in the middle of reading the *Sunday Times*.

'*Right, I'm awake and in the words of Uncle Frank from* Home Alone, *you give the worst goddamn wake-up calls.*'

'Well, I don't know what to do. I mean, technically, it's a fatal road traffic accident and not my department, but it's not right. Something is really wrong, like all the alarm bells and whistles are ringing inside my head kind of wrong.'

'*Do you have proof that it was an accident?*'

'Yes, irrefutable proof. There's dashcam footage of the whole tragic, awful thing.'

'*Then the only thing I can do is fast track the post-mortem and get the bloods sent off to toxicology for a quick turnaround if they can do it that fast. I can't really do anything at the scene if cause of death was by a car.*'

'Van, it was a bloody big delivery van.'

'*Van then. What you'll have to do is get the body brought to the mortuary like you normally would, and I'll take care of the rest. You're still going to need collision investigation to investigate as per usual. Ben, is this a friend of Morgan's too?*'

'Yes.'

'*Then I don't know what to say except that if, somehow, they are being poisoned, which is then leading them to this erratic, hallucinogenic behaviour, we need to watch her carefully. I don't know how they are poisoning them, but someone is putting enough poison into their food or drinks to make them act this way. Whoever it is knows exactly what they are doing, and it's very dangerous because they could actually make themselves really ill with too much exposure to it. Christ, I can't even think straight but you get my drift, don't you? What's to stop whoever this is doing the same to Morgan?*'

'I don't know, nothing probably. But why would they want to poison her?'

'*That's the question, isn't it? Why did they want to poison anyone? There's your answer. Find the motive and you've found the killer. Seriously, Ben, I don't know what this is leading up to but it's not good. You need to get your finger out and get it sorted soon as.*'

The line went dead, and Ben pushed his phone back in his pocket. There was nothing he could do here; it was in the hands of Traffic now. What he needed to do was to sit with Morgan and try to work out what was happening.

CHAPTER TWENTY-EIGHT

2016

Lara hiked her backpack over her shoulders, the two bottles of vodka clinking together so loud she turned around to make sure no one was looking.

'Lara.'

She looked up to see Jess waving at her from the corner of the Co-op car park. She had a carrier bag in one hand and her backpack in the other. Hurrying she crossed the road to get to her.

'What have you bought?'

Jess opened the bag and showed her two family sized bags of Monster Munch, a large bar of chocolate and a box of cupcakes. 'I thought we better get cake for Brittany with it being her birthday, but she's not having the Monster Munch. They're for us.'

Lara laughed. 'Nope, I'm not sharing my crisps with anyone except you.'

Jess held up her little finger. 'Pinkie promise?'

They clenched little fingers, and both laughed. 'Pinkie promise.' As they walked along the road to get to White Moss, there was a lone figure in front of them, and Jess whispered, 'Be still my beating heart. Brad, oh Brad, where art thou?'

Lara elbowed her in the ribs. 'Shh, he'll hear you, don't be a dick. I wonder where Morgan is. Wasn't he supposed to meet her?'

Jess shrugged. 'Well, if she's not here that leaves us with a better chance of a drunken snog, wouldn't you say?'

'No, oh my God, definitely not. He's not going to give us a drunken snog when there's Queen Bee Brittany and Sienna there to tickle his tonsils.'

Jess began to laugh, the loud belly laugh that Lara loved, and they both stopped to catch their breaths. Brad stopped and turned around; their voices must have filtered down to him. He grinned and waved at them. They waved back, and Jess whispered, 'It's nice to dream though. If he fancies Morgan, who's to say he wouldn't prefer us over those two Barbie dolls when he's drunk? I mean I'm not going to say no if he drags me into the cave for a snog and anything else.'

'Shh, he's coming, and you're awful, Jess.'

'Tell me you'd say no, Lara.'

Lara shook her head because she wouldn't say no at all.

'Hey, how are you both?'

'Good, how about you, Brad?'

He shrugged. 'Morgan's grounded.'

'What, she's actually going to stay home and not sneak out? I thought she hated Stan, and he's going to be drunk as a skunk in another hour or so. She could sneak out and join us then.'

'I said that, but she still didn't want to do it.'

Jess shook her head. 'God, she's better behaved than me then, because if my mum had grounded me when she knew I was looking forward to going to a sleepover, I'd probably go mental and storm out of the house.'

'And me. My mum can be a right cow but she's not that tight.'

Brad's face looked genuinely sad. 'I know but I suppose she feels a bit sad. It's not that long since her mum died. Maybe she didn't want to come camping just yet. I feel bad for her. It can't be easy.'

Jess smiled at him and linked her arm through his. 'Well at least you're here. The birthday girl will be overjoyed to see you make the effort, Brad. She fancies you, so does Sienna. Do you like them?'

Lara felt her cheeks go red for him. God, she hadn't even opened the vodka and she was embarrassing him.

He laughed. 'Erm, yeah. I like them both, a lot, as friends. You know I like you all.'

Lara took his other arm. 'Good answer, Brad. That has earned you lots of brownie points.'

'Yeah, very diplomatic, Brad. Who do you fancy the most though? Come on, you can tell us. We won't say anything to those two.'

'Jess, stop being so mean to him.'

Jess shrugged. 'Just putting it out there, Lara, so we can clear the air and have a good time without worrying about anyone's feelings getting hurt.'

His cheeks were pinker than Jess's backpack, but he looked at them both and spoke.

'Morgan, I like her a lot but don't tell the others, please.'

Lara smiled at him, and Jess shrieked. 'I knew it, damn I'm good. Why are you here then if she's not?'

He shrugged. 'I'd already lied to my mum and told her I was sleeping over at Jake's house. I felt bad because Sienna has done nothing but text me for days, telling me how excited Brittany is that I'm coming camping out with you guys, so I didn't want to let her down.'

'Aww, Brad, you are so sweet. What a cutie. For a big tough rugby lad, you're a right softie inside. I like that. Well, don't you worry, your secret's safe with us, isn't it, Lara?'

Lara nodded, wishing she had a Brad in her life, just until she met her rich husband of course. They carried on walking and chattering all the way until they reached the steep path to the caves, where Brad offered to carry the heavy bag containing the vodka, and Lara passed it to him gladly because her shoulders were aching, and her calves were burning.

CHAPTER TWENTY-NINE

Ben got into his car and turned to look at Morgan.

'This is a shocking mess, isn't it?'

She nodded. 'It's awful. I can't get her broken body out of my mind. It keeps flicking between Jess and Brittany like some stupid slideshow.'

'Morgan, who else was in your group of school friends? We need to speak to them, warn them.'

'There's only Sienna and Lara left, oh and me, but I don't need warning because I'm living this nightmare. Ben, I don't know what to do about it. We have nothing, no leads, no suspects.'

He took hold of her hand, gently squeezing it, and the warmth from his fingers felt so good they were so numb.

'Why would anyone want to do this? Can you think of a reason? No matter how big or small or how insignificant it might seem. I have a hard time believing in coincidences when they happen naturally, but I do not believe that a group of your friends are being poisoned to the point of killing themselves accidentally. Did anything happen at school that this could be a repercussion of? Did you all bully some kid so much it's made them hold a bitter grudge until they had to seek revenge?'

She let out a harsh laugh. 'Bully, no. Until Brittany decided to take pity on me and take me under her wing it was her and Sienna who were the school bullies. For some reason after my mum died, they changed their tune and were no longer mean. I have never in my life bullied anyone, Ben, nor would I.'

'Did you tell anyone how they used to treat you? Could they be harbouring a grudge for you?'

'Who was I going to tell? My mum was dead; Stan was a raging alcoholic who barely knew I was around most of the time. A part of me wonders if it was the right or wrong thing to do. If I'd been there, I could have stopped Brad from having that accident, but because I wasn't there wasn't much I could have done about it. At least I haven't had to shoulder the guilt. It's probably the one thing Stan ever did that did me a favour. Who do you think could be harbouring a grudge on my behalf? Ettie? Well, that's impossible because I didn't even know who she was back then.'

'What happened to Brad, what kind of accident was it?'

Morgan closed her eyes. There was something there at the back of her mind just out of reach. Circling around, tantalisingly close yet so far away it was impossible. Then she looked at Ben.

'I think it might have something to do with Brad. It was five years ago; he fell to his death. He was drunk. He'd climbed to the top of Rydal Caves and got too near to the edge. He must have slipped, and he ended up smashed to pieces on the rocks below. A walker found his body the next morning. There was no sign of any of the others. They were all home tucked up in bed.'

'Who were the others?'

'Brittany, Sienna, Jessica and Lara,' Morgan whispered the names aloud. 'We were all going camping for Brittany's birthday. I was supposed to be there too, but Stan grounded me.'

'Jesus, Morgan, why didn't you mention this earlier?'

'I wasn't sure, it was only a hunch. But with Jess now…' She shrugged miserably.

'So they were all camping, why did they go home? Was it before or after Brad fell?'

'They said it was too cold and Brad was too drunk to go with them, so they left him, but…'

'But?'

Morgan looked at him. 'What if they didn't leave him there? What if something went wrong that night and they covered it up? Maybe his parents found out something that we don't know. Although they'd be quite old now. He had a younger brother, but he was only five or six. He might be seeking revenge for them leaving Brad that night. If they'd stayed, he probably wouldn't have fallen.'

Ben grimaced, and Morgan felt a rush of grief for Brad so strong it almost made her cry out; she had really liked him and never even had the chance to tell him. All those teenage emotions had been bottled up and pushed to some far part of her mind, so she didn't fall to pieces, but right now she felt as if the bottle had been smashed to smithereens. 'We better check out Brad's family. Although if his brother was five that would only make him ten. This seems like a pretty complicated way to seek revenge if you ask me. In the meantime let's get you home, you're shivering. Morgan, I have to ask you: do you think there could be a chance that someone would want to see you kill yourself like the others? Is there anyone who would want you dead?'

'How can I answer that, Ben? Who would want that to happen to another person? That's so fucked up it's beyond belief.'

'I know, but whether we believe it or not something really wrong is happening here, and I don't know where to start. Do you want to come back to my place? At least we know what little I have in is safe for you to eat and drink.'

'Why, what makes you so special?'

'Because I'm way older than you and was already a seasoned detective whilst you were having the shittiest year from hell at school.'

She looked out of the window and saw her car. 'Oh, I almost forgot I drove here. I don't know what to do. I can't keep running to your house every time something goes wrong, can I? You're not my dad; you're not supposed to be the one taking care of me. We're colleagues, and you don't owe me anything.'

'I'm definitely not your dad and yes, we are colleagues, but I thought we went deeper than that, Morgan. I thought we were friends?' He smiled at her, and she found herself wishing, not for the first time, that they didn't have to have such a complicated relationship.

'I think I'm okay tonight, Ben, thanks. I'll go home and not eat or drink anything, besides I just want to curl up under the duvet and pretend all of this had never happened.'

'If you're sure. You know where I am, and you know that you're welcome anytime. I quite like it when you stay. It makes the place seem lived-in again, and you always do the cleaning, which I hate, not to mention you make a great bacon sarnie.'

'Thank you.'

She got out of his car and hurried back to hers, not looking behind at the dreadful scene which was lit up like a football pitch now CSI and the collision investigation team were here. She wasn't lying; she was still shivering and just wanted to get back in bed where she was safe, and her friends weren't dying in the most horrific of ways.

CHAPTER THIRTY

Ettie couldn't sleep. Something was wrong and she had no idea what, but she'd known as soon as she'd opened her eyes it was bad and it involved Morgan. She had lain there for some time trying to close her eyes and go back to sleep, but it hadn't worked. She had an ache in her right knee that always signalled something bad was about to happen. She wondered if they had found what had happened to those women. She had only met Brittany a couple of times. Sienna had sent her to Ettie's cottage, looking for some relief for her stomach spasms, and she had been glad to help her. Sienna had been a godsend for her the last two years. She'd first visited the cottage looking for some of her Sleep Well tea, and it had then turned into a friendship that had done nothing but be advantageous for Ettie. Sienna had loved the tea and begged her to let her sell some in her little shop, though Ettie had been reluctant at first, not wanting to get her hopes up that she could bring in a nice little income as an addition to her pension; but the teas had sold out within the first day, and Sienna couldn't replenish the stock quick enough for her liking. Sienna had asked her many times to share her secrets to tea making with her, but she wasn't about to divulge her recipes to anyone except Morgan. Morgan was family, and this was a tradition that was passed down from mother to daughter. In Ettie's case she had no daughter to share them with; she had never been blessed with a husband or children. Most of the time she was happy with this: things happened for a reason. Occasionally when she heard the laughter of small children it filled her heart with joy, and it would be a bittersweet memory for her; the longing she tried to ignore would raise itself from the depths of her root chakra where she had buried those feelings long ago. She had wanted so badly to take Morgan and Taylor who went by the name Dan when he was adopted when they were very young, but it hadn't been allowed. Gary had ruined all of their lives with his own selfish desires. She lay awake some nights wondering why her brother had turned into a monster when he had such a perfect little family.

When Morgan was ready, she would share everything she knew with her. Until then, Sienna would have to be happy taking what she could get, which was a little cruel, she knew that, and if her niece hadn't walked back into her life she probably would have shared everything with Sienna, but she had and family was family. If Morgan wasn't interested in any of this, then she would tell Sienna everything she knew, as she wasn't about to let all her knowledge and years of healing die with her. That would be a terrible waste. She got out of bed and went into the kitchen, where she began to boil the kettle. She brewed a cup of nettle tea, which was good for her arthritic joints, and added a spoonful of honey and a slice of lemon. She might swear by her recipes, but it didn't mean she thought they tasted very good without a dollop of something sweet and runny to take away the bitter edge. Things weren't right though, and she could sense this, not just with her foresight or magical abilities, but her instinct too. Maybe it was her worry over Gary's whereabouts seeping through. Where the hell was her brother hiding out? She tried to keep that fear at bay. The worry that he was waiting and watching them all from the sidelines somewhere. Maybe he had taken his chance to start afresh when he'd escaped from prison, but somehow, she didn't believe this one little bit. He was out there and up to something. She had never been able to tune into Gary's thoughts or wavelength no matter how hard she used to try; he could block her like no other living soul could.

Taking her tea to the kitchen table, she sat down and stared out into the blackness outside. A gentle tap, tap on her window made her hand twitch, and she spilled a little of her tea. Smiling, she stood up and opened the window enough for the bird to waddle through.

'Good morning, my friend, where have you been all night?'

It dipped its head and fixed its eyes on her, then it flew to the table and perched on the chair opposite her. She stood up and went to the fridge to pour out a little cream into a small dish. Placing it on the table she watched as he dipped his beak in and out. There was a loud miaow from the sofa, and she turned to the cat. 'Shush, you know he only takes the tiniest bit. There's plenty left for you.'

The cat stretched out and closed its eyes again. Ettie looked at the raven and back at the cat. 'Look at me, the best friends I have are a greedy cat and a bird that thinks it's a cat.' But she chuckled. On the whole she was happy with her life; it was simple, and it worked. She was about to go and take a shower when there was a loud knock on the door. The bird squawked and began flapping its wings.

'It's okay, I knew they were coming back. I'm ready for them, don't worry.' She finished sipping the last of her tea, then walked to open the front door. There were three police officers standing on the other side, and a man in a suit who she recognised.

'Bit of an early start for you, Tom, it's only just past seven o'clock. What brings you here?'

She smiled at him, but she knew fine well why he was here. He thought she was a killer, and who was she to argue with him? Let him have his moment. It had been a long time since she'd seen him, and he'd never quite forgiven her for not going out with him when he'd had a teenage crush on her.

'There's a situation, Ettie. I think you're aware of it and I can't sit back and watch the whole town go to pieces when all roads lead to you. I'm sorry, and I know you were interviewed yesterday, but I'm not satisfied. We have another victim and I need to put a stop to this now. I have a search warrant for your cottage, and I won't let my team leave until they have turned this place upside down. If we find nothing and there isn't anything to link this mess back to you, then I'll leave you be.'

'I'm not sure that's going to be possible; of course you are going to find something here. I make herbal teas; I use fresh herbs picked from the woods including belladonna, which is what I'm pretty sure you're looking for on that search warrant. So, where am I going to stand here, Tom? Are you going to lock me up and accuse me of witchcraft and murder? If I'm not mistaken those times are long gone. Who are you, some distant relation to Matthew Hopkins the witchfinder general?'

'No, I am not, Ettie, and this isn't some witch hunt. What I'm trying to do is to find out why and how three young women have died in the most suspicious of circumstances.'

Ettie gasped. 'Three? Who are the other two?' She felt the room begin to spin; she was going to faint.

'Two, sorry, my mistake. One of them survived, thank the Lord.'

'Who is the third victim, Tom? Is Morgan, okay?'

He nodded. 'Morgan is just fine, and I'm not at liberty to say who this victim is. It only happened a few hours ago and the family haven't been notified as yet. Morgan has been up all night working the scene. She doesn't know I'm here. This has nothing to do with her.'

'Poor girl, she must be so fed up with all the death that follows her around. I wish I could help her.'

'You can help her by coming to the station without a fuss and answering the questions you're asked this time, instead of opting for no comment.'

She shrugged. 'Are you still mad I turned down your offer to accompany you to the leavers' dance, Tom?'

The two officers standing behind him had all been watching with stony faces, but every one of them broke into a smile.

'Don't be ridiculous.'

She shrugged. 'Let's get this over with then, but first let me feed the cat and the bird.'

At this the raven began to clack loudly, and Tom jumped. 'Jesus, is that alive, is it a raven? I thought it was stuffed. Why would you let that in your house?'

'It's very clean, and I just let you into my house and look how that turned out. The bird has good enough manners not to shit where it eats, which is more than could be said for you.'

A loud snigger came from one of the officers standing behind Tom, and he turned to glare at them. 'Hurry up, these two will be staying behind to search the house. Is that okay? Not that I need your permission because I have a search warrant.' He waved the piece of paper in the air, and she had to stop herself from telling him to go and shove it.

CHAPTER THIRTY-ONE

Morgan had given in and let Ben follow her home and then on to his house. She'd insisted on sleeping on the sofa, and he hadn't argued. Instead, he'd come downstairs with a huge duvet and pillows which smelt faintly of his aftershave. They smelt safe and, right now, as she snuggled down into them, that was what she needed. Now as she lay there, her eyes wide open and her heart pounding, she realised she'd had an awful dream. In her dream she had been there that night camping with the others; she hadn't been grounded, and she had snuck off to meet them. Brad had looked so damn handsome, his grin cheeky as they'd sat together swigging neat vodka from a bottle they were sharing. He'd been laughing and joking, and then somehow, he was no longer next to her but was standing at the top of the cave. She'd begged him to step away from the edge, but he'd laughed and then she thought she saw a dark shadow behind him for a fleeting second and then he came crashing down, and she'd woken up screaming. Or at least she'd been screaming in her dream. As she lay there with cold beads of fear forming on her forehead and her heart feeling as if she was about to have a heart attack, she'd realised, thankfully, that her dream scream hadn't followed her into reality, and if it had, Ben hadn't heard it. She turned on her side. What if Brad hadn't slipped like everyone had assumed? Maybe he hadn't been that drunk. She couldn't remember the details: at the time she was almost eighteen and too lost in her grief for the boy she would never get to kiss or hold hands with. The more she thought about it, the more she was convinced that something had happened that might be far more sinister than she had ever contemplated. Taking her phone from under the pillow where she'd stuffed it last night, she began typing out a message to Declan.

Morning, I know you've been a pathologist for forever, but were you working here back in 2016?

She sent it, hoping that Declan might be able to give her the answers she was looking for. If not, she could go searching through the records at work, but that was time-consuming, and the computer systems had probably been updated at least a couple of times since then. She might be totally off-track, but there had been a niggling feeling inside of her since she saw Brittany's broken body that somehow this all went back to that fateful night.

Her phone began vibrating almost immediately and she answered.

'Hello.'

'*I love you, Morgan, and Ben, very much, but I wish the pair of you would bugger off and stop disturbing my beauty sleep. Do the pair of you not need sleep or something?*'

'Sorry, I didn't realise he'd already rung you. I also didn't think you'd answer my message so soon. I had a bad dream and woke up wondering about something that you might be able to help with.'

'*Go on, I'm intrigued, and yes is the answer to your question. I was definitely working here.*'

'Amazing,' she whispered.

'*Why are you whispering?*'

'I don't want to disturb Ben.'

From the loud screech that almost burst her eardrums, Declan didn't mind.

'*About time.*'

'I'm on his sofa, and he's in his bed.'

'*Bugger. Oh, right, well what did you want to know? I've got to say it, Morgan, you two are just plain weird.*'

She giggled. 'I've been called much worse, thanks. Do you remember the boy who was found dead on the rocks at Rydal Caves?'

'*I could never forget. That was so sad, brutal and a complete waste of a young life. Why are you asking?*'

'He was my friend. I liked him a lot and he called for me that night. I was supposed to go camping with him and some others. The three recent victims, Brittany Alcott, Sienna Waters and Jessica Bell, were all there. I was grounded by Stan who, for some weird reason, decided to act like my dad that night and wouldn't let me go.'

'*Wise man, he did you a favour I think, although I don't suppose it felt like it at the time.*'

'They all said that they left him there alive; he was drunk and wouldn't go home with them. I was just wondering how much alcohol was in his blood and whether he was really that drunk? Enough to fall to his death? Or could someone have pushed him off?'

'*Hmm, you and your boss certainly do give the worst wake-up calls. Let me see, I can't tell you off the top of my head what his blood alcohol level was, but it was sufficient enough to have impaired his thinking that night. He may have considered standing over the top of Rydal Cave as a wonderful idea and wouldn't have taken into account the dew on the grass and how slippery it could have been. We've all been there, a few drinks and suddenly we're invincible. I can tell you one thing, there were definitely no drugs in his system.*'

'No, Brad was into his rugby. He wasn't into drugs at all. What about his injuries, were they consistent with a fall?'

'*Morgan, I'm going to pretend that you're not questioning my ability as a pathologist in determining his cause of death.*'

'Oh God, not at all. Sorry, Declan, I get a little carried away. I'm just trying to figure it all out. I'm convinced that Brad's death and what's happening now might be connected. I just don't know how or why.'

'*Okay, that's a good enough reason for me. I'll check his pathology reports out when I get to work and let you know.*'

'Thank you, sorry for bothering you.'

He laughed.

'*Morgan, there are a lot of people I mind bothering me, but you aren't one of them, so you're forgiven. I know that Ben has probably told you this, but please take care.*'

'I will, why do you think I'm on Ben's sofa? He didn't want me to go home on my own.'

'*Well, if that isn't just the sweetest thing. I'll speak to you later.*'

He hung up, leaving Morgan puzzled. She yawned but there was no getting back to sleep now. She was awake for the second time. She may as well put herself to some use. She began to collect all of Ben's used mugs and plates, carrying them into the kitchen. The house wasn't dirty; it was messy, lived-in and she kind of liked that he wasn't a super clean freak. Des was. The one time she'd been to his house with Amy it was like a show home, and she had been afraid to sit herself down on his sofa in case she crushed his cushions. After she'd washed the pots and then hunted down a tin of polish and a duster, she'd given the whole of the downstairs a once-over. She went into the lounge that Ben never used. There was a single photo frame above the fireplace. She picked it up and smiled to see a photograph of a very fresh-faced looking Ben in a three-piece suit with his wife, Cindy, who was absolutely stunning. They looked so young and so gorgeous, with their whole lives ahead of them.

'I got a whiff of something I didn't recognise and was hoping it was some kind of exotic breakfast, but I guess you found the antique tin of furniture polish.'

Morgan jumped at his voice. She put the photo down feeling like the world's biggest creep. 'I'm sorry, I didn't mean to be nosey but well, that's such a lovely photo of you both.'

He crossed the room and picked it up, then chuckled. 'Oh, how young and foolish we were, back in the days when I believed in happily ever afters.'

'How old were you?'

'Twenty-three.'

She laughed. 'My age then.'

'Somehow, I don't feel as if you've ever been twenty-three, Morgan. You seem as if you're so much older and definitely wiser than I ever was.'

'I think it's sweet that you and Cindy married so young and were so in love. I don't think I'll ever get married at this point in my life. I can't even find a half-decent boyfriend.'

He put the photograph down and turned to her. 'Marriage isn't everything. I mean it's nice and all that but at the end of the day it doesn't mean sod all really. You'll find the right person when the time is right. Did I hear you on the phone, it wasn't work, was it?'

She shook her head. 'No, well sort of, but it was me doing the work. I had an awful dream about the night Brad died and it got me thinking about his post-mortem results. I messaged Declan, not really expecting an answer until midday at least, and he rang straight back.'

'Was he a right grump? I'd already disturbed him.'

'No, he was okay and said he'd check the report when he gets to work. What if Brad didn't fall that night? What if he was pushed or got into a fight? Maybe someone knows or knew more than they were supposed to and somehow it got back to whoever killed him.'

'Crikey, Brookes, you have been busy, and you've managed to clean my house in the process. I like it, Declan said something very similar earlier. I was going to ask your opinion when we got to work.'

'I think something went on that night and the witnesses were Jess, Brittany, Sienna, Lara. Oh my God, we need to get hold of Lara and make sure she's okay. And what about Sienna? She survived her attack. Are they going to come back and try again?'

'Let's get officers to Lara's address for a welfare check. Do you know where she lives? How do you feel about her stopping with you for a little while until we can figure out what the hell is going on? I'm hoping that they'll leave Sienna alone for the time being in case she's being watched. I can't imagine whoever this is being brazen enough to try again.'

'She lives at, I don't know the number I just know the house.'

'Right, well then we're going to have to call and speak to her on our way in to work. I'll go get dressed. Do you need to go home for anything?'

'No, these clothes were fresh on a couple of hours ago. I shouldn't smell too bad. You would tell me if I did, wouldn't you?'

He smiled at her. 'I would, but you always smell amazing so no worries there.'

He turned and ran up the stairs. She took out her phone and searched for Lara's name on Messenger. She typed a quick note and sent it, hoping that she might still be safe in bed asleep and unaware of the senseless death of her best friend.

CHAPTER THIRTY-TWO

Tom wasn't sure if this was the right thing to do. All he knew was that he had to do something and make a stand before the press got hold of this absolute cock-up of an investigation and ripped them all to shreds. As much as he didn't want to, it was leaving him with no choice but to be the bad guy. He had never pegged Ettie as a cold-blooded killer, then again when they had arrested her brother, Gary, for being the Riverside Rapist that had been a shock. He was a nice guy or at least he'd come across as being a nice guy. Two women were dead though, they needed a suspect, and all fingers were pointing towards her. He glanced in the rear-view mirror at her. She was the perfect model of composure. She wasn't nervous or chattering like some suspects did when they were arrested, trying to get the point across to the arresting officers that they weren't criminals and were nice folks deep down. Not Ettie, if anything she looked a little bemused at the whole situation, and he didn't know what to think. He knew he should have waited for the briefing this morning and discussed this plan with Ben and the rest of the team, but when he'd listened to the voice message from the control room in the early hours he knew he had no choice but to take action, and so on his head be it. He would ride the storm if it broke, but at least he could say he tried, even if he did upset everyone in the process.

By the time Ettie had been booked in officially this time and had her prints taken, DNA swabbed, and photographs done it was almost time for the day shift to start rolling in to the station. Ettie had requested a solicitor, so God knows how long it would take to get one down here, which gave them some time to play with. Her cottage wasn't big. He was hoping that the two officers he'd left there to search it would come up with something to justify what he'd just done.

He waited in his office for the approaching tsunami to hit. That was how he felt, like a disaster of a great magnitude was about to knock him over. His phone began to ring.

'*Boss, what are we doing with all these jars of herbs?*'

He ran his hand across his jaw. He should have thought this through. 'How many are there?'

'*Hundreds.*'

'Are there any labelled poison, toxic, deadly?'

'*Sir, we're not in the Halloween section of TK Maxx.*'

'I bloody well know that. Are there any labelled deadly night-shade or belladonna?'

'*I'll look.*'

The line went quiet, and he waited for something, anything.

'*Boss, we found an item of clothing in a brown paper bag hidden in the shed.*'

'And?'

'*Well, it's a bit odd, don't you think, that it's out in the shed in a bag. And I'm not being judgemental or anything but...*'

'But?'

'*It doesn't look like the kind of thing the woman who lives here would wear. It's a size ten and, hang on, it's got a Zara label.*'

'Please, put me out of my misery and explain what the hell a Zara label is, because it sounds like a different language to me.'

There was a snort on the other end and then a cough.

'*Well, it's a women's clothing store that's very popular with the younger, skinnier women. My girlfriend is always moaning she can't fit into anything from Zara.*'

Tom closed his eyes. He wanted to groan out loud, but he didn't. 'So, we have a top that doesn't fit and what else? A hundred jars of herbs.'

'*Er, yeah. That's pretty much it.*'

'Have you found a book or diary with a hit list in it?'

'*Lots of books and notebooks. If you want us to go through them all you're going to have to send another couple of officers.*'

'Fuck.'

'*Sorry, boss.*'

'Bring me the shirt and anything that looks dodgy.'

'*Hang on, I think I have something.*'

Tom closed his eyes and placed his palms together as if he was about to pray.

'*There's a jar here with Bella on it and it looks pretty fresh; it's not all dried out like the others.*'

'Bring it in and anything else that looks remotely suspicious.'

He ended the call, not exactly hopeful that they had found anything worth testing.

CHAPTER THIRTY-THREE

Morgan left in her car to go to visit Lara while Ben followed behind in his. For the entire journey she hoped desperately that Lara was going to open the door to her and be safe. They knocked on her door. It was early, not even eight o'clock, but there were signs of life behind it and for that she felt eternally grateful. When the door opened Lara was standing there, her blonde hair in a messy bun, her mascara smudged, and she was wearing a pair of Barbie pyjamas that made Morgan smile.

'Morgan, is that you?'

She nodded. 'It is, can we come in, Lara?'

Lara rubbed her eyes then fixed her gaze on her. 'No, I don't think I should let you.'

'You're right, you shouldn't, but you need to. We need to talk to you, and you don't want to hear what we're about to say here on your doorstep like this.'

She shook her head, and a deep male voice called from somewhere inside the house. 'Who the hell is knocking at the door this time in the morning?'

Lara shook her head; turning, she shouted back, 'It's the police.' Then she looked at Morgan. 'Are you here to tell me something awful or have I done something wrong? I suppose you'd better come inside.'

They followed her into the house which was painted in the boldest dramatic colours, lots of black and gold with touches of emerald green. It was like something out of a magazine, and

Morgan immediately had a case of house envy until she thought about why they were here. Lara's boyfriend appeared at the top of the stairs. He was dressed in a suit, and she remembered he was a solicitor. She looked at him, trying to smile sympathetically to convey something awful was wrong, and realised she probably looked like a grinning goon and stopped immediately. He came down the stairs and followed them into the large kitchen. Lara pointed to the chairs and both Ben and Morgan sat down. Lara sat opposite and for the life of her Morgan couldn't recall his name and then it came to her Greg, but her boyfriend stood behind her, his arms protectively wrapped around her shoulders. Morgan didn't wait for Ben to talk.

'Lara, we have some dreadful news to tell you.'

'No.'

'I'm afraid there's been terrible—'

'No, Morgan, don't you dare.'

'Jess is dead. She was killed instantly last night.'

Lara pushed her chair back and stood up. 'Get out and don't come here telling me that because I don't believe you.'

Ben stepped in. 'Morgan is telling the truth. I'm very sorry to tell you this but your friend is dead, and we think that somehow someone managed to poison her, which means you could be next.'

'What, what the hell are you talking about?'

Her fists were curled into tight balls, and she was standing with her legs wide apart, looking as if she was about to throw a right hook in any direction. Her boyfriend was behind her, patting her back like some kind of dog. Lara turned around and shrugged his hands off her and hissed, 'Stop that, it's really annoying.'

Morgan agreed. If someone was patting her like that she'd probably turn around and punch them. She carried on talking. 'Jess was standing in the middle of Riverside Road in the early hours, in the dark, when she was hit by a delivery van.'

Lara clasped her hands over her ears. 'No, I don't want to know.'

Morgan felt a rush of anger towards the woman standing there denying what they were telling her because it wasn't in her plan, it didn't fit with her way of life, and for a fleeting second she wondered if Lara could be responsible for all of this sadness, then she stopped herself. She was so close to Jess there was no way she would hurt her. Morgan couldn't help herself. She stood up and crossed the room until she was standing directly in front of her. Reaching out she grabbed her hands.

'This is important, your life might be in danger. You need to listen to what I'm about to tell you, Lara. You could be next, or I could. Someone is managing to poison our food or drinks with what we believe is belladonna.'

Greg looked at Morgan. 'Are you telling me that someone is lacing your food or drinks with deadly nightshade? Are you being serious because it sounds absolutely ridiculous to me.'

She glared at Greg. 'I don't give a shit what you think, Greg, it's true. And now Brittany and Jess are dead. Sienna almost died but we got to her in time. Lara, I also need to ask you about Brad. What really happened the night he died? Because I don't believe that it was as innocent as it all seemed.'

Greg stepped in front of Lara. 'Lara, don't say anything.' He turned back to Morgan. 'Do you have any proof that it wasn't an accident? Anything that is going to stand up in court?'

Ben stood up. 'Not at the moment. We're here because there is a serious risk to your life, Lara, and we don't know why or how but it's serious enough for us to be here now talking to you. We're not pointing fingers at anyone. We are simply trying to figure out what the hell is going on before someone else dies.' He turned to Greg. 'I suggest you step down off your corporate judicial pedestal and take note. We need to figure out what Jess was doing in the hours before she began to act erratic and decided it was a good idea to stand in the middle of a road in her pyjamas in the dark until she got hit by a vehicle. Is that standard behaviour for her, was she suicidal as far as you know?'

Lara sat down, all the fight had left her, and she looked around at Greg.

'You're going to be late for work. I'm okay.'

'I can't leave you here like this with these two. They might stitch you up. I can make sure you don't say anything that could incriminate you.'

'That's very kind of you, but seriously I have done nothing that would incriminate me in a court of law, Greg. I want to talk to Morgan about Jess and help them to figure out what's happened. You have an important day ahead of you. Please leave me to talk and grieve. I'll ring you if I need you.'

He flicked his wrist and peered at his watch. 'Oh shit, I have to go. I can call in, Lara, if you need me to?'

She shook her head. 'No, I don't need you to. I'll be fine.'

He bent down and kissed her cheek, glaring at Morgan and Ben as if they were the enemy, and Morgan felt like telling him to go screw himself, but she didn't. She kept her composure. The fact that Ben had a tight hold of her arm under the table also helped. He was silently telling her not to stoop to Greg's level, and she knew he was right. They sat in silence as he grabbed his briefcase and coat. Plucking a set of car keys off a key-shaped hook on the wall he turned to Lara.

'Are you sure you don't need me, sweetheart? I'm so sorry about Jess.'

She shook her head, tears welling in the corners of her eyes. 'Thanks, I'll be okay.'

He nodded and walked out of the kitchen door, leaving them to it, all three of them staring at each other in silence until they heard the sound of a car engine turn over and it drive away. Lara let out a loud sigh.

'I'm sorry about him. He gets a bit defensive, and I'm sorry for being an idiot, Morgan.'

Morgan smiled. She reached out and took hold of Lara's hand. 'You're allowed to be an idiot. I'm so, so sorry about Jess. I know how close you both were. I couldn't believe it myself when I saw her.'

'You saw her, it was definitely her?'

She nodded.

'What the hell was she doing there? I phoned her last night. Hang on, I'll tell you the exact time.' She reached for her phone and opened the call log, turning the screen to face Morgan: it said 19.21.

'Are you friends with her on Facebook, Morgan? She put this awful picture of a disgusting smoothie on there and said it was her dinner. I rang her to tell her she was taking being a bridesmaid too far.'

'I might be, I don't really use social media much. I tend to scroll through Instagram if I'm really bored. When are you getting married?'

'Eight weeks, three days and twelve hours.' Lara smiled. 'Not that I'm counting or anything. Although I don't know if I want to now Jess isn't…' She began to cry, loud hitching sobs, and Morgan didn't stop her.

Ben was looking at his feet. His phone began to vibrate in his pocket, and he took it out, then whispered to Morgan, 'I have to take this; it's Tom. Excuse me, Lara.' He walked out of the kitchen and headed towards the front door.

Morgan wondered if he was glad of a genuine excuse to leave the oppressive kitchen as she stared after him.

Lara grabbed a tea towel and began to dab her eyes with it. 'Sorry.'

'Don't be sorry, it's so sad and such a terrible waste. Was Brittany a bridesmaid too?'

There was something at the back of her mind, but she couldn't grasp it yet.

'No, I don't really see a lot of Brittany, or Sienna. I only stayed close to Jess.'

Whatever it was slipped away when she didn't get the answer she was hoping for.

'What about you, Morgan, do you keep in touch with them?'

'No, I kind of kept to myself after Brad died. I can't stop thinking about him. I really liked him, you know.'

Lara smiled at her. 'It's so sad. He really liked you too.'

Morgan sat up. 'What? How do you know that?'

'That night we met up with him on the way to the caves, and you know what Jess is like, she was asking him a million questions and whether or not he fancied Brittany or Sienna. He said he didn't like either of them; he liked you. We promised we wouldn't tell them. He'd said that he was gutted you couldn't go that night. I think he'd been hoping to pluck up the courage after a couple of drinks to ask you out.'

It was Morgan's turn for her eyes to tear up and she blinked them furiously. A sharp, stabbing pain in her chest took her breath away. Lara stared at her.

'Oh God, you didn't know. All this time you never knew it was you who he really fancied, and you were the reason he went on that trip. We asked him why he didn't change his mind when he found out you were grounded, but he didn't want to let Brittany down because Sienna had been bugging him for days, telling him how excited she was he was going.'

'I didn't. I kind of hoped that he did, but I always thought he felt sorry for me because of my mum and was just being kind. He was such a nice guy; I wish he hadn't gone, or I wish that I had. Maybe if I had, I could have stopped him from falling.'

'Hindsight is a wonderful thing. None of us knew what was going to happen. If it makes you feel any better, he ended up getting steaming drunk and going off with Brittany. I don't know what they did or got up to, but I think they could have done something. God, what a fucked-up life it is being a teenager: all those hormones and emotions raging around and we're too bloody stupid to know what to do with it all.'

Morgan wanted to go home, throw herself on the bed and cry for Brad and their lost relationship that ended up with Brad's death.

She heard another car engine outside, and her phone beeped with a message from Ben.

Got to go to the station, hope you're okay. Let me know if you need anything, I'll see you when you're ready, take your time.

Confusion filled her mind. What was going on at the station?

'Lara, what really happened that night? I have a feeling that whatever did is the key to all of this, but I wasn't there, so I don't know.'

Lara sucked in a deep breath. 'Nothing. We decided it was far too cold to sleep in the caves and went home. Brad wouldn't come. He was drunk so we left him, and we should never have done that, but we were all drunk, so none of us were thinking rationally.'

Morgan nodded. 'I guess we all act a little strange when we've been drinking. I'm worried that whoever is doing this is going to come after you next. Have you ever bought any herbal teas from Sienna's shop?'

'No, I can't abide herbal teas. I don't drink tea full stop. Why are you asking?'

'I need to figure out how whoever is doing this is doing it.'

'Jess did though. She'd try anything if she thought it would help her lose weight. I kept telling her she was gorgeous just the way she was.'

Morgan felt her heart ache for the loss of another young life and also at the thought of her drinking herbal tea. None of it was looking good for Ettie.

'I'm worried about you, Lara; you were there that night. There might be a very real chance you're next.'

'What, what do you mean? Why would I be on someone's hit list? This is so messed up.'

'I don't know, but what I do know is that out of the five of you who went to Rydal Caves that night, there are only two of you left.

Are you sure there's nothing more, nothing you can think of that would give someone a motive for targeting you all now?'

Lara shook her head and began to cry once more.

'I was going to see if you wanted to come stay with me until we had this all figured out, but I didn't know about Greg. I'm pretty sure you'll be okay with him. The others both lived alone. If I was you, I wouldn't eat or drink anything that you already have in your house though. I'd buy completely fresh from the supermarket; don't take any chances, Lara.'

She stood up. She had been a little harsh with Lara, but she needed her to understand how serious this was. This wasn't some stupid teenage game gone wrong. It was full-blown murder.

CHAPTER THIRTY-FOUR

Morgan drove back to the station feeling emotionally drained. She was washed out and exhausted. Lara had still been crying when she'd walked out of the door, but she had to leave. She had no idea why Ben had upped and left without a word, and there was that heavy, churning feeling inside her stomach again that she wished would bugger off and leave her alone. She walked slowly into the station, her feet in no desire to rush anywhere. As she reached the door, Cain came striding out of it with his student officer in tow. He grinned to see her, and she felt a genuine feeling of warmth fill her insides.

'Morning, Morgan, you look like crap. Rough night?'

And the warmth was gone. She laughed. He was right, she probably did look like crap, and she had no mascara on, which always made her look as if she was ill when her eyeliner, eyebrows and lashes weren't as black as her soul.

'Thanks, Cain, yes you could say that.'

'Hey, do you need a hug?' He opened his arms, and she stepped sideways.

'I'm good, thanks, maybe later.' She realised who he reminded her of, and it was Buddy the Elf. He even had similar hair to Will Ferrell, and now she didn't think she'd ever quite get that image out of her head.

'Well, like I said I'm your guy when you need a bit of comfort.'

She laughed and walked through the open door; her mood lifted slightly. By the time she'd made it up to the CID office she felt better, until she walked in to see Tom and Ben mid argument. Amy and Des were watching, horrified. Ben took one look at her and muttered, 'Oh fuck.'

'Charming.'

Amy was actually grimacing and looking as if she was ready to escape; Des was already standing up pulling on his jacket.

'What have I done?'

Ben shook his head. 'Nothing, sorry, I didn't mean that how it sounded.'

'Oh, that's good to know.'

Ben turned to Tom. 'I think you should explain what's been happening, sir, seeing as how you're currently running a one-man team.'

Tom's cheeks had two small red circles on them, and he looked as if he was ready to explode. 'Morgan, there have been some developments overnight.'

Ben was shaking his head. She didn't say anything, so Tom continued, 'I know this is a bit of a shock for you, but I decided to bring Ettie Jackson in under arrest and search her cottage. The search team have found a woman's white T-shirt that doesn't belong to Ettie, and also a large jar of fresh herbs labelled Bella which have been sent off for testing. I'm sorry to have to do it this way but it was for the best. As of now, because of the family involvement, I'm going to have to ask you to step off the investigation.'

She didn't quite know what to say to him. She'd known deep down that they would bring Ettie in again. She was still the most viable suspect, but why the sneakiness and why was she being kicked off the case? Did they think the T-shirt belonged to Sienna? Ben was still shaking his head, and Amy said, 'Boss, I think you're going to give yourself some kind of brain aneurism if you keep shaking your head like that. It's not normal.'

He stopped, looked at Amy, but didn't reply. Everyone was watching Morgan, waiting for her reaction, expecting her to explode. For once, though, she didn't have one. She felt as if she was fighting a losing battle and had been from the beginning. The air was fraught with tension, and they were all ready for her to have a meltdown. Well they could wait forever because she wasn't going to give it to them.

'That's fine, do what you must. What should I work on then?'

Tom looked confused, but not as much as Ben. He had finally stopped shaking his head. 'I, erm, I think there's been a break-in at a shop in Kendal. You could take it on if you get in touch with Mads downstairs. It would take the pressure off Response if you're happy to deal.'

'No problem; I'll go speak to him.'

Morgan walked out of the office and left them to it. She wasn't sure what to do and then she stopped in her tracks. What could she do? This was out of her hands. All she could do was to try and make sure Lara was safe. Maybe she should pay Sienna another visit, to tell her to be careful too, but the thought of talking to her made her shudder. The girl had changed into an older but awful version of teenage Sienna, with the same attitude. She'd always looked down on Morgan at school, and even now, though she wasn't that same scared, sad girl, Sienna had still made her feel like crap.

'Morgan.'

Ben's voice called over the railings of the floor above her. She stopped and looked up at him. 'Yes.'

'Hang on, I'm coming down.'

She shook her head but waited. His cheeks were flushed, and he looked harassed.

'I didn't know about this.'

'It doesn't matter though, does it? You brought her in yesterday without telling me. Now Tom has done the same. You guys are obviously in charge. It's not down to me.'

'It's not like that.'

'I don't care.'

'Don't say that. Where's the feisty don't-mess-with-me Morgan?'

She smiled at him. 'I'm tired and sad. I don't know what I'm feeling at the moment about any of this.'

She turned and walked away; Ben's hand reached out for her arm, tugging her back. For a startling moment she thought he was going to pull her to him and kiss her right there on the stairwell of the nick, but then he let go and turned away, his cheeks burning bright.

CHAPTER THIRTY-FIVE

Mads waved her into his office. Morgan hadn't even had to knock, so she knew he must be desperate.

'Ben sent me to see if you needed a hand.'

'First time he's actually been useful. Yes, if you don't mind that would be just dandy. Here's the log.' He passed her a printout of the call log.

'She's not having much luck this week, poor lass.'

'Who is it?'

'That girl who you rescued from the caves the other day, wasn't she called Sienna Waters?'

Morgan's mouth dropped open. 'You're shitting me?'

'I haven't got time for that, so are you dealing or what? Cain and his student are supposed to be on their way, but they've been diverted twice so far: once to a traffic accident and then sheep on the road.'

She really wanted to tell him to send Cain and she would gladly chase the sheep in his place, but there was this niggling feeling that she needed to check on her anyway. It was strange how this had happened in the middle of the sudden deaths. Was it all connected? And she desperately wanted to be able to clear Ettie's name, so she might as well kill two birds with one stone and deal with them both.

'That's fine, I'll sort it.'

'Cheers, Morgan, much appreciated.'

She left him as his radio began to ring, calling at the storeroom to pick up some gloves, protective clothing and evidence bags.

*

Morgan parked on the double yellows outside Sienna's shop and put her hazard lights on. If she got a ticket, it would finish her off, but she wasn't about to spend forever looking for a parking space. The front of the shop looked intact. Snapping on a pair of gloves she looked to see if there were any cameras pointed in this direction. She saw a couple on the building society opposite and hoped they were working. Sucking in a deep breath, she walked into the shop. It was a mess. There were broken jars scattered all over the floor, and the bookshelves, the best thing in the shop in her opinion, were tipped over and books were strewn everywhere. Sienna was sitting behind the counter, black mascara trails down her cheeks.

'What a mess.'

She looked up at Morgan and there was a look of confusion on her face.

'What are you doing here?'

'Commercial break-in, CID are dealing with this one. How did they get in? The front of the shop looks intact.'

'Through a window at the back. There's a brick in the kitchen sink along with broken glass. I haven't touched anything in case the police want to take it.'

Morgan walked through the narrow door leading to the small kitchen area, where there was indeed a shattered window and a large brick on the kitchen sink unit. She looked to see if there was any dried blood but couldn't see anything. She took out her phone and rang Wendy.

'Morning, have you been asked to attend a commercial break-in? I'm here now if you're on your way.'

'Yes, it's on my list. If you're there I'll head over now. Is there anything promising?'

'Not for me to say. I'll leave that for the expert.'

'Haha, you mean there's nothing obvious?'

'How did you guess?'

'See you soon.'

She turned around and almost jumped out of her skin, Sienna was standing so close behind her.

'How are you feeling now?'

'What about? The fact that someone tried to kill me, or that some arsehole has broken into my shop and trashed it?'

'Have you heard about Jess?'

'No, why, what's she done now? She was moaning on Facebook about her diet the other day.'

'She's dead.'

Sienna was scrolling through her phone, but she looked up at that, shock written on her face. 'What?'

'I said she's dead. She got killed by a van last night.' Morgan felt bad being so abrupt about it, but Sienna just annoyed her so much and she had wanted to shock her, to see what her reaction was.

Her hand flew to her mouth. 'Is this some kind of sick joke, Morgan, because that's so not funny.'

'It's no joke. Why would anyone joke about something so tragic? I had to attend the scene; it was awful.'

'Oh, my God. So then, my poisoning... Is someone trying to kill us off? But why? I don't get it. Who would be doing this? Surely you must have some kind of idea. Aren't you the hotshot detective? I Googled you, and you're always in the paper.'

And just like that Morgan wanted to swing her fist right into her nose. Her arm twitched it was so hard to control the anger she felt towards the woman standing in front of her.

'I'm not working the case currently, which is why I'm here dealing with your minor break-in. So, can you tell me what's been stolen?'

'Well, nothing that I can see. It's all damage; they trashed the place.'

'CSI will be here soon, so don't touch anything until they've taken what they can. In the meantime, talk me through what time you locked up last night to when you opened up this morning.'

Sienna was still open-mouthed, no doubt trying to process what she'd been told about Jess.

'I shut the shop at five, like always. I didn't actually leave until around six though. I was cleaning because the woman who comes once a week rang in sick. What a waste of bloody time that was now. Then I went home. Oh actually I called in at Sainsbury's, then I went home, and I came here an hour ago to open up and found it like this. That's it, nothing more to it.'

'Does the shop have any CCTV? Has anything been stolen or have you upset anyone lately?' Morgan thought that this was the understatement of the year because the woman was truly horrid and probably upset almost everyone she came into contact with.

'No.'

'But this week someone tried to poison you and now your shop has been broken into and vandalised. Can you think of anyone who would do this to you?'

She shook her head. 'No, I honestly don't.'

Morgan looked up from her notepad where she'd been writing everything down. 'Look, I can't prove it right now, but I think this may have something to do with the night Brad died. Brittany and now Jess are both dead in the space of a couple of days, you were poisoned, so that leaves Lara. All of you were there that night. Was there anything that happened which maybe wasn't told to anyone else? Have you all been keeping some huge secret that has come back to bite you all on the arse?'

'Brad? But that was years ago. No, it was an accident. He was alive when we left. It got too cold and once the alcohol began to wear off, camping in the caves didn't seem like such a great idea. We left, and he wouldn't come with us.'

Morgan sighed; she had so wanted it to be something else, but Sienna and Lara had both stuck to the same story. Maybe she was wrong about the connection? Sienna turned away from her, and she caught sight of a small bruise to the side of her head that she'd tried to cover with her hair.

'What happened to your head?'

'Nothing.'

'How did you get that bruise? You didn't get it at the cave the other day. There wasn't a scratch on you.'

'I banged it on the corner of a cupboard. It's nothing. I'm so clumsy. I do stuff like that all the time.'

'Hello, CSI.'

Wendy's voice called from the front of the shop, and Sienna hastily made her escape to greet her.

Morgan took another look around. Unbolting the back door she went out into the small yard and then the alleyway behind it to look for cameras. There weren't any that she could see. Whoever did this must have known there weren't any because it was quite secluded out here. She walked back through the shop where Wendy was talking to Sienna, who was like a different woman with her. Maybe it was only Morgan she had the problem with, some long-fuelled grudge from their school days that she didn't understand in the first place.

'Thanks for coming so quick, Wendy. I really appreciate it. I've taken a first account from Sienna. I'll get it typed up back at the station. I'm not sure what's going on here but there's been nothing stolen.'

'You're very welcome. Morgan, are you okay?'

Morgan felt as if Sienna was way too invested in her and Wendy's conversation. She was watching them both wide-eyed.

'Great thanks, I'll speak to you at the station.'

And with that she walked out of the door. She turned back to look at Sienna one last time. 'If I were you, I'd be very careful and vigilant. You've already been hurt once; you don't want it to happen again.' Turning back, she walked away, unable to be in Sienna's company for much longer. A voice inside her head whispered, *it could be her.* Maybe that's why she couldn't stand her because she was a killer.

CHAPTER THIRTY-SIX

2016

Lara was knackered by the time they reached the caves; it was steep, and she hated walking. Jess was still flirting with Brad but only in a friendly way. She could hear Brittany's and Sienna's voices in the distance, giggling, and Jess asked Brad, 'Are you sure you want to spend the evening with Eddy and Patsy from *Ab Fab*?'

Brad had chuckled. 'A man's got to do what a man's got to do.'

Lara had looked at him and asked, 'What's that mean?'

Brad had laughed. 'It's a saying that John Wayne was famous for.'

'Who's John Wayne?'

'You never heard of him, seriously, Lara?'

She shook her head. 'Nope.'

'My grandad loves his films. He's an old movie star. Was in a lot of westerns.'

'Oh, right. Still no idea but okay then.'

Jess rolled her eyes. 'It's a joke, Lara, don't be a dweeb. He's saying that he's only staying because it's what he has to do, not what he wants to do. Aren't you, Brad?'

Brad shrugged. 'If you say so, Jess. To be honest I don't know what it meant; it just sounded good.'

Jess and Lara began to giggle. 'Come on then let's get this over with.'

Brad looked puzzled. 'I thought you were all BFF?'

Lara smiled at him. 'It's difficult, we are but those two are in a league of their own. There's a pecking order. Brittany is the leader because she's beautiful and fearless; Sienna wants to be the leader but she's not fearless and, well, a bit of a bitch to be honest, so she kind of hogs all Brittany's attention with her private little jokes and trying to be a right cow to the rest of us. Me and Jess here are like their little servants that follow them around because it's easier to be a part of their group than it is to break off and be on your own. It also helps because the bullies tend to leave us all alone. So, it's a kind of self-preservation thing. You're either with them or they make your life a misery. We just want easy lives, don't we, Jess?'

Jess shrugged. 'I suppose so.'

Brad was shaking his head. 'Wow, I had no idea it was so complicated. Where does Morgan fit in to all of this? She's kind of like the odd one out?'

'Morgan is Brittany's pet project. Before her mum died, both her and Sienna were giving her a bit of a hard time and then that happened, and I guess Brittany has a guilty conscience. She apologised to her and kind of took her under her wing, but Sienna hates her still and is only putting up with her because we think she's got like a major girl crush on Brittany and loves her.'

All three of them were standing huddled on the top of the fell just before the small descent down a rocky path to get to the caves, where the faint voice of Carly Jepsen singing 'Call Me Maybe' was fading in and out on someone's phone.

'Lara, I can't believe you just said that out loud.'

'Brad won't say anything, will you? And besides, he fancies Morgan not either of those two, so he's good, aren't you?'

He was nodding. 'Should we turn back? Do we really want to be here with them if they're so awful?'

'Oh God, no, we can't do that. Absolutely not. If we leave now and they think we didn't turn up, there would be hell to pay at school. We're all in this together, Brad. Let's go get drunk and maybe they won't seem like such cows.'

They laughed and walked single file down the rocky path, Jess leading the way, then Lara followed by Brad. Brittany and Sienna were sipping from a vodka bottle, and both screamed out loud when they saw them approaching and began jumping up and down. Lara turned back to Brad and whispered, 'Sorry, I didn't mean to put you off. They can be okay really.'

He smiled at her, nodding his head. 'I can do this; I just wish that Morgan was here.'

The sky from the patch of damp, mossy grass outside of Rydal Caves looked as if it was cloaked in thick black velvet. They all sat around a tiny fire at the mouth of the cave, taking it in turns to listen to crappy playlists until their phones died, swigging vodka and talking rubbish. Brittany couldn't take her eyes off Brad, neither could Sienna, and they had made him sit in-between them, where the pair of them were pressing as close to his body as they could. Lara felt bad for him. He looked as if he was in pain, and the only way to ease it was to keep on drinking the neat vodka that was being passed around.

Sienna said, 'Should we play strip poker? I bet you'd like that, wouldn't you, Brad? Seeing me and the other girls in our underwear.'

The look of horror that filled Brad's face made Lara spit the mouthful of vodka out all over herself as she began to cough and splutter. Wiping her mouth with the back of her hand she looked at Sienna.

'What are you trying to do, traumatise him? He doesn't want to see any of us in our underwear, do you, Brad? And anyway, it's too fucking cold, Sienna, to be running around half naked.'

Brittany was leaning close to him, whispering into his ear, and Lara felt a twinge of something. It wasn't jealousy exactly; she knew he was out of her league. Maybe it was annoyance that Brittany and Sienna loved themselves so much they thought he was going to want to screw around with them. They carried on drinking and chatting until almost all of the alcohol had been consumed. Jess was describing the dress she wanted to wear to the leavers' prom when Brittany stood up. 'I need the toilet. Where can I go that's safe?'

Brad stood up, stumbling a little, and Lara could tell he was more than a little drunk. 'I'll show you. I come up here all the time.'

Brittany grabbed hold of his hand and dragged him away from the circle, grinning. He didn't let go but kept tight hold, and Lara wanted to tell him not to go with her, to think about what he was doing. Then she took a swig of vodka and giggled. Who was she to spoil his fun, and anyway, weren't they only going to look for some place for Brittany to pee? That wasn't exactly the most romantic of situations to be in. They carried on talking about the leavers' prom and who was going with who. Sienna was adamant that she was going with Brad, and Jess kept grinning at Lara, clearly dying to reveal that he was as good as asking Morgan. Then Sienna stood up.

'I need to pee. Which direction did they go? They've been ages.'

She stumbled off, and Jess whispered, 'Imagine if she catches those two at it behind a bush. She'd flip her lid. I'm so drunk, I feel as if the world is spinning.'

'Bloody hell, Jess, do you want to lie down on the sleeping bag?'

'No, I don't, thank you. I'm good.'

There was a lot of loud trampling through some bushes, and Brittany appeared, flushed and out of breath. Her top was unbuttoned, and Jess looked up at Lara. 'Did she pee out of her tits? Or has Brad copped a bit of a feel?'

They both began giggling as she reached where they were sitting. On closer inspection, Lara could see some twigs in Brittany's hair.

'What have you been doing? You've been ages? Did Brad give you a birthday shag?'

'Hey, look at me. I'm king of the world.'

Brad's voice echoed down at them from the hillside at the top of the cave. It was really high up, so high up he looked like a small dark shadow. He was standing there with his arms and legs wide open, and Jess screeched, '*Titanic*, I know that one. I've watched it loads; Leonardo DiCaprio is well fit.'

Lara scrambled to her feet. He looked dangerously close to the edge of the cave.

'Brad get back, it's dangerous.'

She screamed at him, but a gust of wind took her voice in the opposite direction.

'What?' He stepped closer to the edge. 'I can't hear you.'

Jess and Brittany stood up. 'Get down, Brad.' They shouted in unison, waving at him. He waved back and then it happened in slow motion. One minute he was there laughing and waving at them, the next he stumbled, lurching forwards. They were screaming at him, but he didn't seem to be able to stop himself and then he was mid-air, free-falling through the sky, his arms and legs flapping in the wind. The thud as he hit the jagged outcrop of rocks at the entrance to the caves was deafening, and all three of them screamed and rushed towards where his broken body lay face up. The mouth of the cave, seeped in blackness, made it look as if it was stretched open in a never-ending scream.

Lara wanted to scream along with it.

CHAPTER THIRTY-SEVEN

Morgan had no idea what to do next. She didn't want to go back to the station and the mess that was happening there. She crossed over the road to the building society and went inside. The woman on the desk smiled at her, and it was so warm and friendly that she immediately felt better.

'Good morning, how can I help?'

'Hi, I'm Detective Constable Brookes and I'm investigating a break-in at the shop across the road. I was wondering if it would be possible to get a copy of your CCTV?'

'Oh, I wish I could help you. I can't for the life of me access the system, but I can ask Emma when she comes in later to take a look for you, if that's any good. What are you looking for?'

Morgan felt a bit bad; it was a pointless exercise because it was clear the offenders had gone in through the back, but they might have been hanging around outside the front whilst they decided what to do.

'That would be amazing, thank you. If I give you my details, could you phone if you find something?'

'Of course, what time are we searching from?'

'Probably from when the shop closed until this morning. So about 5 p.m. until 8 a.m. Sorry, that's a long shot, isn't it?'

'Emma won't mind. It's better than being out here most days anyway.'

Morgan scribbled her phone number down. 'These are my contact details. Thank you, I really appreciate it.'

'Is she okay? Sienna, I think she's called?'

'Yes, just a little shook up. It's been a bit of a week for her. I'm sure she'll appreciate your help.'

Morgan left her to it. That was one thing ticked off the list. Now all she had to do was figure out what was going on.

She decided to go grab a coffee and sandwich before heading back to the station, and for the first time in forever she chose to sit in the café and sip a latte in peace, alone. She didn't think she was in any danger from whoever was doing this because she didn't have anything to do with that night. Still, she wasn't taking any chances with her food and drink. She didn't know anyone who worked here, so that was fine. She took out her notepad and began writing lists whilst waiting for her chicken salad sandwich to be brought to the table. At the top of the list was Brad's name, then below that Brittany, Jess, Sienna, Lara. She put a line through the ones who were dead. That left Lara and Sienna. How had someone got close enough to them to poison them? That was the big question. How were they doing it? Everyone was blaming Ettie's tea, which was one thing they had in common. Brittany drank it for her stomach problems; Sienna sold it and drank it. Did Jess drink it? Had anyone been to search her house yet? They probably had. She took out her phone to ring Wendy and ask if she'd been there when Declan's name flashed across the screen.

'Hello.'

'Morgan, I've taken a look at the records for your friend, Brad. He did have enough alcohol in his system to impair his judgement; in fact he had more than twice the legal alcohol limit with seventy-five milligrams in his bloodstream. However, he was a big lad, wasn't he? Not big as in chunky but big as in a strapping, fit rugby player build, which might mean that it wasn't enough to cause him to be drunk as a skunk for want of a better word. There were no signs of foul play that I could see. He really did die from his injuries from the fall; they

were catastrophic. The height he fell from and the impact when he hit those rocks, well, death would have been instantaneous.'

'Bless him, he didn't deserve to die like that. Do you think he jumped?'

'Definitely not. There were skid marks in the damp grass where it looks as if he lost his footing and slid right off the end of the cave. It's a long way down.'

'Could he have been pushed?'

'Well, I suppose that he could have been, but I think that whoever investigated would have taken that into consideration.'

'Does it say on the report who the investigating officer was?'

'Hang on, let me look.' There was the rustling of papers. *'Yes, I thought it was, but I didn't want to say until I'd double-checked. It was DS Tom Fell.'*

All the pieces were coming together. She just needed to figure out how to slot them into a whole. 'Thanks, Declan, you're the best.'

'Ah, it was nothing and you're very welcome. Don't go giving your DI a hard time, will you?'

'Me? As if I would.'

'Speak later, Morgan.'

She put her phone away. Tom was an excellent copper. Surely, he would have picked up on it if there had been any suspicion of foul play. She ate her sandwich and watched as the world went by, wondering, no, wishing she could see Brad one last time. Tell him not to go to the caves that night, to stay with her. They could have watched a movie on the small TV in her bedroom. The last mouthful of her sandwich was too hard to swallow because of the lump that had formed in the back of her throat. She blinked back the tears and looked out of the window and saw the outline of a familiar figure across the road, head down, walking so fast he was almost scurrying. She stood up, grabbing her jacket, the adrenaline pumping around her body. She almost ran out of the door. It looked like him, like Gary Marks. His head disappeared around the corner, and she had to dash across the road. A car horn blared at her and she waved an apology, taking out her radio ready to shout for urgent assistance to apprehend him, but there was no sign of the guy. She stood still, her hands on her hips, looking around to see if there was a side street he could have snuck down to escape her. There was a small alley with a dead end and no sign of him. If that was the case he had to have gone into a shop or a property. She began to slowly walk past the few shops that were dotted along this small road. Maybe it hadn't been him. She'd only seen him twice in prison. How could she be so sure? But she knew that her instinct was strong, that she was right and that somehow Gary Marks was here, back home, hiding in plain sight right under their noses.

Her phone began ringing and she answered it. 'Yes.'

'*What's up, have you been running, Brookes? You sound out of breath.*'

She was about to tell Ben about Marks and changed her mind. He was her burden to bear. If it was him then she would bring him in by herself, but first she wanted to make sure it was him.

'No, I'm just excited to hear your voice.'

Ben laughed so loud down the phone she had to hold it away from her ear.

'*You're such a crap liar. I thought you'd want to know that Ettie has been bailed.*'

'Jesus, Ben, sent home on bail, why?'

'*Pending further investigation. There's not much we can do in all reality. There was a hair on the T-shirt which has been sent off for testing, but even if it comes back as a match for Brittany or Sienna it's not enough evidence, is it? If the T-shirt had been covered in dried blood that might have been another matter. I think Tom panicked. He thought he was doing the right thing, but he has no motive. Why would Ettie want to poison people with her tea out of the blue and not just any people, a specific group of people who are all linked together from an incident years ago. It has to be more than that. It's something to do with the night your friend died. You said that, and I'm convinced too.'*

'Oh, is it the T-shirt Sienna lost? Thank you. Poor Ettie, I should go see her.'

'It may well be. I'd give her some space; she wasn't best pleased with her time spent in our company, and I know you had nothing to do with it, but still, I'd hate for her to take it out on you when none of it is your fault. She's bound to be pissed off and angry with the world right now. She didn't say much in interview, but one thing she mentioned was that the tea she makes is bitter and needs to be sweetened with honey to make it palatable. She said that the minute quantities of belladonna that she uses wouldn't be sufficient to send a person into full-blown psychosis. What she did say, which I think is interesting, was that the berries from the plant are far sweeter and that they could easily be eaten in a large quantity without anyone being any the wiser that they were highly toxic until it was too late.'

'Wow, that's very interesting. What does this mean then? Can I come back? Am I allowed to work the case?'

He paused, and she knew that they didn't want her involved. It stung, but she also kind of understood that it was a conflict of interest.

'I'm sorry, Morgan, not just yet. How did you get on at that break-in?'

'Did you know it was the shop owned by Sienna Waters?'

'No.'

'I thought you didn't; otherwise you wouldn't have sent me here either. To be completely fair it's all a bit weird. The shop was trashed, they broke a window out the back, but nothing was stolen. She's acting weird too. I'm not sure if she hasn't got something to do with all of this, Ben. Don't you think it's strange how she survived when the other two didn't? Maybe she's trying to throw us off her trail by distracting us.'

'You think it's Sienna who is the poisoner?'

'I'm just putting it out there. She could have planted that T-shirt at Ettie's, couldn't she, or put it somewhere for her to find? I think we should be focusing on her.'

'Sounds plausible. What's the motive for her though? And why frame Ettie?'

'I haven't figured that out yet, revenge maybe. I'll think about it some more.'

'Well do it from a safe distance and don't do anything stupid. Run it by me and I'll take any actions that need to be taken so you're out of this and safe. Is that okay with you?'

'Yes, boss. It's fine by me.'

'No, Morgan, it's not just fine. I need to hear you say that you'll keep on feeding the information back to the rest of the team, but that you won't take anything into your own hands.'

She tutted, loudly. 'I promise not to take anything into my own hands, which is more than can be said for the rest of you sneaking around behind my back like you have been.'

'I know, I'm sorry about this whole investigation, Morgan. It's been a shitshow from day one and you deserve better.'

'Thanks.'

She hung up, looking around the area to see if she could spot the man she could have sworn was her biological father.

CHAPTER THIRTY-EIGHT

Morgan was driving home. She'd decided to avoid the station, and she had nowhere else to go. She was searching her mind for the idea she knew was hiding at the back of it. It kept surfacing for a millisecond to tease her then would disappear again. She remembered the picture of the smoothie Jess had posted on Facebook. Flipping heck that was it. Brittany was into being healthy. Hadn't someone mentioned she drank a lot of smoothies? She turned her car around at the next junction and began driving back to Brittany's house. What had they made the smoothies from, or where had they bought the ingredients? She parked up and opened the gate to the house, looking at her watch. It was mid-afternoon, so it wasn't likely that anyone would be in, but she hammered on the front door hoping for an answer, nonetheless. But no one came to open it. Pressing her ear against the door. She couldn't hear any signs of life in there. *Damn it*, she muttered. If she hurried to the school, she might catch Paige; otherwise she could spend the next two hours chasing ghosts.

The school playground was empty. Morgan walked past the tarmac where Brittany had landed. The blood had been washed away, of course, but she was positive the ground was stained a deep, dark colour, as if Brittany's essence had seeped into the floor. It was a permanent reminder of the tragic, brutal way she had died. A cold shudder ran down the full length of her spine, and she stopped to look up at the staffroom window that Brittany had thrown herself out of. It was boarded up. She wondered if the staff were still using that room. Would they still want to take their breaks and eat their lunch, staring at the large piece of wood reminding them that their friend had launched herself through it and killed herself? God, she hoped not, and that Andrea had found them a temporary place to kick off their shoes and relax.

'Hello, Morgan, how are you?'

She jolted back to the present moment at the sound of Andrea Hart's voice.

'Andrea, I'm good. How are you? How's everyone doing?'

'I'm not going to lie, Morgan, things are extremely difficult at the moment. As you can see, there are too many reminders of what happened here a couple of days ago. I thought they should shut the school, but the board of governors said it would make things far worse and draw far more attention to it. I think the Chair's exact words were: "As bloody awful as this is there is nothing we can do but keep calm and carry on. We'll ride out the storm which will pass in a couple of weeks".'

Morgan pulled a face. 'What did you say to that?'

'I told him he was a pompous prick who needed to go screw himself and stop being so heartless.'

Morgan began to laugh. Then, realising how inappropriate it was, she lifted her hand to her mouth and began to cough, trying to stifle the laughter.

Andrea smiled at her.

'I bet that went down really well.'

She shrugged. 'Actually, it didn't but you know what, I'm past the point of caring. I lost a dear friend and a valuable member of my staff. The children lost a warm, wonderful, loving teacher who nurtured them; even the ones who are little swines behaved themselves for Brittany. Life is so cruel; she didn't deserve to die like that.'

'No, she didn't, and she sounds like she was the most amazing teacher.'

Andrea nodded. 'I'm sorry, I'm not in a good place at the moment. When things like this happen, they have you questioning your own mortality and every single life choice that you've ever made. How can I help you, Morgan? Won't you come inside and take ten minutes? I hope you don't mind me saying but you look washed out and exhausted.'

'That would be wonderful. I'm so sad about all of this and it's bringing up a lot of stuff for me too.'

'Then come in and have a soothing cup of lavender, camomile and lemon balm tea. It's wonderful for calming us the fuck down. I think we could both use some of it.'

Morgan grinned at her. 'Well, that sounds like it might be perfect. I suppose you can't really drink neat vodka when you have a school to run.'

'Trust me, if I could get away with the vodka I would, but I fear I may not hold back what little values I have when the next idiot doesn't take my suggestions on board, and if I get sacked who is going to run my queendom? So, for now, until I can let go of this place I'll stick to the tea.'

They went inside, Andrea leaning forward and pressing the small black fob on her lanyard against the keypad. The door clicked open, and she pushed it back, holding it for Morgan. Sandra looked up from her phone. Immediately tucking it under the desk, she stood up and opened the sliding glass window.

'Hello, Detective Brookes, what brings you here?'

Andrea looked at her. 'Sandra, please be a darling and make two mugs of the tea with the tea bags from the purple box, then bring them into my office.'

Sandra pulled a face but didn't answer back, slamming the sliding glass windows shut.

Andrea tutted. 'One of these days she's going to end up either chopping her own fingers off or her nose. Probably her nose because it sticks out more than Pinocchio's; she's so damn inquisitive.'

Andrea walked into her office, and Morgan followed. She sat down on the leather sofa, too tired to even attempt sitting on one of the world's smallest chairs that were reserved for the pupils. Andrea sat behind her desk and let out the world's loudest sigh. 'Am I allowed to ask how the investigation is going?'

'Yes, as long as it's between us and Sandra doesn't know. I have a feeling she'd spread the update quicker than a case of gastroenteritis.'

Andrea began to laugh, so loud neither of them heard Sandra knock on the door. She walked in carrying a tray and stared at Morgan as if to ask *what's up with her?* Andrea stopped herself by smothering her hand over her mouth.

'Thank you, Sandra, that's all for now.'

Sandra was positively glowering at Andrea now, and Morgan felt a little bad, but Sandra slammed the tray down and walked out, slamming the door even harder.

'Ouch, she's angry. Do you think she heard what I said?'

'I'm afraid she spends most of her time being angry. I don't know if it's an age thing or what but never mind. I'll feed her a few snippets of gossip after to appease her; obviously not what we've talked about.'

'Have you heard about the other tragic accident in the early hours, and the incident at Rydal Caves?'

'No, oh my gosh, there haven't been more?'

'A woman who both Brittany and I went to school with was found acting in a, I think the best way to describe it was, hallucinogenic state. We managed to get her medical help before she did anything life-threatening. Then another of our friends was killed in a tragic road traffic accident last night.'

Morgan picked up one of the mugs from the tray. She blew the hot steam and was relieved to see a tea bag inside the mug. Not that she believed Ettie's tea was the culprit, but she wasn't taking any chances. She took a sip, expecting it to taste vile and was pleasantly surprised. 'This is actually okay.'

Andrea smiled. 'It is, I drink it regularly. Oh my gosh, those poor women. What on earth is happening? I've never heard of anything like this in my life.'

'To be brutally honest with you neither have we. What I'm trying to do is to figure out how they were given something so toxic that it could affect them in the way it did. At first we thought it may be a herbal tea.'

Andrea took the mug away from her mouth and stared down into the cup, a look of horror on her face.

'But not this kind of tea. I'm assuming this is from the super-market and mass produced.'

'I assume so. I buy it from Booths.'

'The tea we were looking at is of the loose kind. We know that Brittany and the other victims drank it but…'

'But?'

'That line of enquiry is no longer valid. I've been trying to figure it out and I've realised that both Brittany and at least one of the others drank smoothies. I don't know what sort, but I've been told that by a reliable source.'

'Oh my God, Brittany did. She was on some healthy eating kick and always brought one in with her for breakfast. If you ask me, they looked disgusting, but she raved about them and said they were really great and full of vitamins. She never said they were full of poison though.'

'She wouldn't have known; apparently we think the berries used are highly toxic though they taste very sweet.'

'Hang on, she might have brought a flask of it in with her that morning and put it in the fridge. It could still be in there if she didn't drink it all.'

Morgan felt a rush of adrenalin and hope course through her veins. 'That would be amazing. I could get it sent off for forensic analysis.'

Andrea stood up. 'The staff leave all sorts in the fridge in the staffroom. It's disgusting. The cleaners have a rule they won't even

open the door because it looks as if it's some kind of bacterial labora-
tory on the bottom shelf.' She raced out of the room, and Morgan
almost threw her mug onto the tray as she jumped up to follow
her. Sandra's eyes nearly popped out of her head as the two of them
rushed past her tiny office to the concealed stairs that led up to the
staffroom. Morgan's heart was thudding loud in her ears. She could
clearly picture the last time she ran up these stairs and hadn't been
able to save her friend. Andrea threw open the staffroom door so
hard it crashed against the wall, leaving a large dint in the plaster.
She strode to the fridge and opened the door, scanning the interior.

'Bingo.' She pointed to a clear drinks bottle that contained a
slushy, green mess.

Morgan stared at it, praying this was the break they needed. If
this contained the poison, they could hopefully trace it back to where
the ingredients came from. Andrea began to reach inside the fridge.

'Don't touch it.' Morgan shouted so loud Andrea jumped and
pulled her hand back as if she'd been burned.

'Sorry, didn't mean to scare you. I need to seize it properly,
photograph it where it is and bag it up.' She took her car keys
from her trouser pocket. 'I know this is cheeky, but in the boot of
that battered old VW Golf outside the funeral home is a box of
evidence bags and gloves. Could you go and get me some gloves
and a clear plastic bag, please?'

Andrea nodded. 'Yes, of course.' She took the keys and left
Morgan staring inside the fridge at the congealing mess that looked
like something from a nuclear waste plant. Taking out her phone
she began to video it and snap photos, then she rang Wendy.

'*Yes, Morgan.*'

'Sorry, Wendy, are you busy?'

'*Always busy, what's up?*'

'I think I've found the stuff the poison is in. It's in a clear
container in the staffroom fridge.'

'*Where at?*'

'Priory Grove.'

'Right, I'm in the middle of documenting the house of the victim from last night. Do you have gloves and an evidence bag with you?'

'Yes.'

'You can seize it then but wear the gloves. If you think it contains poison, double glove then double bag it and bring it back to the station. I'll meet you there. What's in it?'

'It looks like a mouldy smoothie. Apparently, Brittany was on a health kick and lived off them. So did Jess, the woman whose house you're at now. Can you see if you can find any of the ingredients that could be used to make a smoothie? You're looking for small black berries in particular.'

'I'm on it. I'll meet you at my office when I'm done here. Good effort, Morgan; have you told Ben yet?'

'Not yet, I'm technically not supposed to be working this case. I only came here on a hunch.'

Wendy laughed.

'Excellent hunch, I won't say anything. He's on his way here to take a look around.'

'Actually, if you sort of broke the news to him about the berries in the smoothies, he might not be so angry with me by the time I get back. I'll owe you big time.'

'Morgan, you could never repay me all the favours I do for you. I don't suppose this will make much difference.'

'Thank you, Wendy, you're amazing.'

'Yeah, I am, aren't I? Make sure you document, double glove and double bag. I don't want to have to be attending your flat if you manage to poison yourself. Can you seal off the fridge too?'

Andrea came back with a box of gloves and several different sized bags. 'Sorry, I wasn't sure which ones.'

'Those are perfect, thank you.'

Morgan wrote out the information on the evidence bags to protect the chain of custody and then did exactly what Wendy told her to, carefully picking up the container of what she hoped was in it as if it was a stick of explosive. Andrea watched holding her breath. When it was safely sealed inside the bags, she muttered, 'Blimey, that was intense. Thank God for the lazy staff and stubborn cleaners. I hope that is of some use to the investigation, Morgan, and we can find out what really happened to Brittany. She doesn't deserve to be known as the crazy teacher who threw herself out of the window, because up until it happened, she was the kindest, sanest person I'd ever worked with.'

Morgan nodded. 'I hope so too, thanks, Andrea.'

Andrea smiled then led the way downstairs, opening the doors for Morgan so she didn't have to risk spilling the evidence. She even walked her to her car, opening the door.

'Did you see Sandra's face? Bless her, she was staring so hard at what you were holding. Where are you going to put it?'

She pointed to the cup holder. 'It should be okay inside that. Even if it spills it will stay inside of the bag.'

The door shut and Andrea gave her the thumbs up, mouthing *good luck* through the window. For the first time today, Morgan couldn't wait to get back to the station and hand this over to Wendy.

CHAPTER THIRTY-NINE

Morgan waited inside Wendy's office for her to get back. She didn't even bother going to tell Ben or the rest of the team what she'd discovered, in case they took it from her and said thank you, bye. She put the evidence bag on the side and then sat in the corner, not moving so the automatic light switched off. She was tired and leaned forward on the desk, laying her head onto her crossed arms. Closing her eyes, she didn't think it would hurt if she just had a five-minute nap. She wasn't superwoman and couldn't survive off very little sleep. She drifted off but not for long because her phone began ringing, jolting her out of her slumber.

'Yeah.' She yawned loudly.

'*Oh, I'm sorry did I disturb you? Is that you, Morgan?*'

She sat up, unsure of who this was. 'Yes, it's me, who is this?'

'*It's Lara, we need to talk.*'

The tiredness left as fast as it had arrived. 'We do? What about?'

'*About Sienna and what happened that night at the caves. I've been thinking about it a lot and I don't want to be a grass but...*'

'But?'

'*I'd rather speak to you in person, alone. Not here when there's a chance Greg could come home at any moment. He's forever wearing his corporate lawyer head and thinks he knows what's best for me all the time.*' She sighed. '*It gets a bit much, you know. I love him but he forgets that I'm an adult with a mind of my own.*'

'Where do you want to meet?'

'If we met at White Moss car park we could hike up to the caves, and I could show you exactly what happened and why I need to talk to you about Sienna.'

Morgan's entire body was tingling with tiny jolts of electricity. She knew there was something that Lara had been holding back.

'Yes, I can be there in an hour. There's something I have to do at work first.'

'I can't now. Like I said, Greg's on his way home, so I can't just tell him I'm going out for a hike for old times' sake. I haven't been out for a walk in forever. He's always asking me if I want to go on some ten-mile hikes with him and I always tell him no thanks.'

Morgan felt deflated. 'Oh, that's a shame but I don't blame you. I wouldn't want to go on ten-mile hikes either.'

'Greg has to be at work extra early, so he'll be leaving at seven. Should we say seven thirty tomorrow morning, before it gets too busy? You know how popular that route is, everyone walks that way.'

'Brilliant, see you then, Lara.'

Lara ended the call, just as Wendy walked in clutching an assortment of evidence bags.

'Are you hiding in here?'

Morgan nodded. 'Yep, can't go into my office. I'm like a naughty kid who isn't allowed in.'

'Surely not? They can't treat you like that.'

'No, maybe it's not that bad but I'm not supposed to be anywhere near this investigation because it's a conflict of interest. It's so not fair.'

Wendy smiled. 'No, it isn't, but you don't have the best track record. Maybe this is Ben's only way of trying to keep you safe and as far from it as possible. He really cares about you; I can tell.'

'So everyone keeps telling me, that is except for Ben. He doesn't say a word, so maybe you're all wrong.'

Wendy laughed. 'Erm, I don't think I'm ever wrong about who fancies who in this place. I also have it on good authority that Cain is a little bit besotted with you.'

'Oh, blimey, no way. Why would he even be interested in me? It's not as if I'm the catch of the day. Bless him, he's been so nice lately as well.'

'Do you ever look in the mirror at yourself, Morgan?'

'Of course, I do, these wings on my eyeliner are a work of art.'

'No, I mean actually look at yourself. What do you see when you do?'

'What are you, my therapist?' She smiled at Wendy. 'I see a geeky Goth girl who lost everyone she ever loved and is a sad loner with no life outside of work.'

'Wow, that's just wow. You have some shit going on there. Maybe you do need a therapist; it might help you to work through all of that. Do you not see the beautiful woman you are staring back at you?'

Morgan laughed out loud.

'Morgan I'm serious, you are flipping gorgeous, and you don't even realise it. No wonder all the guys are wanting to take you under their wing and protect you.'

'Thanks, Wendy, that's kind of you to say, but come on I don't need anyone to protect me. I'm quite capable of looking after myself.'

It was Wendy's turn to laugh out loud. 'I bet the A & E Department beg to differ with you there. You've had a few run-ins with some violent criminals since you joined. Take my advice, when you look in the mirror next time take a good, hard look at yourself. You're definitely not a geeky teenager any more. Now, pep talk finished, what did you do with my nuclear smoothie?'

Morgan pointed to the side where she'd left it.

Wendy put the rest of the bags down on the counter.

'Lord that looks vile. Why anyone would want to drink that stuff is beyond me.'

'Did you find anything at Jess's house?'

'Only an empty bag of frozen smoothie mix in the bin.'

'No way, that's amazing.'

'It is. I'm going to get these sent off to the lab right now and fast tracked. If they come back as a positive then all you have to do is find out where they bought the stuff from. It has to be somewhere local.'

Morgan jumped up and high-fived Wendy. 'What a team.'

'Yep, what a team. Are you going to go and tell Ben? It might take the pressure off your aunt.'

'I don't know. She's already been bailed pending further investigations, but Ben doesn't think it's her. If I go and tell them now, I'll get told to keep my nose out. Can I wait until you get the results back, so I know we're on the right track?'

'Fine by me, as long as you don't get yourself into any bother. I don't think it would hurt.'

'Thank you.'

'But I will have to tell them when and if I get a positive result.'

'I know, that's fine. I will too.'

Morgan waved goodbye and walked out of the office. She paused. She could go up and see what they were getting up to. Instead, she decided to go home but first she was stopping off at the supermarket for some groceries that didn't include smoothie mix. She ran back to Wendy's office, bursting through the door and almost giving her a heart attack.

'Is there a brand name on the bag you found in the bin?'

'No, sorry. It's a clear Ziploc bag with nothing on it except the words "Berry Blast Smoothie Mix".'

'Damn, that would have been too easy, I guess. Never mind, thanks.'

As she walked out to her car, she felt happy that she was heading in the right direction with the investigation. She wondered if she should phone both Lara and Sienna to warn them not to make any smoothies, but Lara had already said that she didn't eat that crap so she should be safe. As much as she disliked Sienna, and that had increased a thousand times the last few interactions she'd had with her, she didn't want to see her die an awful death like the others. She went to find a response officer to go and visit Sienna to warn her about it, Morgan had a feeling she might not listen to her if she went.

CHAPTER FORTY

The supermarket was busy; she hated busy. There were far too many people, but she wasn't going to risk eating anything she already had at home. Not that she had frozen smoothie mix or fresh fruit in because she wasn't that kind of girl, but she wasn't taking any risks. As Wendy reminded her, she was pretty prone to getting caught up in disastrous situations. She picked up a couple of pizzas, a few bottles of rosé, crisps, chocolate and fresh milk, steering clear of the fruit and vegetable aisles, not that she needed an excuse to eat crap, but this was a legitimate one if ever there was. As she queued for the checkout her phone began vibrating in her pocket and for once she felt like ignoring it. It had rung nonstop all day like some hotline, but she couldn't. Taking it out, she saw 'unknown number' and almost silenced it but thought she better answer. Unknown was usually work.

'Hello?'

'*Is this Detective Brookes?*'

'Yes, it is. Can I help you?'

'*It's the building society, well not the actual building, it's Emma who works there. My colleague asked me to go through the CCTV for you, and the only thing I found was an incident around one a.m.*'

'Thank you, Emma, that's amazing.'

'*There's a guy who comes out of the shop I think you're asking about. Fifteen minutes later the woman who owns it comes out. If you want to come and take a look, I'll wait for you. If you need the footage actually downloading, then I'll have to put a form in and request it from head office. It could take some time. They're not the quickest.*'

'I'm on my way now, thanks.'

Morgan paid for her shopping and almost threw it all into the back of her car. As she drove back to Kendal and the building society, she realised just how little she knew about Sienna. She said she didn't have a boyfriend, so who else could this man be? Morgan also realised she knew very little about the group of women who'd been her friends back at school and this made her sad. She'd gone her own way and followed her own path, not needing anyone, but was that any way to live your life? At least it wasn't complicated. She only had her work and herself to please.

It was past five, so she parked outside the building society. Sienna's shop was in darkness. If it had still been open, she'd have driven somewhere else. She didn't want her to know what she was doing until she had to confront her. The door was locked, and she knocked on the glass window. A woman around the same age as her opened it.

'Detective Brookes? I'm Emma.'

'Please, call me Morgan. Hi, Emma, thanks again for doing this.'

'It's no problem, please come through to the security office.' She bolted the door behind her, then Morgan followed her through three sets of doors to what must be the security office. It was cramped and full of TV monitors. There was a desk and an ancient chair that looked as if it had been here since the building was first constructed.

'Please take a seat.' Emma pointed to the dilapidated chair, and Morgan, not wanting to appear rude, sat, hoping it wasn't going to break.

'I went through it from when the shop shut at five yesterday until the woman who owns it appeared to open it the next morning.' She grabbed a notepad and looked at it. 'A man comes out at 1.03 and then I'm sure it's the owner around 1.16. She locks up and hurries off.'

Leaning forward, she pressed play on the paused monitor that captured the street and shops opposite. Morgan watched as a tall man wearing a suit came out of the shop. It was a very good quality recording, just in black and white. He had his head down, and he hurried off without glancing behind him.

'Stop, sorry can you rewind that again?'

She leaned in as close to the screen as she could get and watched once more as the guy walked out of the shop. She knew him, well she didn't know him, but she recognised him. She was pretty sure it was Lara's boyfriend, Greg. What the hell was he doing in Sienna's shop in the early hours of the morning?

'Should I fast forward to when she comes out?'

'Yes, please, that would be fab. Does it capture them going in?'

'No, it's weird. Just this. I double-checked, unless they went in the back way.'

Emma was right: at 1.16 out walked Sienna. She shut the door behind her, locking it and scurried off in the opposite direction to where Greg had gone.

Morgan leaned back. 'Wow, thank you so much. That is very interesting. Would I be able to record it on my phone, do you think?'

Emma shrugged. 'There's only me and you here and it's police business, so I don't see why not. If I play it from the beginning, I'll just nip to the loo and you can do what you want, then I'm not actually here whilst you do it, if that's okay?'

'Perfect.'

Emma rewound the disk and left Morgan to it. Morgan took out her phone and began recording. She would ask Emma to put the paperwork in to get an official copy of the footage but for now this would do just fine. Just what were those two doing together in that shop at that time in the morning? She had her suspicions but couldn't go around saying that they were having an affair behind Lara's back when she was only weeks away from her wedding. She'd come looking for answers and was now more confused than ever. A heavy, dull ache behind her eyes told her it was time to call it a day. She needed to take a break from it. Outside in her car she tried phoning Ben to tell him about the CCTV footage but it went to voicemail; leaving him a message explaining, she ended the call. Tomorrow she would pass on everything she had to Amy if Ben was still in a bad mood with her. Hopefully Wendy would have the results back from the smoothie mix as well.

But not until she'd met Lara and she'd told her everything that had happened that fateful night that had changed all of their lives.

CHAPTER FORTY-ONE

Lara was pacing up and down. Greg was late again. He had promised her he'd be home early. They had a meeting with the vicar at six for the final run through of the wedding, but all she wanted was to forget about the whole thing now. She hadn't stopped thinking about Jess. How could she have been speaking to her last night and then be told today that she was dead? It was awful and sad how a life could be taken away like that and, at first, she'd thought Morgan was wrong, or she was being a bitch, but she'd had that other detective with her. She couldn't lie about that, and then she'd got a phone call from Jess's mum, who had sobbed down the phone at her for twenty minutes without actually speaking. She felt like telling them all she was done; the wedding was off. How could she get married without a chief bridesmaid? It was never going to be the same without her best friend by her side. She'd argued with Greg last night. He'd stormed out of the house and hadn't come back until the early hours, and she had no idea where he'd been. She should have followed him to see, but she hadn't, and now she was told that Jess had died in the early hours of the morning. It was weird, too weird. Not that he had any reason to do anything to Jess. He liked her, probably liked her a lot more than he should, he flirted with her that much, but that was Greg. He thought he was God's gift to women and flirted with everyone. It was the way he was, or at least that was what she kept telling herself.

The door opened and he came in carrying the hugest bouquet of flowers she'd ever seen, all white: her favourites.

'I'm so sorry about Jess and having to dash off this morning and leave you. Am I forgiven?'

She took the flowers from him, nodding. She was wrung out, emotionally and physically, too tired for any more arguments and too upset to care about him.

'What's for tea?'

She looked up from the bunch of flowers into his eyes, searching for an ounce of genuine compassion and saw none. He flinched, then smiled.

'Sorry, that was insensitive of me. I wasn't thinking. It's been a busy day; I didn't get time to eat. I was being selfish.'

Her head moved up and down. She was lost for words.

'How about we order a takeaway and cuddle up on the sofa?'

'We have to be at the church in twenty minutes.'

'Bollocks, ring the vicar and cancel. We can go again.'

'No, Greg, we can't. It's eight weeks until the wedding. Tonight is the only time we can all get together for the rehearsal. As much as I want to lie on the sofa feeling sorry for myself, I can't. We can't let everyone down.'

He tutted. 'Suit yourself, Lara. I'd have thought you were too upset to be bothered about whether you're walking down the aisle the right way and where everyone is sitting. All this fuss, we could have buggered off to the registry office with a couple of witnesses and be done with it in less than an hour.'

He walked towards the stairs, shrugging his suit jacket off and hanging it on the balustrade at the bottom, and she stared after him. The urge to rip his bloody expensive jacket off and throw it on the floor was overwhelming. He was such an insensitive pig at times. The voice inside her head asked her for the hundredth time *why are you marrying him, Lara?* She couldn't answer it. Truthfully, there were lots of reasons why: because it was the right thing to do, because he'd asked her to, because her mum was more excited about seeing her daughter married in a big fancy wedding than she was, because he had plenty of money, because she liked the thought of having a rich, successful, handsome husband. All of these thoughts rushed through her head, but not one of them whispered *because you love him and can't live without him.* She took the flowers to the large Belfast sink in the kitchen and put them in water to soak. They smelled too sweet and overpowering. She stared out of the kitchen window, onto the formal garden that had been designed especially for them when they'd moved in, and felt the tears begin to roll down her cheeks. Her life was not turning out as she'd imagined, and Greg was definitely not the man of her dreams. She thought about Brad. Handsome, cute, funny Brad who had died in the cruellest of ways far too young. She'd never told anyone how much she'd really fancied him, because for a start he was way out of her league, and you didn't go after the boys Brittany and Sienna fancied. Then when he'd told her he had a thing for Morgan, she'd felt her heart almost break in two, but she'd much rather prefer he went out with Morgan than the other two. Life was so cruel it could almost be unbearable at times.

CHAPTER FORTY-TWO

2016

The moonlight illuminated the rocks enough that she could see Brad wasn't moving. His eyes were wide open, fixed. They looked as if they were staring directly at the full moon. His body was bent, his back arched across the sharp jutted rocks and boulders. Her hands shaking, Lara leaned closer and saw that the side of his head was completely crushed, and the pale grey rocks were stained with a river of his blood. Jess reached her. She grabbed her arm and asked, 'Is he okay?'

'No, does he look okay, Jess? He's fucking dead.'

Brittany let out a scream, so loud it pierced the night sky and some birds, which had been nesting in a nearby tree, took off into the air in a flurry of flapping wings and loud cries.

'Oh my God, what are we going to do? He can't be dead, he can't be. It's my birthday.'

Lara shook her head. She wasn't a doctor, she had never even done a first aid course, but she knew that his body wasn't supposed to be bent at that angle or that his head shouldn't be so crushed. She stepped forward to feel for a pulse, she knew that much, and pressed two fingers against the side of his neck, whilst holding her head near to his mouth to see if he was breathing. There was nothing, no movement in his chest or throat, and she wasn't sure what his pulse should be, but she couldn't feel anything.

'He's dead.'

Brittany was rocking backwards and forwards. 'Oh my God, oh my God, we are going to be in so much trouble. None of us were supposed to be here. We're going to go to prison.'

There was a loud noise from the bushes, and Sienna fell out of them onto her hands and knees groaning. 'I'm so ill. I've just puked my guts up.'

They turned around to face her, and she lay there groaning. 'What are you doing? Why are you screaming?'

All three of them were sobbing and crying. They turned back to Brad's body. Sienna called to them. 'What's wrong, why are you crying?' Forcing herself to her feet, she stumbled towards them as they parted from the group. They were huddled in so she could see him.

'Is he?' She didn't finish her sentence. 'Is he? Is he?'

Lara finished it for her. 'He's dead. Where were you? Did you not hear him fall?'

Sienna was shaking her head. 'No, no, no, he can't be. What happened?'

'He fell off the top of the cave.'

Brittany was making a high-pitched keening sound that sounded like some wild animal.

'We're going to prison for the rest of our lives.'

Sienna sank to her knees, clutching her stomach. 'No, we're not. I feel so ill, this isn't our fault. What was he doing up there?'

They all shrugged. 'He was laughing and joking about being the king of the world. What were you and him doing, Brittany, what took you so long?'

Sienna's voice was accusing, and Brittany sobbed. 'We were holding hands and then we started kissing and one thing led to the other, but we were only halfway up the side of the cave. I swear we didn't go to the top; I came back to see you, and he carried on climbing.'

'This is your fault, Brittany.'

Lara looked at Sienna. 'How is it her fault? She was down here when he fell. I'm sorry, but it was his own fault. We yelled at him to get down, and he slipped. It's an accident, an awful accident. We didn't do anything.'

'That's not what the police will say though, is it? And look at us, our parents will ground us for the rest of our lives. That's if we don't get thrown in prison first.'

'Then what do you think we should do, Sienna?'

Brittany cried. 'We need to get to a phone and ring for an ambulance. They might be able to help him.' She was still making that awful keening sound, and Sienna stood up and slapped her across the face.

'Stop it, he's dead. There's nothing an ambulance can do to help him. We need to think about ourselves now. I'm so sad to see him dead but it was his own fault. He's had too much to drink and had a terrible accident. That doesn't mean we should ruin the rest of our lives because of his drunken decision. I think we should grab our stuff and go home.'

'What, are you for real? You think we should leave him here all alone like this?'

'What else can we do, Lara? He's dead, there's nothing we can do now except get out of here and pretend it never happened; otherwise we are going to ruin all of our lives.'

Brittany was staring at Sienna. 'We can't, we just can't.'

'What else can we do? None of us were supposed to be here. My mum will kill me if the police don't get me first. We can't ruin our lives over this. I'm sorry, I liked Brad a lot, but this was his own stupid fault.'

Lara slapped Sienna's cheek so hard it left an imprint on it. 'You cow.'

Brittany was shaking her head. 'Stop it, you two, fighting isn't going to help. She's right; we can't admit that we were here, we'll ruin our whole lives.'

Jess stared at them. 'Selfish bitches, look at him.'

'Fine, you two stay here and call the police, but we're going home and if you grass and say we were here, I'll never forgive you both for ruining our lives.'

Lara looked at Jess. As much as she didn't agree with them it was true. They would end up arrested and locked up. They'd never be able to get over the stigma of it all and would always be known as the girls who killed Brad Murphy. She took hold of Jess's hand.

'They're right, I don't want to leave him here like this on his own, but he's gone. If we phone the police, our whole lives are ruined.'

'I'll do what you do, Lara.'

Lara turned away from Brad's broken body. 'We get our stuff, go home.'

Sienna added. 'And tell no one. This place is really busy in the daytime. He won't be here long before someone finds him. We tell our parents we felt ill so came home early, and don't speak to each other at all, no phone calls or text messages.' They were all huddled in a group. Sienna asked, 'Are we all agreed this is between us and we don't tell another soul as long as we live? I need to hear you say it, because I'm certainly not wasting my whole life on a tragic accident that wasn't my fault.'

They took hold of each other's hands and said in unison, 'Agreed.'

They set about gathering up their sleeping bags, and the three empty vodka bottles that were strewn on the grass. Making sure there was nothing left behind, Brittany and Sienna left first, both of them clutching each other's hands as they walked off.

Jess turned to Lara. 'Are we doing the right thing?'

She shook her head. 'No, we aren't, but she's right: there's nothing we can do for him now. I guess we should look after ourselves.'

They both turned back to stare at Brad one last time. Jess blew him a kiss and whispered, 'I'm so sorry, Brad, so sorry to leave you here on your own.'

And then they began the long walk back down the fell, and back to the safety of their homes. Lara's legs were trembling so much it was difficult to keep on walking; all she could do was take one step at a time and hope that she made it home without collapsing.

CHAPTER FORTY-THREE

Ben walked out of the station feeling as if he'd been there forever. He hadn't but it had been a long day and made even longer by the fact that he'd had to send Morgan off on her own, to keep her away from this investigation. He thought about calling to see how she was; maybe she would fancy a takeaway. She liked pizzas; he could eat a juicy meat feast pizza right now. So he got in his car and drove to her apartment. Her car wasn't there, and he felt a tightness in his stomach that he got whenever she wasn't where she was supposed to be. Not that she was supposed to be home: he had simply assumed she would be. He got out and rang her doorbell, anyway, just in case she was in and had left her car somewhere else. She had one of those fancy bells that she could answer and speak to you from anywhere. So, he leaned into the camera grinning like an idiot, waiting for her voice to filter out of the intercom, asking him what he wanted. She didn't answer. He pressed it again, still grinning at the camera, when the front door opened, and Emily, who was on her way out, screamed, 'Christ, you gave me a fright. What are you smiling at?'

He jumped up. 'You gave me a heart attack screaming like that, what's up?'

'Well with you lot, I scream a lot more than I used to. This was sold to me as a quiet, restful place to live. I've never seen so much drama since I used to watch *Casualty* on a Saturday night.'

He laughed. 'Sorry about that; although technically it's not my fault. You can blame your neighbour. Have you seen her this afternoon?'

Emily crossed her arms. 'No, I've not long got in from the college. Why don't you get her microchipped and then you could put a tracker in her, so you know where she is and who she's with?'

'Bit extreme. She's my colleague not my pet dog.'

She laughed. 'Sorry, that was mean. Do you want to come in for a coffee whilst you're waiting for Morgan to come back? I've phoned you a few times the last couple of days, but you haven't answered. I'm assuming you're very busy and not trying to ignore me.' She winked at him, and he felt bad because it was a combination of both of those things. He liked Emily, she was funny, kind and very attractive, but she was also very forward which he wasn't so keen on. Then again, he wasn't very forthcoming either, so if she was waiting for him to make the first moves, she'd be waiting forever.

'Coffee would be great, thanks.'

He followed her inside, ignoring the feeling of mild panic inside his chest, wondering what Morgan was up to and if she was okay, as he walked up the stairs past her front door. Emily's apartment was the complete opposite to Morgan's; it had a ginormous corner sofa that dominated the whole room, covered in more soft furnishings than the entire aisle at the B&M Bargains in Barrow that Morgan had dragged him to last time they were down there. Everything in here was painted pink, white and grey; it was very, what was the word Morgan had used? shabby something. Morgan's was almost empty compared to this, and she only had that oversized chair, no sofa and definitely no cushions. The most things Morgan had in hers were the books stuffed onto the bookcase.

'Tea, coffee, glass of wine maybe? Are you off duty?'

He looked at her. 'Oh, sorry. Yes, I am. I don't know. I should probably stick with coffee; it's been a long day.'

Emily had already unscrewed the cap on a bottle of red wine. 'Don't mind me, I'm having a glass after the day I've had. I'll stick the kettle on.' She turned away from him to fill up the pale pink kettle.

'Actually, I'll have a small glass of wine. It has been a bit rough.'

She smiled at him and took another glass out of the cupboard, pouring out a large glass and handing it to him. He didn't say anything. He could just have a few sips and leave it when Morgan arrived home.

'Sit down, Ben, you're making the place look untidy. Are you hungry? I was about to order pizza.'

At the mention of pizza, his stomach let out a loud groan and he nodded. 'I'm starving. I was just thinking about pizza. Let's go halves and order enough so Morgan can have some.'

'You're such a sweetheart, always thinking of her. It's so nice, but you know that she won't come up here and eat with us, don't you?'

'She might, you don't know that.'

'I do, she's not the mixing kind. Do you know how many times I've asked her up for coffee, a glass of wine, a takeaway? I ask her all the time, and she always replies, maybe next time. She's a bit of a loner, isn't she? Not that there's anything wrong with it, but you know I think she prefers her own company and her nose in a book. Not me, I'm the complete opposite. I hate being alone.'

She smiled at him, and he tried not to sound irritated with her when he replied.

'She's been through some tough times this last year. You need to cut her some slack, Emily. She's not weird or a loner.'

'Sorry, I didn't mean it like that. Of course she isn't, she's lovely, and yes she has had a rough time. It's just I'd be the complete opposite if I'd been through what she has. I'd never want to spend another night alone.'

She sat on the sofa next to him; a bit too close for his liking, but he smiled at her.

'We're all different, I suppose. It's a good thing really.'

She took a large sip of wine and nodded. 'Yeah, it is.'

She placed her hand on his thigh, and he almost spat the mouthful of wine he'd just swallowed all over her cream sofa and her white shirt that was unbuttoned a lot lower than when she'd answered the door. His eyes stared right at her cleavage, and he began to cough, looking away. She took his glass from him and, putting them both down, she leaned forward and began to rub his back.

'God, don't go choking on me. I don't want to have to explain that to your mates when they turn up.'

Her hands were kneading at his shoulders now, rubbing across them, and she was leaning dangerously close to him – he could smell her perfume – and there was no way he could avoid looking at her.

'I better go, Emily.'

She pulled herself even closer to him. 'Why? You know you want me as much as I want you. Let yourself go for a couple of hours. Enjoy being Ben the man and nothing else. Forget about your responsibilities and let me help you feel better.' She clambered onto his lap, and he groaned. He closed his eyes, knowing he should push her off and get out of here, but he didn't, and when her mouth closed in on his, he pulled her to him, crushing his lips against hers, pushing away everything except the burning desire inside of him.

CHAPTER FORTY-FOUR

It was dark when Morgan finally drove through the gates to her apartment. The car headlights illuminated Ben's car, and she shook her head. Surely, he wasn't sitting waiting for her. Getting out she grabbed her shopping from the boot and walked along the crunching gravel to knock on the driver's window. She realised the car was empty and wondered if he was waiting inside. Letting herself in, she'd expected to see him sitting on the large sweeping staircase, but the automatic lights flickered on as she pushed open the front door, and she realised with a sharp pain in her chest that he must be at Emily's. She glanced up the stairs then quickly looked away again. Letting herself into her flat, she locked the door behind her. She didn't want to see either of them; it was way too awkward.

She went into the open-plan kitchen and put her shopping away. Turning the oven on, she opened a pizza and slid it onto a pizza pan. Whilst she waited for it to cook, she checked her phone. It was dead. The doorbell hadn't alerted her that Ben had called because it must have died after she'd filmed the CCTV at the building society. No wonder: she'd spent most of the day answering calls. Plugging it into the charger, she left it alone; at least until she'd eaten. The thought of Ben getting it on with Emily right above her head was the biggest insult she could think of. Today at the station she had been sure he'd been about to kiss her. Well that just proved how crap her concept of the opposite sex was. She was doomed to a life of a spinster, on her own for all of eternity because she was too naïve and slow to know when a guy was flirting with her or not.

Fuming, she poured herself a large glass of wine and drank it before the timer had a chance to go off on the oven. She pulled out the pizza and sighed, telling herself it was okay, this was the life she needed. But her heart didn't quite agree with her, and there was a dull ache in it that she couldn't shift. The pizza was good, but it was too stodgy, and she found herself struggling to swallow it. Forcing herself to eat two slices, she covered the large plate with tinfoil and refilled her wine glass. Her bedroom was directly below Emily's. Christ what if she could hear them having sex? It would finish her off, and she'd never be able to look Ben in the eyes again. Instead of going in the bedroom, she showered, slipped on a pair of warm pyjamas and grabbed the book she was reading, *The Rules of Magic* by Alice Hoffman, off the top of the microwave where she'd left it. Losing herself in someone else's world seemed like a far better idea than having to deal with the shitshow that was fast becoming her life. She sipped her wine and found herself immersed in the streets of New York City with her two favourite characters, the aunts from her favourite movie *Practical Magic*. Despite the heaviness in her chest, her eyes began to close. Today had been so difficult and before she knew it, she was asleep, her book fluttering gently to the floor.

*

She woke up a couple of hours later, cold and with a stiff neck. Letting out a groan she stood up and stretched. She needed to get into her bed, and if she could hear those two still having sex, she'd put a pillow over her head. Grabbing her phone, she saw she had two notifications for missed calls at her doorbell and another three from Ben. She didn't ring him back; he'd made his bed, he could lie in it. He was forever complaining about how forward Emily was, yet there he was in her apartment yet again, doing God knows what. She peered out of her bedroom window down onto the drive and his car was still there. She checked the time on her phone: it was two a.m. At least she knew where she stood now. She could get all those stupid ideas about the two of them out of her head for good. From now on it was work and the pub quiz. She needed to get herself a life.

As she lay in bed, she wondered what Greg was doing with Sienna at that time in the morning. Had they had some kind of fight in the shop, was that why it had been trashed? Then had she tried to cover it up by pretending she'd been broken into? It was possible, but why would they be fighting at her shop? The obvious reason was they were having an affair. It seemed that everyone was having affairs except her. She turned over onto her stomach, pulled a pillow over her head and tried to breathe deeply to send herself back to sleep, praying she wouldn't hear any noise from above.

Her alarm went off, and Morgan was amazed that she'd drifted back to sleep. It was early: only six a.m. but her first thought was Sienna. She had to ask her, and she didn't particularly want to speak to her face to face, so she did the next best thing and phoned her, not expecting an answer, but a croaky voice answered.

'*Who is this and why are you phoning me so early?*'

'It's Morgan, I have to ask, are you having an affair with Lara's fiancé, Greg?'

She paused for a second, wondering if this was the right thing to do, but it was too late to stop now. She wasn't doing anything wrong. It was a simple question and if she couldn't answer it that was her fault, not Morgan's.

'*What?*'

'I said are you sleeping with Greg?'

'*I know what you said, I'm just trying to get my head around why you're even asking me that at this time in the morning.*'

'I'm asking you because it's pertinent to the investigation.'

'*What do you mean, am I having an affair with Greg? That is the most preposterous thing I've ever heard. Is that it, is that all you have?*'

Our friends are dying one by one like in some awful horror film and all you're concerned about is that? How is that relevant to anything?'

'It's relevant to the break-in you're reporting at your shop, or should I say allegedly reporting. I have the pair of you on CCTV leaving the shop in the early hours the day you said it had been broken into.'

'Are you calling me a liar?'

Morgan sighed. 'No, I'm just trying to figure out what is going on and all I keep coming across is more secrets and lies. None of it makes any sense. I have to go. Why don't you have a think about that question and when you're ready to speak the truth ring me back. I'm going out walking.'

'What? You're just hanging up on me, leaving me wondering what the hell you're insinuating whilst you go out for a jolly old walk.'

'It's work, not a jolly, and I'm going back to the caves where this whole mess began.'

She put the phone down determined not to get into a full-blown argument with her main unofficial suspect for the murders. She had a voicemail and listened to it; the officer she'd sent to speak to Sienna had been unsuccessful and would try to follow up again later.

When she looked out of her window, Ben's car was gone, and she wondered what time he'd snuck off. She could check the doorbell app on her phone, but she didn't want to know. It was clearly his business and none of hers, besides she had to meet Lara at seven thirty, so she should stop wasting time and get ready. Should she ask Lara about her smarmy boyfriend's activities with Sienna? She couldn't imagine she would be pleased to find out they were caught on camera. Dressed in her best active wear and a big thick jumper, because it was bloody freezing on Loughrigg Fell this early in the morning, she put her trainers on. The last time going up and down it in her Docs had almost killed her feet off. She would play it by ear, see how open Lara was before she dropped that bombshell on her about Greg.

She drove to the car park and waited for Lara to join her.

CHAPTER FORTY-FIVE

Sienna was furious with that little bitch Morgan; they had been nice to her at school and look at how she was repaying them. It was unbelievable. She was sitting at the breakfast bar, drumming her long perfectly manicured acrylic nails on the granite surface. She hadn't spoken to Greg since the other night: that had been a hell of an argument. He thought he could phone her whenever he wanted a quick shag, then leave her hanging for days afterwards. She closed her eyes. The anger had radiated from him in waves. When she'd asked him to decide what he wanted, to marry Lara or be with her, he'd laughed at her so hard. And what had he called her? 'A stupid little whore who was so desperate for attention she'd sleep with her mother's boyfriend if she had to.'

She'd been raging, fully red-mist raging, at his condescending attitude and had slapped his face so hard it left an imprint. Her fingers had been numb and had tingled for ages. Greg obviously wasn't used to being spoken to that way, but he had not slapped her back; no, he'd pulled his fist back and punched her in the side of the head, where her hair would cover the bruise, the sneaky little bastard. She'd lost it then and had begun picking up jars of tea and throwing them at his head, followed by the books off the bookcase. He called her a lunatic and scurried out of the shop, leaving her crying tears of rage with a pounding headache and ruined stock that she couldn't afford to replace. She had decided to break the kitchen window, then she could put in an insurance claim. She had texted him to tell him she was calling the cops on him; she wasn't, but he didn't have to know that. He could sit and stew, worrying about them coming to his house to arrest him in front of his fiancée for assaulting her, the creep. Why she had let him seduce her in the first place was beyond her; he wasn't even good in bed. Actually, she'd done it because he was marrying Lara and she'd been jealous. The first few times it had been okay, exciting. And the thrill of being the one having an affair under miss goody two shoes' nose had been just too much of a perfect opportunity to resist. Now though, things were out of hand, and she didn't know how to put a stop to it all. And why was Morgan going back up to the caves? Something was going on; she had to try and find out what before she ended up in a really sticky situation that she couldn't get out of.

She didn't want to, but she had to try and smooth things over with Greg. He could make her life awkward. Sucking in her breath she wrote out a quick message.

I'm sorry, I miss you please forgive me.

Almost instantly it was read.

You're forgiven, come to my house now for a kiss and make-up fuck you'll never forget.

Don't be daft, where's Lara? You come here.

She's gone out on some hike. She'll be gone a couple of hours and I haven't screwed you in our bed yet. It's still warm.

Sienna suddenly found it hard to breathe. Her lungs felt as if they were constricting, and she couldn't gulp in enough air. Where the hell was Lara going on a hike to? Morgan was going up to the caves: what if Lara was going there too? What were they going to talk about? She didn't answer Greg. Instead, she rushed to get ready to go up to the caves. She was going to have to take the route from behind the caves, so they didn't see her. Panic was settling inside of her along with an impending sense of doom. She had to get there before them. Or at least be there hiding somewhere, so that if they arrived together she could hear what they were talking about. Paranoia was setting in big time. She wasn't going to prison; she'd never survive inside a women's prison.

CHAPTER FORTY-SIX

Ben had showered. There were a myriad of emotions running through him. He sat down at his kitchen table and realised that he didn't have a clue how he felt. Last night had been amazing; Emily wasn't shy, and it had been such a long time that he'd been unable to say no to her. When he'd woken up in her bed though, the feeling of euphoria had quickly turned to remorse. He'd left without waking her, writing her a note and leaving it on her bedside table. He liked her, he definitely liked the sex, yet he felt as if he'd cheated on Cindy and let Morgan down. She was bound to have noticed his car there when she got home. It was pretty hard to miss and then she had that stupid bloody doorbell that recorded everything, so it probably had him grinning at her then disappearing with Emily, only to reappear hours later, after sleeping with her neighbour. He buried his head in his hands. Why was this so bloody complicated? Now he was not only a crap husband, but a crap boss and even worse friend. How many times had he stressed to Morgan that he was her friend, only to do this to her because he was too afraid to admit how he really felt about her.

He slammed his fists down on the table so hard the coffee mug that had been perched dangerously close to the edge vibrated off and smashed all over the floor. He didn't even care; it could stay there. He checked his phone to see if Morgan had called or messaged him: not one, not even a text. He didn't blame her. What was she going to say to him, 'come down and see me when you've finished screwing around with my neighbour'?

His phone beeped, and he saw Morgan's name. A rush of relief ran through him; she wasn't mad. He opened the message and read.

Morning, I might be late in. I'm meeting Lara and we're going for a walk up to Rydal Caves. I need to clear my head, and I think she might know something about the night Brad died. Hopefully she'll tell me, and it might have some relevance to what's happening now.

He let out a groan, *what the hell, Morgan, you're not supposed to be anywhere near this investigation.* He didn't know what to say. She was an adult and if she wanted to go for a walk with her friend who was he to stop her? But, and there was always a but when anything involved her, what was to stop either of them being followed by whoever was killing their friends? He phoned Amy, who answered sounding rougher than he did.

'*What?*'

'Morning to you too. I need you to come with me.'

'*Where?*'

'Rydal Caves.'

'*Sod off, are you having a laugh? It's not even seven. I'm not due in work till eight.*'

'It's an order.'

'*Well now you're really taking the piss, boss.*'

'I'll pick you up in ten minutes.'

She let out a loud groan that sounded very much like a muffled, 'go screw yourself'.

He had no idea if he was doing the right thing, but it was better than nothing. He'd rather she went mad with him for acting like an overprotective friend, instead of the pair of them getting into any difficulty. He couldn't afford to take that risk under any circumstances.

*

Fifteen minutes later he was waiting outside Amy's address. He couldn't beep his horn, it was far too early, but if she didn't get a move on, he would. He saw the curtains open, and Amy press her face against the window, holding two fingers up. He was assuming she was telling him two minutes, but it looked as if she was giving him the Vs and, knowing Amy, she probably was. He had sent Morgan a text asking if she thought this was a good idea, she hadn't answered him. He hadn't wanted to get into an argument with her as well; it was far too early. Amy finally came out of the house carrying a mug and eating a slice of toast. She got in the car.

'Don't speak to me, it's too early.'

He smiled, turning his face away so she couldn't see.

'Yeah, honestly you're not welcome. I never get why you don't ring Des whenever Morgan is out on the loose and, by the way, you need to get her under a bit better control. You complain about me being wild, but she's another level.'

'I thought you weren't speaking?'

'Sod off, I'm not.'

He began to drive in the direction of White Moss car park.

'I don't ask Des because I like getting abuse from you and—'

'And he's a fanny. He'd probably have to do his yoga workout and eat a tofu-laden goats milk quiche before he could even think about leaving for work.'

Ben laughed so loud it made her jump, sloshing coffee everywhere. She glowered at him.

'You might be my boss, but you're an arsehole.'

'I'm not disagreeing with you.'

They drove the rest of the way in silence. He let Amy finish her toast, and he even drove a little slower, so she didn't spill her coffee again. It wasn't as if Morgan was doing anything dangerous. She was going for a walk with a friend. He was just going to be around and in the area, should she need a hand.

CHAPTER FORTY-SEVEN

Morgan was already out of her car and ready to go. The sky was full of thick grey clouds, and she hoped the rain would hold off until they at least got back down onto the path to the car park. She hated wet soggy feet and was regretting her choice of footwear. Trainers were great for walking and jogging, but the minute it rained the water soaked through. A car pulled into the car park, and Lara got out of the brand-new white BMW and waved at her. Morgan waved back, feeling a little envious of Lara's choice of footwear; she was wearing a pair of sturdy walking boots and a very nice pink Berghaus waterproof jacket. Morgan had her best Primark special on and she felt a little self-conscious; it must be nice having a rich fiancé. Then she stopped herself. She knew very little about Lara. She might be the wealthy one: it was so presumptuous of her to assume she let Greg pay for everything.

Lara walked towards her smiling.

'Well, if this doesn't blow the cobwebs off I don't know what will.'

Morgan looked at her. There were dark circles under her eyes, and she looked as if she'd been awake all night crying. The skin around her eyes was red and puffy.

'I think you're right. It's a bit cooler than I imagined.'

'You'll be fine once we start walking up that hill. It's a bit tougher now we're not kids. Have you been up here lately?'

She nodded. 'Yes, I did the path a couple of times the other day when Sienna was found up here.'

Lara looked at her. 'How is she now?'

'I think she's okay. Not having a very good week by the look of it.'

'Why?'

Morgan didn't know if she should be discussing this with Lara, but they were all friends and she had asked for a press release to go in the local paper about the break-in, appealing for witnesses, so she wasn't technically telling her anything that wasn't in the public domain.

'Her shop got broken into a couple of nights ago and trashed.'

Lara turned to look at Morgan. 'Did it now, wow that's very convenient.'

'What do you mean?'

'Nothing, I'm being a bitch that's all. I shouldn't be so awful. I try not to, but she just irritates me so much. Do you ever have that sense when you don't really like someone and then just seeing them makes you want to punch them in the face?' She laughed. 'No, you probably don't, do you? Coppers won't be like that.'

Morgan smiled at her because she often felt like punching people in the face, but she wasn't going to admit that to Lara in case she repeated it.

'I'm a human being, I have feelings.'

'What's that supposed to mean?'

'I might work for the police, Lara, but it doesn't mean I don't want to smack a few people.'

Lara laughed. 'That's more like it. I was worried the feisty little Goth had completely disappeared into her shell.'

Morgan glanced at her, trying not to let her see how hurtful that last comment was. They began the ascent up the long, stony path to reach the caves, both of them a little out of breath. It was Lara who broke the silence.

'Do you ever think about Brad?'

'When it first happened, he was all I could think about. I'm ashamed to say that until Brittany died I hadn't really thought about him much at all. I'd kind of pushed him to the back of my mind. When he died though, I didn't think I'd ever be able to get over it.'

'I know what you mean, it was so awful, and he was just the nicest guy ever. I think we all fancied him, and I think we were all hoping that one of us would get off with him that night. Were you mad that your dad wouldn't let you out that night?'

'Mad, I was fuming, and when Brad called for me, I very nearly climbed out of the window to go with him.'

'He was in your bedroom?'

She laughed. 'No, on the flat roof directly below it for around five minutes. He climbed up the drainpipe to try and talk me into going.'

'Why didn't you? How come you did as you were told that night? You normally didn't.'

She shrugged. 'I don't know. I've asked myself that question hundreds of times. I wonder if I knew deep down that something bad was going to happen.'

'What like a sixth sense kind of thing, are you psychic?'

Morgan laughed. 'Definitely not. So, what did happen, Lara? The truth, because I can't quite believe that you all walked off and left him there on his own when he was drunk too.'

Lara's eyes filled with tears, and she carried on walking. They were almost at the very top where the path went down, and the cave that had been hidden until this point was suddenly visible.

'It's such a beautiful place, isn't it? So peaceful, especially when there's no one else around. I come up here now and again and bring some flowers for Brad, leaving them on the rock they found his body.'

'How do you know which rock they found his body on, Lara, if you weren't here when it happened?'

Lara looked at her, misery etched across her face.

'I'll tell you what happened. Will we get in trouble?'

She shrugged. 'I don't know, it depends how serious it is.'

Lara shrugged. She carried on walking towards the rocky outcrop of huge boulders to the right of the entrance to the cave. She stopped at one which was bigger than the others and jutted out at a sharp angle. Reaching forward she placed her hands on the large piece of slate and closed her eyes.

CHAPTER FORTY-EIGHT

Sienna was clambering up the side of the fell in a blind panic. She was terrified of what Lara was going to tell Morgan. This was one big mess and she wished she'd never got caught up in any of it. It had all started the night of Brittany's birthday, and it was still going on five years later. How many regrets did she have now? There were too many to count. They should never have left Brad there the way they did. It had been wrong, she knew that at the time, but had been too scared to do the right thing. She also wished that she'd never set eyes on Greg. She hadn't known he was Lara's fiancé until she'd spotted them out together in a restaurant, where they had been drinking champagne, and Lara had sat staring at the huge diamond solitaire on her engagement finger. Sienna'd left before they even saw her, and the next time he came around like a dog on heat she'd told him to get out of her life. He turned up with a huge bunch of flowers, bottle of champagne and the most grovelling apology she'd ever heard from a man. He'd told her it wasn't working with Lara, but he was too scared to hurt her by breaking it off. All complete bullshit, of course. The man was a sleazeball and she realised that now. How many women was he sleeping with at the same time? And now she was positive that Lara knew about them; she had seen her loitering around outside the shop a couple of times, as if she'd been plucking up the courage to come in and confront her, but then she'd walk away, leaving Sienna's heart racing and feeling even worse than she already did.

Sienna knew she was a cow, that she'd been awful to almost everyone all of her life, but if she could stop this from happening, she might be able to make up for some of her past behaviour. The grass was damp, and the sky was getting darker by the minute. It should be getting lighter, but the huge, ominous dark rain clouds were waiting for the right time to drench her. It didn't matter; she knew she had to keep going and she continued slip, sliding, breathing hard until she reached the caves. She was almost there; her foot went from under her, and she fell forwards, wrenching her ankle so hard she couldn't keep in the scream despite trying her best not to. It filled the air, echoing around the hills, and she fell heavily to the floor, clutching her throbbing ankle.

*

Morgan looked around at the faint scream she'd heard in the distance. Lara turned too. 'What was that?'

Lara laughed. 'Probably a bird or a sheep. They make the weirdest noises. Have you ever walked through a field of sheep in the dark? They actually cough, and it sounds like you're surrounded by lots of people. The first time it happened to me, I almost had a heart attack. I thought I was going to be killed by some group of weirdos in the dark.'

'Yeah, they do sound weird, don't they? Probably right.'

Lara still had her hands on the rock. 'He landed on this one. I've never heard a more sickening noise in my life than that loud thud when his body smacked onto it.'

'Did he die instantly?' Morgan had to know; if he'd still been alive and they'd left him there dying, she didn't know if she would be able to keep herself from attacking Lara. Was this the reason someone was killing them, because they left him here to die when they should have got help?

'I'll show you exactly what happened.' She began to clamber up the side of the fell that led to the roof of the cave, and Morgan followed her. She had to know what had happened and how it happened so she could figure out what to do about the situation now. After several minutes of scrambling through the bushes and steep ledges, the first drops of rain began to fall. Big, round splotches hit Morgan's face and the rocks around her. Pretty soon they would turn into a downpour, but they were so near, and she had waited all these years to know the truth, she wasn't going to let a bit of rain stop her from finding out. Lara was at the top, waiting for her, and she pushed herself on as the raindrops began to pelt them both. Lara held out her hand to pull her the last few feet, and she took it. Then they were both standing on the grassy bank which led down to the roof of the cave. Lara walked towards the edge, and Morgan felt her knees wobble a little. She didn't particularly like heights.

'Don't go any further, it's dangerous.'

'I just want to see how it looked to Brad; I've wanted to do this for a long time, but never been brave enough.'

Despite her fear, Morgan edged a little closer too.

Lara turned to her. 'It was so awful, Morgan. One moment we were all huddled together swigging neat vodka and laughing, the next Brittany decided that she needed to pee. Brad being the gentleman he was offered to escort her to a safe place. Here's the thing though, they were gone for ages. Much longer than it takes to pee. I think they were having sex. Well actually I know they were.'

Morgan was stunned by this revelation. 'Oh.'

'Sorry, I know you fancied him, and you know that he really, really fancied you because he told me and Jess on the way to the caves. I honestly think if you'd have been here that none of this would have happened, and he'd have been having sex with you in the bushes.'

'He would not have. Yes, I really liked him, but there is no way I would have lost my virginity in a bush on the side of Loughrigg Fell.'

'Well either way, he wouldn't have ended up shagging Brittany and then, because he was on some drunken, sexual high, he wouldn't have thought it was a great idea to stand at the edge of these bloody caves. All our lives could have been a lot different if you'd come that night. Damn you, Morgan.'

'What, what do you mean? How dare you put it on me. None of this was my fault.'

'No, you said yourself he'd been below your bedroom window. He was probably as horny as hell after looking and had to settle for a quick shag with Brittany.'

Morgan stepped closer to Lara; she was fuming at the mean accusations she'd just tossed her way, as if all of this was her fault.

'She got pregnant, you know.'

'What? No, I didn't.'

Lara was smiling at her. 'You didn't know an awful lot, did you? Yes, she was pregnant with Brad's baby after their brief encounter.'

'Did she keep the baby?'

Lara shook her head. 'How could she? Her parents would have had a fit and demanded to know who the father was. If she told them who the father was, they would have known that we were there the night Brad died, and we couldn't risk them finding out.'

'What did she do?'

'Well, she couldn't tell Sienna because she'd have been raging with her. Sienna has a lot to answer for. She came to me instead. She said she didn't trust Sienna because she was acting all weird. Which she was by the way. When they were missing, Sienna got up and said she needed to pee and stumbled off in the direction they went in. She was nowhere to be seen when Brittany returned; she was missing for quite some time in fact.'

'Was she with Brad?'

'I think Sienna saw Brad and Brittany together and was furious with them. She fancied him as much as the rest of us. When Brad was standing on the edge of the cave shouting he was the king of the world, there was still no sign of Sienna.'

'Do you think she followed him up here?'

'Yes, I do. I also happen to think she pushed him off. She turned up a few minutes later out of breath and saying she was really ill. And I also think she's the one who poisoned Brittany and Jess. Then she must have given herself enough of a dose to make herself seem innocent.'

Morgan was shocked. She was having a hard time processing what she was hearing, though it was all confirming what she'd been thinking about.

A voice shouted up to them from down below. 'Don't listen to her, she's lying.'

Both of them looked down to see Sienna hobbling towards the entrance of the cave. Lara's face changed into a mask of anger.

Sienna shouted, 'Morgan, I don't know what she's told you, but I haven't done anything wrong.'

Lara put her hands on her hips. 'Really, Sienna? You mean you haven't been sleeping with Greg then? Because I know you have. You're nothing but a jealous slut, Sienna, always mad because you get second best and are never good enough for first prize. How does it feel to be such a loser? Brad slept with your best friend, and you pushed him off the cliff because of it. What were you planning to do to me so that you could have Greg to yourself?'

Sienna shook her head; the rain was lashing down now, and her hair was soaked, sticking to her face. She pushed it back.

'I'm sorry about Greg. He's a dick, Lara.' The wind took her voice away and all they heard was, 'Sorry, dick.'

Morgan glanced at Lara, who was now staring at Morgan. Their eyes locked, and she realised that there was nothing there. Any shred of rational thought had gone. They were wide, dark and staring straight through her; there was no emotion in them. As she thought through all she had learned over the last few days, it struck her that Sienna wasn't the killer: Lara was.

Lara shouted, 'She's the killer, Morgan, you need to arrest her. She pushed Brad off here, then she found out about Brittany being pregnant to him, then aborting his baby. She's twisted. She didn't like that Brittany told me everything and her nothing, and she decided to kill her and Jess all to get at me, so she could have Greg all for herself. She'd have killed me next or tried to frame me for everything.'

Sienna was hobbling closer; she cupped her hands to her mouth.

'Lara, you're a hateful, spiteful, bitter woman. You never got over Brittany being pregnant by Brad. You've been jealous of us all since school. I had no idea Greg was your fiancé when we got together. When I found out, I broke it off with him and he hit me, Lara. Does he hit you too? Morgan, Lara bought bags of frozen smoothie mix from my shop, and I know that both Jess and Brittany used them, because they came back to buy more. She must have slipped the poison in, resealed them and then given it to them.'

Morgan felt an ice-cold chill race down her spine. No one knew about the smoothie angle she'd been investigating, and the officer hadn't got hold of Sienna to warn her. It was only her and Wendy; she hadn't even had the time to mention it to Ben yet. Sienna had just given her the final piece of evidence. Morgan could hear Sienna screaming from below, but had no idea what she was saying, because the rain was lashing so hard now it was difficult to hear anything but the pounding of the blood as it rushed through her brain. The realisation that she was standing on a cave edge with a stone-cold killer wasn't lost on her, and she took a step away from Lara. She was far too near to her. Lara was watching her every move with a small smirk on her face.

'Well, this is a bit of a conundrum for you, isn't it, Morgan? Who do you believe? Crazy, bitter whore Sienna or me, poor Lara, whose fiancé has been sleeping with the slut of the century behind my back.'

The rain was making it hard to see properly. She was squinting her eyes against it, but there was no mistaking the look in Lara's eyes: they were wild and darting all over. Every nerve ending in

Morgan's body was screaming at her to run away from her as fast as she could because the woman was edging on the brink of insanity.

'I think we should go down and talk it out, get out of this rain and discuss it somewhere warm, dry and safe.'

Lara took a step towards her. 'I agree, it's far too wet and slippery up here. Either of us could fall right off the edge, and we know how that ended for Brad.'

Morgan's heart was racing. There was no mistaking the threat in her voice, and she wished she was back at home, tucked up in bed, ready to start the day all over again, but she wasn't. She was here, facing a killer in the most dangerous of places she could ever wish to be.

CHAPTER FORTY-NINE

Ben and Amy reached the top of the stony path and both of them said 'Shit' at the same time.

'What the hell is she doing up there?' Amy screamed at Ben, who felt as if his whole world was about to collapse. He began running towards the woman standing below them screaming Morgan's name. As he got closer, he recognised Sienna.

'What's going on?'

'That crazy bitch is the killer.' She was pointing her finger at the two women and, for a fleeting second, he thought she was pointing at Morgan.

'You have to get up there. Lara won't let Morgan leave. She's in danger.'

Amy was already scrambling up the side of the fell. Ben followed her.

*

Lara glanced down and saw the two people with Sienna. Morgan saw them out of the corner of her eye, but she didn't dare take her eyes away from Lara. She saw that she was distracted and made a run for it, but the wet grass was like ice and the trainers she was wearing gave no traction whatsoever. Instead of making a quick getaway, she slipped to her knees, ending up falling towards the edge of the cave. Reaching out she tried to grab hold of a rock, anything to hold on to, but she kept on slipping and, as she reached the edge, all she could hear was screaming from every direction.

She had never in all her life imagined she would die like this. Her fingers tried to grip anything to anchor her, but they just left trails in the mud. She had gathered up speed and was unable to stop herself. In a last-minute attempt she found a small rock, jutting out, and reached out for it with both hands as her legs went over the edge feet first. Fear unlike anything she'd ever felt as she clung on to that small rock coursed through her veins. She could feel her legs kicking thin air. There was nothing below her; she was going to die just like Brad, smashed to bits on the rocks. And then suddenly Ben's face was in front of hers.

'Look at me, Morgan. I'm going to take hold of your arms. It's okay; you're safe. I won't let go.'

She looked in Ben's terrified eyes. He was staring at her, smiling.

'I promise. I won't let go.'

She felt his strong arms clasp around her wrists. He tried to pull, but her jacket was soaked through, the material too slippery for him to grasp properly, and she slid even further down. A scream ripped through the air from below, and then Amy was there, lying on the grass next to Ben.

'I'm going to push your sleeves up, Morgan, so we can grip your wrists. Hang on.'

Morgan's arms and wrists were burning, in pain. She didn't know how much longer she could keep hold of the rock; her fingertips were going numb. She felt her jacket sleeves pushed back and then both Amy and Ben were gripping her wrists. They began to tug her towards them, and she thought they were going to rip the skin straight from her wrists they were gripping her so tight, but then her knees were touching the edge of the cave. Another giant heave and they dragged her back onto solid ground. She lay there panting, tears rolling down her cheeks as Amy and Ben got onto all fours, breathless.

'Christ, Morgan, what did you eat for breakfast, lead weights?' Amy asked her, and despite the harrowing situation she began to laugh. Glad that she was still alive and able to laugh at it all. A few seconds longer and it could have been a very different matter.

Ben stood up. He was smeared in grass and mud. 'Where did she go?'

'She's the killer, Ben, we need to find her.'

Morgan, who looked as if she'd just finished a Tough Mudder assault course, scrambled to her knees. Despite the pain in her wrists, she saw Lara making her way down the side of the fell.

'Christ she's going to go for Sienna. We need to stop her.'

'How do you know it was her?'

'Long story, but I'll fill you in as soon as she's cuffed. Have you got cuffs?'

When Ben shook his head, Amy rolled her eyes at the pair of them, pulling a set from her jacket pocket.

'Call yourselves coppers? You're a disgrace.' And then she took off, scrambling down the side of the fell towards Lara.

Ben reached out a hand to pull Morgan to her feet. Reaching out, he touched the side of her cheek. 'That was too close, Morgan, you could have died.'

She clasped her hand on his briefly, savouring the warmth.

'But I didn't, thanks to you two.'

Then they took off, following Amy, who was almost at the bottom. Sienna was standing helplessly watching as Lara barrelled towards her, screaming. Lara had almost made it to her when she was taken down by a perfect rugby tackle from Amy, who was then on top of her, cuffing her hands behind her back. Morgan hobbled towards them clapping.

'Impressive, Amy.'

'Yeah, I always was good at rugby. The lads wouldn't play with me, said I was too rough.'

Morgan laughed out loud. Ben reached them and nodded.

'I have no idea what's going on, what's her full name?' he whispered in her ear.

'Lara Geldard.'

He addressed Lara. 'Lara Geldard, you do not have to say anything. But it may harm your defence if you do not mention when questioned something which you later rely on in court. Anything you do say may be given in evidence. Do you understand?'

Lara let out a scream so loud Amy jumped and almost let go of her arms. The rain had begun to ease off and the five of them looked a sodden, sorry sight.

Sienna grabbed Morgan's arm. 'I'm sorry, Morgan, this is all my fault.'

Morgan lifted her finger to her lips. 'Enough of the blaming ourselves. We need to find out what exactly has happened and why so many people have died in the process.'

Ben and Amy walked either side of Lara. He turned to Morgan.

'Can you call for a van to meet us in the car park to take Lara back and, as much as I love you, Morgan, you are not sitting in my car in that state.'

She grinned at him, took out her phone and rang the control room to request a van to back them up. Her wrists were still on fire, but it was a small price to pay. Sienna was struggling to walk on her swollen ankle, so she hooked her arm through hers to help support her. Sienna smiled at her and whispered, 'Thank you.'

It took them forever to get back down to the car park. When they finally reached it, Cain and his student were leaning against the side of the police van. He eyed them up and opened his mouth.

Ben shook his head. 'Don't even ask, I have no words.'

Cain shrugged, beckoning his student closer. They both took hold of Lara, who had given up trying to fight and was now silent. They opened the cage doors, searched her pockets then helped her inside, slamming the heavy metal doors shut, the sound so loud it echoed around the valley.

'Now what?' asked Cain.

Ben pointed to Morgan. 'Can you give her a lift as well? We'll get the other cars picked up later.' Morgan smiled at Cain who grinned back. 'What have you been doing, Morgan, mud wrestling? You could have invited me; I'd have paid to watch that.'

Ben shook his head and got in his car. Amy pointed to the back door for Sienna to get in, then she got in, leaving Morgan and Cain standing watching them. He whispered in her ear, 'Do you need a hug?'

And she laughed, nodding. Yes, she did, a bloody big one, and Cain obliged. Stepping forward, he scooped her up into his arms, lifting her off her feet and rocked her from side to side. Ben looked away, but Amy opened the window and whooped then shouted, 'Put her down, boy, you don't know where she's been.'

Cain gave her the finger, then gently put Morgan back on her feet. His student was watching the whole thing open-mouthed. Morgan smiled at him. 'Welcome to Rydal Falls and Cumbria Constabulary. You're in for a fun ride. If you thought you'd fallen lucky and this was some sleepy Lakeland village, I'm afraid you'll be sadly disappointed.'

'Jesus, Morgan, don't scare the kid. It's only his second week out with me.'

She got into the back of the van and sat down on the seat. Laying her head back, she closed her eyes, ignoring the earthy coppery smell emanating from her clothes. It didn't seem that long ago since her first day out on independent patrol. So much had happened since then. Thanks to Lara, she had a lot of bridges to rebuild with Ettie and Sienna. As soon as this was over, she needed to go and make sure Ettie was okay. It was obvious that Lara had tried to frame Sienna by using Ettie's tea, to make them think it was how the poison had been given. So many deaths just because Lara had found out Greg was cheating on her with Sienna. So she'd taken that night they'd all sworn each other to silence and used it against

Helen Phifer

them. They would never know who sent the letter to Brittany, but Sienna would be interviewed about her involvement, but Morgan had seen first-hand how easy it was to slip and fall off the top of the cave. She was confident that poor Brad had done just that; too much alcohol and a long drop off a steep, slippery edge were not a good match for anyone. Declan had found no evidence of foul play and neither had Tom. Lara had spent so many years convincing herself that Sienna had something to do with him falling that when she'd found out about her affair with Greg, it had pushed her over the edge. She wasn't sure why she killed her best friend, though, and wondered if Greg had got a little over friendly with Jess as well. Brittany had been the perfect girl to die first because of her connection with Sienna and Ettie. Lara had tried her best to not only ruin Sienna's life but Ettie's as well. It was so sad.

CHAPTER FIFTY

Forty-Eight Hours Later

Lara had been interviewed and then remanded in custody until the court hearing. She had admitted everything, against her solicitor's advice, telling them how she found out that Jess had slept with Greg a couple of times after a few too many glasses of wine, and that Greg had then moved on to Sienna. She had taken Sienna's T-shirt that she'd found on the floor of his car. She knew it was Sienna's because it was too small for her, and she had seen Sienna in the same white T-shirts in the shop. When she'd asked her, Sienna had told her she had several she used as a kind of uniform. She had kept hold of it to plant in the woods near to Ettie's cottage, to try and use her as a decoy to keep them from looking too closely at Lara. Greg had turned up demanding to represent Lara, and she'd told Amy to tell him to go screw himself. A part of Morgan wondered if she had admitted her guilt as a final fuck you to her cheating boyfriend. It wasn't going to do his career much good having a killer fiancée. Sienna had sworn she had nothing to do with Brad falling. She had been sick in the bushes, and she had heard him and Brittany having sex and been so upset that she'd gone off on her own to have a cry about it.

Morgan had spoken with Tom about the investigation, and he'd even pulled up the original file and shown her the crime scene photos. There was a single set of footprints in the damp grass, then a longer one where it looked as if Brad had lost his footing and slipped to his death, confirming what she'd concluded herself on the way back to the station.

Morgan had excused herself and taken the afternoon off work. She walked along the high street to the little florists on the corner called Posh Flowers, where she had gone in and asked Alyson, who owned it, for a bunch of white roses. Alyson deftly made her up a beautiful bunch, and she left the shop smelling them with a smile on her face. The sun was shining, and it was a beautiful spring day. She carried on walking until she reached the small church where she'd spent many an hour as a kid wandering among the graves. She walked past Stan's and Sylvia's graves. Taking out a single white rose for each of her adoptive parents, she kissed each flower and lay it on the ground in front of their headstones. Then she carried on until she found Brad's rugby ball shaped headstone. His handsome smiling face stared back at her from the porcelain plate, and she felt the tears she'd been holding in all these years finally begin to fall.

Kissing her fingertips, she leaned forward and placed them on his picture, then she lay the rest of the roses on his grave and sat down on the grass next to him.

'I hope you're at peace. I miss you so much and I'm sorry I didn't go with you that night. I loved you a lot you know, I just never would have said it out loud or told you because…' She gulped. 'Because I was stupid. And I'll always regret that.' A cool breeze blew across the left side of her head, gently moving her hair, and it felt as if she'd been touched with the softest of fingers. She didn't flinch or turn around. Instead, she closed her eyes, hoping that it had been Brad saying goodbye to her one last time, and she felt as if she'd just had a hug from heaven. As she sat there, she promised him that she would start to live her life a little more, for the both of them, and she felt as if the heaviness she'd been carrying around with her since that night had finally lifted.

Life was far too precious to waste, and she knew that better than anyone.

A LETTER FROM HELEN

Dear reader,

I want to say a huge thank you for choosing to read *First Girl to Die*. If you did enjoy it, and want to keep up-to-date with all my latest releases, just sign up at the following link. Your email address will never be shared and you can unsubscribe at any time.

www.bookouture.com/helen-phifer

I hope you loved *First Girl to Die* and if you did I would be very grateful if you could write a review. I'd love to hear what you think, and it makes such a difference helping new readers to discover one of my books for the first time. I hope you enjoyed visiting Rydal Caves with me, if you ever get the chance to go, they are certainly worth a visit. It's a lovely, slightly hilly walk up to them and the views are outstanding. I wrote in the story that Morgan and Ben carried Sienna's unconscious body down from the caves to White Moss car park; it looked totally doable on Google Maps. Then for some reason I decided to drag Steve up there just to check if it was. I had this niggling feeling and I was also very fed up with being locked down and it was just as the restrictions lifted allowing travel for exercise. Boy was I in for a shock. By the time we'd made it to the caves I realised that it would be impossible for Sienna to be carried down from them. Especially when there was a large, flat area directly in front of them where the air ambulance could land. I learned a valuable lesson, that sometimes you need to research things yourself and not rely too much on the internet. I'm wondering if Morgan should be asked to consult on a homicide in New York next, you know because I'd definitely have to go and research that.

I love hearing from my readers – you can get in touch on my Facebook page, through Twitter, Goodreads or my website.

Thanks,
Helen

Helenphifer1

@helenphifer1

helenphifer

www.helenphifer.com

www.unleashyourcreativemagic.com

ACKNOWLEDGEMENTS

The hugest of thanks to my amazing editor, Emily Gowers, for being brilliant, patient and an all-round amazing person. I love working with you, Emily, thank you for everything.

I'd also love to say a huge thank you to the rest of the fabulous Team Bookouture who work tirelessly to make these stories what they are. I love that I get to work with you all and I'm eternally grateful that I do.

A great big thank you to Alison Campbell and the rest of the Audio Factory team for bringing these stories to life. You're all fabulous and very talented.

A special thank you to the bloggers who so lovingly read these stories and then tell the world about them. You are so very much appreciated in more ways than you could ever know.

I'd like to thank my fabulous family for testing my strength and durability, it's thanks to them I can cope with the crazy deadlines and probably because of them I have crazy deadlines but I love you all so very much and hope that one day you might read these stories and realise how hard your poor mother works in-between the shopping trips, babysitting (which I adore), fast food emergency call outs and anything else that you throw my way.

As always a huge debt of gratitude goes to the amazing Paul O'Neill for his final surveyor's reports, they are literally a lifeline and very much appreciated.

A special thank you to the guys and gals at Costa for fuelling my tired brain on the days I'm struggling with life in general.

A very special thank you to my readers, you are just amazing and I'm so blessed that you enjoy my stories.

A special thank you to Gabby Secomb Flegg, Billelis and Lauren Shadbolt for loving the stories I have forced on you all to read and for the inspiration.

Printed in Great Britain
by Amazon

21862790R00148